Death's Hand

An Urban Fantasy Mystery

The Descent Series - Book One

SM Reine

I0618942

Part 1: Before

Russia – February 1998

James spotted a splatter of blood through the tree boughs. It marked the snow like an ink stain on paper.

He pushed through the pine needles, and her bare feet appeared, blue-toed and limp. He saw the curve of a calf and a knobby, bruised knee. He saw the jut of ribs under her skin and an arm thrown over her face. And the next thing he saw was the twelve other bodies.

Nausea gripped James, but he covered his mouth and maintained composure. His guide was not so lucky. The other man dove behind a bush, gagged twice, and vomited across the frozen earth.

Elise was already dead. He was so certain of it that he almost walked away at that moment. But what would Isaac think of James abandoning his daughter's body? The indignity of leaving her naked on the ice for the birds to devour was too much, and he came so far to find her remains.

Yet he couldn't bring himself to step foot in the clearing. Elise looked peaceful, but the others were twisted in agony. Blood marked their fingernails. They had gone out fighting.

Each of the twelve other bodies could have been siblings. They had pale skin, slender forms draped in white linen, and white-blue eyes—he could tell, because they were frozen open. The snow around them looked fluffy, as though it were freshly fallen. Something about that struck him as wrong. It was cold, but it hadn't snowed in days, leaving the earth a solid sheet of ice.

Taking a closer look, James found it wasn't snow—the clearing was covered in feathers.

His guide had recovered and began babbling in Russian, but he spoke too fast for James to understand. He heard one recognizable word—*chort*, devil.

James hung back in the trees, fighting the urge to leave. He adjusted his balaclava, tuned out the guide's shouts, and stepped into the clearing.

The hair lifted on his arms. His skull began to buzz.

He tried not to look at the other corpses, but it was like they reached for him, pleading for escape. Their teeth were bared. Their tongues were purple and twisted.

That one had been stabbed in the chest.

The body by his feet was disemboweled.

Those two bodies had died clutching hands.

He couldn't look at them anymore. He focused on his feet and forced himself to take a step once, twice. Again and again. When he reached Elise, the buzzing grew so loud that he could no longer hear Maksim's protests.

James hovered a glove over her body. All the energy vanished. The clearing went silent.

He pushed the arm off her face to examine her. Dirty, frayed bandages were wrapped around her hands, so tattered that they looked like they might blow away.

Elise had her father's auburn hair and his strong nose,

but her soft chin belonged entirely to Ariane. Her eyelashes were sealed by ice. How had she died? There wasn't a mark he could see.

He moved to unwrap one of her hands.

Her eyes fluttered.

"Maksim!" he shouted. Her broad lips parted to exhale silver fog. "Maksim! She's alive!" He forgot to speak in Russian, but his message didn't need translation.

His guide shouted and ran to the van. James shed his parka. The cold seeped through his undercoat as he wrapped her in his furs. *Alive.* It was impossible. Nobody could have survived an hour naked in the killing frosts of Siberian spring.

James watched the other bodies, waiting for them to jerk to life and creep forward, but they remained lifeless. Elise was the only survivor, even though it was impossible for one small girl to have survived an attack that killed a dozen others.

Unless she had been the one to do the killing.

He carried her out of the clearing without touching the other bodies. There was nothing he could do for them. He wasn't sure he would have anyway.

The guide opened the van, letting steam escape the back end. As soon as James climbed inside, laying Elise between their extra gas tanks and a rattling space heater, he closed the doors again.

"Hurry!" James said, reverting to his limited Russian.

"She's a demon," repeated Maksim as he climbed to the driver's seat, and then he continued to speak so quickly that James couldn't understand if he tried. He picked up a word here and there—devils and hell, curses and fear—but he was too busy to translate.

He cracked heating packs open and pressed them to

Elise's underarms, her groin, and the back of her neck.

James pulled a glove off with his teeth and touched his bare fingers to her throat. Her pulse was slow but steady. Color began to flush her cheeks.

A demon, Maksim said. Maybe. But she was also Isaac and Ariane's daughter, and James promised to bring her back safely. He kept all of his oaths, no matter how unpleasant.

His driver shouted and gestured. James interrupted him to say, "Town. Take us to town!"

The van bounced and groaned over the path. He had to brace his back against the fuel canisters to keep them from falling on Elise as he searched her body. He found no injuries. Aside from a few bruises, she was unharmed.

Surely a girl that young couldn't have killed so many people without injury. There must have been someone else in the wilds—someone he hadn't seen. It wasn't a comforting thought.

He peeled the bandages off and flipped her hands to look at the palms.

No.

James turned her hands over again, heart racing.

It was the first time James wished Elise had died on the tundra, but it was also far from the last.

Elise woke up five days after James found her in the forests near Oymyakon.

He knocked lightly and entered the room. There were no hotels in the small Russian village, so he had been staying in a house full of laborers under the guise of an ordinary traveler. Since bringing home the girl's body, their friendliness turned to uneasy whispers, and James seldom left Elise sleeping alone in what had once been a tiny closet.

James sympathized with their wariness. Even he had to steady himself when he found her crouched in the corner of her bed, staring at him with eyes rimmed by dark circles, and he was the one who had brought her there.

"The women told me you were awake," he said. "They say you're refusing to eat. Please lay down. You must conserve your strength."

She remained so still that she might have been a painting.

There were three bowls on the rickety table by her bed. It didn't look like she had touched any of them.

"The stew is safe to eat, I assure you. Babushka is an excellent chef. I've eaten a dozen of her meals since I arrived, and she has yet to poison me."

Her gaze flicked to the table and back to him.

James moved to sit on the stool next to her, but he caught a glimpse of something shining amongst the sheets. She had somehow stolen a knife from the kitchen. He froze at the sight of the blade.

Tension hung suspended between them. She didn't move to stab him, and he didn't show his fear.

"My name is James Faulkner," he went on after a long moment, speaking in the voice one might use to soothe an angry hawk. "The woman you were staying with, Pamela Faulkner, is my aunt. I found you three days ago. We're in Oymyakon now."

"Where's Pamela?" Her voice was throaty and hoarse.

He shut his eyes. He could see Pamela's body as he found it in her house: slumped against the wall as though she had decided to rest for a few minutes. Her body was mostly unmarked, but blood stained her ear canals. Her beautiful black hair, streaked with gray only at the temples, was in its perpetual bun with only a single hair astray.

James had been very close to his aunt as a child. She was the high priestess of their coven, and she revolutionized ritualistic magic when she invented paper spells. Pamela had arguably been one of the most powerful witches in the world.

Very little could have caught her off-guard. Even fewer things could have killed her.

"She's dead," he said.

This didn't seem to cause any emotional reaction in Elise. She got to her feet, letting the sheets tumble to the ground, and the sight of her skeletal frame made James's stomach flip. Even swathed in a simple dress borrowed from one of the village women, he could see every curve of every bone in her body.

She took a step toward the door, knife clutched to her side, and staggered. Her hand slipped on the dresser when she tried to catch herself.

James stood to help her back to bed, but the look she gave him burned with sheer loathing, so he hung back without touching her. That glare made her look just like Isaac.

"What are you doing?" he asked.

She carefully made her way toward the door, gripping the frame to lift herself to a standing position once more.

"Please, Elise, sit down and eat. I assure you, we'll leave as soon as you can walk. If He doesn't know where you are yet, then we're a step ahead of Him, and we don't want to lose this brief advantage."

Her nose wrinkled, like the idea of going anywhere with

him revolted her. He was almost offended.

She fumbled for the doorknob.

"You're very weak and it's hundreds of miles to the nearest city. You won't survive alone."

Elise's only response was a silent glare. James was struck by the feeling that she was more of a feral animal than a teenage girl. He probably wanted to be trapped with her as little as she did, but neither of them had a choice in the matter.

She opened the door. James stepped in her path. She tried to shove him out of her way, but even though she was surprisingly strong for someone who looked like she should have been dead, he was stronger.

"Your parents asked my aunt to watch you until they came back. Since she died, the responsibility of your care falls upon me. I've sworn to keep you safe. I intend to keep that promise."

She transferred her grip from the doorway to a fistful of his shirt. He felt metal press against his stomach through his parka.

The knife. He tensed.

He breathed shallowly and forced himself to speak calmly. "I'm not safe now that I've found you, either. We need to stay together. It's the only way either of us will survive."

Elise radiated silent fury. He was struck by her resemblance to Ariane, although he didn't recall the sweet witch who had birthed her ever being so angry.

And then she released him and sat on the side of the bed, stubbornly ignoring his hand. With careful, measured movements, she lifted the stew to her mouth and drank its broth without dropping her gaze from his.

When the bowl was drained, she ate each piece of meat

one by one and set the bowl down again. She already moved without shaking. James doubted he would be able to keep her under control for long. It wouldn't be long before she was much, much stronger than him.

He wondered again if she had killed all those people in the clearing.

"I don't trust you," Elise said. "I will *never* trust you."

It was the last thing she said to him for a very long time.

December 1988

Isaac Kavanagh gave his daughter a pair of twin falchion swords for her seventh birthday. Wickedly sharp and too big for her hands, Elise accepted them with a grave nod before turning to kill her first demon.

She skewered it. The demon shrieked and wailed.

"Good," Isaac said with a proud smile. "Very good."

Later, they will say this day marked the beginning of the end of the world.

This is only half true.

Part 2: Retirement

Chapter 1

May 2009

Steam drifted from the surface of Marisa Ramirez's coffee. She blew on it gently, cupping the mug between her hands to warm her chilly fingers.

Golden morning light rimmed the closed curtains over the sink. The thermometer outside the window read sixty-two, but the swamp cooler clicked on and blew chilled air into the kitchen anyway. Marisa shrank deeper into her sweater.

Augustin Ramirez sat across the table with his face in his hands. The ceiling rattled above their heads as distant screams and sobs peaked in time with fists pounding against the floor.

His left cheek muscle twitched. They exchanged glances, and he found his own haunted expression mirrored in her face.

Hands shaking, she lifted her coffee cup and took a sip.

The doorbell chimed. Their daughter shrieked in response.

"Are you going to get that?" Augustin asked. Marisa didn't respond. His jaw tightened. "I said, are you going to get that?" She ducked her head, lips trembling. The right side of her mouth was darkened with the shadow of a bruise. He made a disgusted noise, shoving his chair back as he stood. "Fine. I'll get the door."

She took another drink and set the mug down.

The living room blinds were shut and covered by heavy curtains, casting the room in twilight. Augustin navigated to the door by memory, unlocked the dead bolt, peeked through the door.

The woman on the other side pushed her sunglasses into her hair to study him with narrowed eyes. A single scar broke the line of her right eyebrow.

"Augustin Ramirez. Right?"

"Yes," he said. "I'm sorry…do I know you?"

She held out a hand. She wore black gloves with a button at the wrist. "Elise Kavanagh. James sent me."

He gave her hand a brief shake. Her grip made his knuckles ache. "James Faulkner?" Augustin asked. "He said he was going to send a—uh, an exorcist to look at our daughter."

Elise nodded. "Yes, right. I'm the exorcist."

"You're not what I…that is to say…"

"Yeah, I know. Can I come in?"

"Yes," Augustin said, stepping aside.

"I'm sorry I'm late. I was on my way to the office, and I wasn't expecting James to ask me to do a job. I haven't been an exorcist in a long time." She indicated her outfit with a sweep of her hand—a black skirt, white blouse, and black blazer. Augustin wasn't sure what he expected an exorcist to wear. Maybe leather and chains. Definitely not business casual.

She handed a business card to him. *Elise Kavanagh, Certified Public Accountant.* It was so absurd he had to

11

laugh. "So you used to exorcise people a lot?"

"More often than I do now," Elise said. "I went into retirement five years ago. Anyway, I'm not going to exorcise your daughter. I'm going to determine if it's demonic possession."

"Demonic possession," he echoed. "You have me at a loss. Frankly, this all seems a little…absurd."

She gave a humorless, thin-lipped smile that might have been a grimace.

"You're here," Marisa said. She hovered in the doorway, arms wrapped around her shivering body. "I'm so glad you came."

Augustin frowned. "You know this woman?"

"She's always at the coven meetings," Marisa said. Her voice trembled slightly. "I think she does James's accounting. And he told me they're, uh, bound. Kopis and aspis."

"*What?*"

Her cheeks colored. "It's Latin."

"Greek, actually," Elise said. "Kopis means sword, and aspis means shield. It means I am—or used to be—a warrior against the forces of Hell, and he's my partner." She wasn't laughing at all. She was completely serious.

Distaste twisted Augustin's mouth. "Coven nonsense. It's taken me awhile to get used to the idea of witchcraft in the first place, and I don't think—"

Elise held up a hand. "I have places to be. I don't have the time to let you get used to it, Mr. Ramirez."

His face grew hot. "I'm not—"

"Augustin," Marisa said softly.

He closed his eyes and took a breath. Their marriage counselor harped on him about counting to ten when he was getting to mad, but he gave it to twenty this time.

Covens and "warriors against Hell." He could count to a thousand and still feel unsettled.

"Sorry," Augustin finally said. "We're stressed."

Elise accepted his apology by inclining her head. "Where's Lucinde?"

"She's upstairs. We'll go with you."

Marisa and Elise headed up the stairs. Augustin followed a couple steps behind, watching the legs of the supposed exorcist. She wasn't wearing nylons. Another scar marred her ankle, like a dog bite that had long since healed into a fleshy white mass, and his stomach turned. *Some accountant.*

Elise spoke to Marisa as they walked, oblivious to the reaction her scars evoked. "I need to ask you some questions. Have you summoned any demons or used a Ouija board?"

"Of course not."

"Any unusual noises or sightings? Animals with glowing eyes, objects flying across the room, strange noises on the telephone…"

Marisa shook her head. "Aside from Lucinde's illness, everything has been normal."

"What about nightmares? Have you experienced sexual dreams of a dark nature?"

"That's a personal question," Augustin interrupted.

Elise's lip curled, but she didn't respond.

"I haven't," Marisa said. Her voice was hardly louder than a whisper. "Augustin?" After a moment, he shook his head. "Lucinde was having nightmares before. Not… sexual. But she kept waking up screaming."

"Did she tell you what she was dreaming about?" Elise stopped to peer at a family camping photo beside an artful arrangement of silk flowers. In the picture, the Ramirezes were tan and smiling. Lucinde's low, croaking moans echoed through the house.

"She told me a monster was eating her heart," Marisa whispered. "I thought...I mean, what a strange thing for a little girl to dream about. She dreamed a monster ate her heart and sat in her chest."

Elise's eyebrows lifted. "Really."

"It's not weird for her to have bad dreams," Augustin interjected. "Especially not about her heart. She has a condition. The doctors don't think it should be fatal, but you know how kids are. Of course she's scared of bad things happening to her heart."

"What kind of heart condition?" They reached the top of the stairs, pausing down the hall from Lucinde's room. All the doors were open but hers.

"I don't think you need to know that to do your job," Augustin said.

"Just wondering. I assume you've already taken her to see a doctor and a psychologist?"

"Those were our first choices. They gave us the option of waiting to see if she would improve or sticking her in an institution. I wouldn't have let Marisa call you unless we didn't have any choices left."

"I see. I'm going to go in and look at her now."

"Be careful. She's gotten...violent," Marisa said.

"How violent can a five-year-old be?" Elise gave an unpleasant smile that didn't suit her angular face. "I'm sure I've handled worse."

"Just be careful. She's in here."

Elise approached the door Marisa indicated, and the Ramirezes hung back. The girl became quieter as she grew near. When she stood before the door, Lucinde became entirely silent.

Elise pushed the door open and went inside.

Lucinde's room was even colder than the rest of the house. Heavy curtains cast the room in near-complete darkness, and a portable swamp cooler made the air chill and muggy. A white canopy bed blocked the back half of the darkened room.

There were multiple obstacles strewn across the floor: an overstuffed comforter, rose-colored pillows in varying sizes, and a toy chest. Possible hiding places included the closet and the shadowed area behind a pink trunk with princess costumes draped over the sides. No girl in sight.

Elise didn't like the room's poor visibility. It felt confined. Dangerous. "I'm going to open the window, Marisa."

"She won't like it."

She moved toward the window, hugging the wall, and stepped over a toy unicorn with blood caking the mane to its neck. Ears perked for any hint of motion, she jerked aside the first layer of curtains, then the second.

Light filled the room. Someone squealed.

Elise rounded the bed in time to see bare feet disappearing under the bed. "Lucinde?"

She dropped to her hands and knees and leaned her cheek close to the carpet. A pair of luminous eyes stared back at her. The girl under the bed looked nothing like Marisa. Her skin was dark, like her father's, and her flat nose was offset by his same expressive lips.

"Cold," she hissed. "Cold!"

Elise's gaze traveled over her bared legs. Her knees were heavily bruised, purple and black and brown on the edges. The flesh on her shins looked like broiled strawberries. "Have you used force to restrain her?" Elise asked.

"She hurts herself," Marisa said. "We can't stop her."

"Colder!" Lucinde demanded again, sinking further into the corner as though she wanted to hide inside the wall. Elise glanced at the swamp cooler. *Colder.*

Lucinde tried to jerk away when she touched her foot, but Elise caught her ankle, pulling her foot into the light. A few remaining flakes of pink nail polish decorated her toenails under caked blood. One nail had been torn out. She released the child's ankle, and withdrew again.

"How are you doing?" Elise asked. "*Quomondo vales?*"

Lucinde froze. Her eyes widened fractionally.

"*Quomondo vales?*" she repeated. "*Loquerisne Latine?* No? ¿*Hablas inglés?*"

"She speaks English," Marisa said, offended.

"Of course."

Elise pulled the chains of her necklace over her head and picked a bronze pendant from amongst the other charms. It caught the sun and scattered gold light on Lucinde's forehead. The whites of her eyes were almost yellow, shot through with crimson veins, and a long, low hiss issued from between her lips.

"*Crux sacra sit mihi lux,*" Elise whispered. Lucinde recoiled, covering her face.

"What are you doing?" Augustin demanded.

Lucinde remained flat against the carpet, fingers spread through the dusty shag as though she feared being dragged away. She whimpered like a wounded dog.

She was so small. Elise was sure she had never been that small.

Elise leaned closer. "Can you speak?"

Marisa stepped forward. "Watch out—"

The girl's foot lashed out and the bedroom exploded into red stars. The pain struck a moment later like being struck in the jaw by a baseball bat.

She reeled, hand flying to her mouth. Lucinde scurried from beneath the mattress.

"Colder! *Colder!*" Her voice was shrill, piercing.

Lucinde's nails flashed. Elise raised her arm in defense—but the little girl stopped short, swiping the hand inches from Elise's face. Lucinde's wrist was roped to the corner of the bed.

Augustin hauled the exorcist to her feet, dragging her away from Lucinde. She shook her elbow free of his grip.

"We told you to be careful," he said, voice rough. "She's not normal anymore." Elise ignored him, meeting the girl's eyes.

"Cold," Elise echoed.

Marisa moved into the room, making soothing noises. Lucinde screamed a long note with the tenor of a beast. Augustin guided Elise out of the room and shut the door. Without windows, the hallway was darker than Lucinde's bedroom, but it felt much less oppressive.

"We won't be held liable for our daughter's—"

"I'm not going to sue you for my wound, if that's what you're getting at. I've had many injuries much worse than this."

"Good." His mouth twisted. "Good. What were you doing in there?"

"Testing her," she said. "This is the pendant of Saint Benedict. He's the patron saint of a lot of things—nettle rash, servants who have broken stuff that belongs to their masters. Spelunkers."

"Spelunkers?"

"He's also invoked during exorcisms. I wanted to see if she would react to Latin because a lot of Greater Demons don't speak any living languages."

"She's been speaking English," Augustin said. "She

keeps saying 'cold.'"

"I saw that."

"So…what do you think?"

"I can't say if she's possessed," Elise said, touching the back of her hand to her mouth. It came away bloody. "She's definitely got an attitude problem."

"She was never like this before," Augustin said.

"I'm sure." She headed down the stairs, leaving Lucinde's screams behind her. "I'll do some research. I've seen my share of possessions and exorcisms, but never one as spontaneous as this. You're sure nothing has been flying around?"

"Completely sure. We're not *freaks*."

"You don't have to be a freak to be targeted by demons; just unlucky or stupid. Since you haven't summoned anything, you could be the former."

"We're not stupid," he said. Her eyes narrowed.

"Don't put words into my mouth."

Augustin puffed out his chest. "Can you exorcise Lucinde or not?"

"I could, if she's possessed," Elise said. "It definitely seems like a demon problem."

"Like in the Bible."

"Yes. 'Like in the Bible.' I'm going to confer with James, after which he'll be in contact with you. What would be the best number to reach you at?"

"Marisa's so-called high priest has it," Augustin said.

"Okay. Keep Lucinde in her room for now. Try to keep her eating and drinking water, because if she is possessed, she'll resist it on her own," Elise said. She touched her bleeding lip. "You already know to keep your distance."

"Yes."

He opened the front door to let in the hot summer air.

The clouds had thickened since Elise's arrival, and it smelled like rain again. "You have my card. Call me when she gets worse," she said, stepping outside.

Augustin was already closing the door. He looked as inclined to give her a call as he was to offer a finger to his daughter's mouth. "Right, thanks," he said.

Elise paused by the Ramirezes' gate. She glanced up at Lucinde's window, half-covered in a heavy drape. As she watched, a hand came up to jerk it closed.

"You're welcome," she muttered. Elise turned on her car, cranked the radio, and pulled out of the cul-de-sac.

Chapter 2

Elise's office was conveniently located one mile from the airport and just across the street from the bad side of town. The toxic green carpet had been bought secondhand from a casino, but the loud pattern was downplayed by yellowing paint and fixtures that hadn't been replaced since the mid-seventies. Since most of her business was done online, Elise hadn't seen the point in spending much money on rent.

The mail room was empty except for a consultant who had moved in the week before. "Good morning!" Felicia sang.

Elise took the mail from her cubby and didn't respond.

Her box was labeled "Bruce Kent." Elise had been retired for years now, but demons had a long memory for revenge. Starting her business under a pseudonym had seemed like a good idea. It worked well enough. In the five years since their retirement, she'd only been attacked twice.

The first envelope on her mail stack proved to be yet another threatening letter from her former employer's lawyer. Elise moved it to the back of the pile. Her roommate would be happy to use the shredded paper in her compost. The rest of it was bills—lots of them.

"That coffee sure smells good," Felicia said hopefully. Elise walked away. "Say hi to Bruce for me!"

Her suite was just as dreary and green as the rest of the building. She didn't have any decorations to lessen the impact; the walls were bare aside from her diploma and proof of CPA certification.

Elise thought Augustin had been right to laugh at the absurdity of her career choice, but when she retired, she had no skills for a normal career. James had job experience from the time before he became a nomad, but she hadn't even completed kindergarten.

At the time, she toyed with the idea of becoming a police officer, but she hated guns. Then Elise learned she had passion aside from the hunt: money. There was probably a joke to be made about going from killer to accountant, but a college education didn't bestow her with a sense of humor. She also didn't learn to be friendly to assholes, which was why her internship with an accounting firm was brief and ended up in court.

Elise settled her chain of charms next to throwing knives in the top drawer of her desk and prepared a fresh pot of coffee. Once she started working, she could go through two pots before lunch.

Her email was as pleasant to read as her normal mail. Elise filled a niche market: financial services for infernal and ethereal businesses. Most demons came to Earth to make trouble, but a few came to get rich. Their scruples— or lack thereof—gave them good business sense. But demons also had no morals, which meant they often didn't pay their accountant.

Elise paged through multiple emails full of excuses. Her

frown deepened at each one.

"Fuck me," she muttered, drinking deep from her mug. It was going to be a three pot morning for sure.

The only highlight was an email from James. All it said was, "Dinner tonight?" Elise responded with, "Sure," and minimized her email program.

The rest of it could wait. Her daily allotment of patience for clients had been expended upon Augustin Ramirez, and the only company she wanted now was math: silent, unemotional red and black numbers.

She glanced at her knives in the desk drawer. Math, and maybe a sharpening stone. It *had* been a long time since she gave proper attention to her arsenal.

Leaning back in her chair, Elise balanced one of the slender knives across a finger. The blade glinted in the fluorescent overhead light. It was shiny enough to serve as a mirror, and the braid over Elise's shoulder was distorted across its surface like the promise of spilled blood.

If she had her clients' lack of scruples, she would bill the Ramirezes for services rendered. Why shouldn't she make money off her knowledge like any other consultant? The only problem was James. He would never approve of profiting off a five-year-old girl's life.

Elise tested the edge of the blade with her thumb. Maybe instead of billing families in need, she could start threatening her pre-existing clients with violence. Yeah. That could work.

She speared the stack of mail with her knife. It gave a satisfying *thunk* as the knife's point bit into the blotter.

The only warning her door was about to open was a single knock. Elise jerked the blade out of her desk and dropped it in the drawer just in time for a blonde tornado to sweep in.

"Good morning, gorgeous!"

"Morning, Betty," Elise said. "How did you get here?"

Betty was the exception to Elise's steadfast refusal to develop a social life. Her roommate liked to describe herself as the sexiest research scientist in the West, and she played into that image with a dangerously low-cut blouse and what barely passed as a skirt.

"I'm just popping by. Cassandra and I are on our way to the university. I need a revision to my taxes!" Betty set her folder on Elise's desk with all the flourish of bestowing a gift upon her.

"No, you don't. I prepared your taxes three months ago. They were perfect."

"Yeah, but I think I found more deductions. Would you take a look? Please? I don't want to have to pay the IRS this year."

"You know every month you don't pay incurs a half-percent fine, right?" Elise asked. "And aren't you worried about splashing caustic chemicals on your cleavage?"

"I'm not doing work in the lab today. I have to see my mentor about my thesis," Betty said, giving Elise a knowing grin.

"I'll take another look at your taxes if you promise not to get kicked out of graduate school for sexual harassment. Nobody else is paying me anyway."

"Great! Well, except for the part where you're not getting paid. Are you going to make your half of rent this month?"

"Probably," Elise said. She silently added, *I hope.*

Betty wasn't fooled. She gave Elise's hand on the desk a comforting squeeze. "We're doing okay. Don't stress about it. But maybe it's time to hire some goons to have a talk with them, huh? Make them an offer they can't refuse?"

"Would you believe me if I said I'm seriously considering that as an option?"

"I'll believe anything with you, Elise. So what happened with your mail? Taking out your frustrations with a letter opener?" She wiggled a finger through a hole in one of the envelopes.

Elise shrugged. "They showed up like that."

"Yeah? I wonder if it was the postal service or the mailroom guy," Betty said. She lowered her voice to a whisper. "Ooh, you know, I bet it was that guy that does the credit counseling services. He's such a creeper. He always gives me looks when I go by his room."

"I think he's surprised anybody likes me enough to visit. It could also be your amazing disappearing wardrobe. I've seen strippers wear more than you."

Betty laughed. "Elise! Why are you seeing strippers in the first place?"

"I've got some weird clients." Understatement of the year. Betty didn't know that most of the people she worked for weren't people at all.

She swiped Elise's coffee, took a sip, and set it back down with a sigh. "Hate to demand deductions and run, but Cassandra's outside and my mentor is waiting." Betty wiggled her eyebrows. "You going to be home for dinner tonight?"

"No. I'm going to go see James."

"Oh *really*. So you're planning on *eating out*? Get it? You know, like—"

Elise didn't let her finish. "Not everyone lives in a porno like you do, Betty. It's not like that."

"I don't know why," Betty sighed. "If James was inviting me over for dinner, it would definitely be 'like that.'"

"Uh huh. I'll let you know about your taxes tomorrow."

"Thanks, love," Betty said. "By the way, you got some ketchup on your blouse." Elise glanced down, touching her injured lip. The smear of red on her collar wasn't ketchup. "See you later!"

"Bye, Betty."

She turned back to her computer, where the emails full of excuses were still waiting. Her smile slowly faded.

A lifetime of killing demons could never have prepared her for the ugly reality of being unable to pay her bills. It seemed cruel that she could be a skilled accountant creeping toward debt, but she didn't think many demons would be impressed by phone calls from debt collectors.

Elise's gaze wandered to the drawer with her knives again. Demons only responded to violence.

Screw discretion. Maybe it really was time to start speaking their language.

Click. The sign outside Motion and Dance Studio flickered and turned off. Rain tapped against the control box on its side, dripping onto the brown grass and running off into the gutter.

Elise locked the door on the control box and headed inside. Her footsteps echoed through the main hall as she moved from window to window to shut them. Elise's reflection on the mirrored wall behind her mimicked her actions, a dark silhouette of a long-haired young woman in an open blazer and low heels.

She peeked into the second, smaller dance hall. It wasn't quite as nice as the main one, since it had recently been converted from a garage. The studs were exposed on one side and boxes with branded t-shirts were stacked against the wall.

The windows were already locked, so Elise turned to leave again. Her own motion in the mirror caught her eye. She hesitated in the center of the dance hall.

A scar on her left breast peeked over the neck of her blouse, glowing pale white in the light from the street lamps. That injury had been delivered by a stone knife in the hands of a woman claiming to be a death goddess. She tortured Elise for hours by chaining her to a wall and drawing lines in her flesh. Most of them healed cleanly, but the one over her heart had been deep enough to scrape bone.

It was the last time Elise hunted a demon. She prevented apocalypse that day, but the costs had been too high.

She clicked off the flood lights before locking the front door, wiggling the handle to make sure it was secure. She hugged the side of the building to avoid the rain as she took the stairs to the second floor.

The door upstairs was ajar. She hung her coat on the hook beside James's jacket and shook out her hair.

"James?" she called, stepping into the kitchen.

All of the lights in the apartment were off. Elise flipped the switch to the stove's overhead light. Golden potatoes simmered under a glass lid, and two wine glasses were waiting nearby on the counter. The wine itself was still on the rack.

Her eyes scanned the arrangement of the furniture, the appliances. The table had been moved from the informal dining area to the living room. Half-melted candles marked with pentagrams and anointed with oil were arranged on low stands around the edges of the room. A large crystal had been set on a velvet cloth in the center of the table, and the last edition of the Sierra Witch's Almanac lay by its side.

It looked like James had been preparing for a ritual, but she heard no sounds in the house beyond the occasional hiss of steam and clicking as the stove's temperature shifted. He would never leave dinner unattended.

Where was he?

Elise slipped off her shoes, a thread of adrenaline thrilling through her stomach. She turned off the light again and approached the hallway. Lifting her skirt over her knees to free her legs, she lowered into a half-crouch.

"James?" she called again, softer this time.

Creak.

Danger.

Elise spun too late. The closet door slammed open, and a tall, dark form flew at her from its depths. Her hip hit the arm of the couch and sent the side table crashing to the ground. She let herself roll over the side, and the assailant flew past her.

She was on her feet again in a heartbeat, sweeping her leg high to strike his back. He cried out, stumbling forward, and Elise kicked again, lower this time. Her foot connected with a muffled *thump*.

He lost balance, barely catching himself on the half wall. He threw his arms up to block Elise's next kick, catching her ankle. She jerked and broke his grip.

Her attacker's fist flashed through the darkness. Elise twisted away. The blow landed on her right shoulder instead, and her arm numbed.

The blows between them were fast, smooth, like a choreographed dance. He swung at her, and she blocked him with her forearms to strike low, seeking a hole in his defense. Kick, kick, punch—Elise caught his arm and threw him against the opposite wall.

She grabbed him by the throat and pushed his head back. She tightened her fingers around his esophagus. It didn't take much force to hold him in place, even though he was nearly a foot taller than she was; one wrong move and his airway would collapse.

"Got you," she growled.

A frozen moment hung between them, his struggling breath hot on her face. He smelled of breath mints and aftershave, and a little bit like summer grass, and he all but radiated heat. He had been inside—waiting—for quite a while.

Her assailant gurgled. Elise relaxed her hands.

"Oh, sorry. Are you okay?"

He coughed once and cleared his throat. "Yes...I think so. You haven't lost your touch, have you?"

"There's no chance of that happening with your help." Elise backed off, allowing her aspis to step away from the wall. She flicked on the living room light, and James rubbed his neck.

"You could have pulled your punches," he said. "Didn't you recognize me?"

Elise smiled. She would have recognized him in total darkness. "It would be insulting to go gentle on you. What's that I smell in the oven?"

"Prime rib roast with red wine sauce."

She picked the side table back up. "Sounds great. What would I do without you?"

"Starve, I imagine," he said as he pulled an apron that said *Kiss the Crone* over his head.

James returned to his cooking while Elise fixed the mess she made in the living room.

The apartment was small, but he made good use of the space; James's sense of aesthetics was far superior to hers.

All his furniture matched in a Pottery Barn kind of way, his walls were decorated with fine photography, and he even had some kind of fancy throw rug. Elise's idea of decorating was putting up movie posters with thumb tacks.

"It took you a long time to get up here," he remarked from the stove. "I hid for ages. What were you doing downstairs?"

"Locking up. Someone forgot to shut all the windows."

"I was busy making dinner." James turned on the oven light and peeked through the window. "Just a few more minutes, I think. Are you all right?"

"I'm fine."

He gave her the kind of look that said he knew she wasn't, but didn't feel like arguing it. "Did you see the Ramirezes today?"

"Yeah. *That* was fun. They're a mess."

James uncorked a bottle of wine and poured it into the waiting glasses. "Is it possession?"

"Maybe. Lucinde didn't like having St. Benedict flashed at her. She also kicked me in the face."

Elise picked up the Sierra Witch's Almanac and peered at the bookmarked page. James's coven published a new almanac every year with lunar correspondences and seasonal spells, and they always included an excerpt from their Book of Shadows in the back. The spell he was looking at seemed complicated.

He handed her one of the glasses. She dropped the book. "Your bruises look painful."

"She's got a nasty kick for a five-year-old. Nastier than yours, anyway," she said. He opened his mouth to protest, but she went on. "Marisa mentioned she was having nightmares. It's possible Lucinde was attacked by a mara or an incubus instead."

"But you don't think it's possession?" he asked, serving dinner using puffy blue pot holders.

"Probably not."

"Good. That will make it easier."

Elise shrugged. "It's not my problem. I'm not an exorcist anymore."

He turned on the radio on the windowsill.

"—other *spooky* news, a temp guard by the name of Richard Czynski disappeared from a cemetery in the north side of town," the DJ said in a voice far too perky to be discussing a missing persons case. "Curiouser and curiouser, he's not the only thing that's disappeared. The grave of notorious Amber Hackman, one of the only people to escape this black hole of a town, has also been raided. Obviously she didn't like having to spend her death here anymore than she did her life. Zombie attack? Your run-of-the-mill grave rob gone wrong? You ring in and let us know on *Spooky* News, your favorite—"

"What trash," he muttered, switching it over to a classic rock station.

She felt the motion before she saw it. James's hand whipped toward Elise.

Side-stepping his reach, she jerked his wrist forward and trapped his arm under hers. A twist, a hard shove, and she had him against the wall.

Elise grinned at him, and his returning smile was softer, but no less affectionate. It softened the coldness of his eyes. Ten years, and he hadn't won a fight against her once.

"Damn, you're fast," he said when she dropped him. He rubbed his elbow. "I'll get you someday."

"Sure you will," Elise said, mostly to be nice.

They sat down together at the table. James hesitated

over a piece of potato, pushing it through the prime rib's juices with his fork. "I think you should keep working with the Ramirezes."

"Why? The coven can handle it, and I have too much work to do. Real work. The kind of stuff that pays the bills." Elise smiled over her wine glass. "Unless you think the Ramirezes would pay me a consultation fee?"

"You can't charge them money."

"And I can't pay the rent with gratitude." She tried to ignore his disapproving stare, but she could feel its weight as she picked at her salad. "I'll investigate. Maybe I'll find out something helpful."

"Thank you."

She grunted. "Do you still have my falchion?"

"It's in the locked case where you left it. Why? Did you want it back?"

"Not really. I was just thinking about it earlier."

"I've been thinking about it a lot lately, too," he murmured over his glass of wine. He didn't mean the sword.

The sounds of classic rock intermingled with the soft pattering of rain on glass, making for a peaceful meal. Elise made a good show of picking at her dinner to appease James, but as good as it tasted, she left her plate half-full. She cleaned up her place at the table, shoveling her barely-touched potatoes into a container.

James wasn't finished, but stood to help her anyway. "Eager to escape?"

"No, I just have to follow up on some clients that aren't paying."

He touched Elise's chin, his thumb hesitating over the gash. "Are you certain you're all right?"

Elise gazed up at him, momentarily breathless. James

was a handsome man. He also had absolutely no interest in her romantically, which he had made *very* clear over the years.

"Yeah." She turned from him to put the leftovers in the refrigerator. "I'm fine."

He caught her elbow—a less violent gesture than their earlier fighting. "Let me take care of you," he said.

All she had to do was nod, and James ran his knuckles down her cheek, and his power flowed around them, gentle and warm. It breathed through Elise, and she felt as though she was sinking into the sky.

An instant later, it was over. Elise touched her lip. The wound was gone.

James held up a yellowed note card with a single, prominent rune inscribed on the blank side—an old healing spell.

"Found this in my fire safe yesterday. Might as well get some use out of my old paper spells. I don't plan on using them ever again. This, on the other hand..." He took a knife of the cabinet and handed it to Elise. It was as long as his forearm and intended to be worn in a spine sheath.

The corner of Elise's mouth twitched. "Hiding weapons in your kitchen? I'm visiting a client, not going on safari." She jabbed the dagger into an invisible enemy, and the muscles in her arm rippled.

"Yes, but between Lucinde's demon problem, and some of the other news I've been hearing..." He trailed off. "I would appreciate it if you humor me."

Elise led him to the entryway and showed him the throwing knives hidden in her blazer pocket. "I'm miles ahead of you."

James's smile was sad. "Be careful."

"Always," she promised.

Chapter 3

Elise didn't deal with many local clients, and of those nearby, only one would provide information as well as a paycheck: Craven's, a small demon-owned casino with six months of outstanding debt to their accountant.

Craven's wasn't one of those big hotel casinos that booked Cirque-style shows and courted high-rollers. It was a little dive a few blocks off downtown with boarded windows and no flashy lights. Elise only discovered it wasn't condemned when one of her oldest clients, a cambion that could barely stand, informed her that their racks of ribs were the best kept secret in the city. And they did have great ribs—but it wasn't always from the kind of animal Elise was willing to eat.

Her contacts worked in the basement nightclub beneath Craven's. It was the kind of place a kopis couldn't visit unless she wanted a fight, and it wasn't much safer for someone in a business suit, either. Instead, she went home to change into something club-appropriate. Elise didn't go anywhere except work and the gym, so all she had was a black halter top and Lycra pants left over from Halloween. The pants were skin-tight, with nowhere to hide a weapon, but she fit an ankle rig under her right boot and a small knife under her belt. It wasn't a fast draw, but it would have to do.

Elise was doing her makeup in the mirror when Betty got home.

"You look like you're ready for a hot date," she said, invading their shared bathroom without knocking. Betty was still in her barely-decent skirt, but her lip gloss was a pink stain at the corner of her mouth.

"How was dinner with your mentor? I take it your hunt was successful." Elise gestured at her own mouth. "You're messy."

Betty wiped what little lip gloss remained off on her finger and laughed. "Successful? Yeah, right. He only wanted to discuss biomedical sciences, and not the naked kind. You using the sink?" Elise stepped aside to give her room, and Betty bent to wash her hands. "You didn't answer when I asked about the hot date, I noticed."

"My mission for the night is far more innocent than yours. I'm going to drop in on a client."

"Really."

"Yes, really. Why?"

Betty folded her arms. "How often do you visit your clients wearing skin-tight Lycra?"

"Any time my client happens to work at a casino nightclub and it's a Friday night," Elise said, tossing her sponge in the trash. "I can't show up in business casual. I'd get laughed out of the place."

"That might happen if you try to seduce the money out of your client, too. I've seen the way you dance."

Elise pushed Betty away from the sink with her hip. "Out of my way. I'm an accountant on a mission."

"Uh huh. Sure. I'll keep my phone on me tonight, so

give me a call when you're too drunk to drive yourself home."

"I appreciate the offer, but I'm taking the bus." She applied eye shadow with her fingers.

"Taking the bus and *not* planning on getting drunk? A likely story."

"The casino is downtown, Betty," Elise said. "There's no free parking."

Betty snorted. "Okay, have fun with your 'client.' I'm going to collect the withered scraps of my dignity and read research papers on the couch."

She left. Elise ran her fingers through her thick hair to detangle it and appraised her looks. The look wasn't "accountant," but she wasn't sure she would pass as an ordinary clubber, either. Elise didn't *feel* convincing.

Elise grabbed her jacket off the back of a chair. "See you in the morning," she called as she passed through the living room. Betty waved a hand over the couch.

She passed Betty's cousin on the way down the sidewalk. Anthony occupied the other half of their duplex, and he worked multiple jobs, so he was always coming and going at weird times. It looked like he had just left his job at the car shop. His jeans were covered in oil.

"Hey, Elise," Anthony greeted, pausing on the sidewalk. "How are you? Did you—"

"Have to catch the bus. See you later," she said, brushing past him without stopping.

She jogged down the street and around the corner. A breeze moist with distant rain washed into her face and down her shirt. The storm had passed, but the weight of the air promised more to come. A man in a bulky coat was slumped over the bus stop bench, holding the schedule over his head as though it was still pouring.

Right on time, the bus groaned up the street and paused at her curb. Elise took a seat near the back door. No amount of fresh, rainy wind could make the inside of the bus smell good—despite being cleaned frequently, it still smelled of sweat and the hundreds of people who rode it every day.

The lights turned off and the bus rumbled down the street again. It jerked and swayed with every bump in the road. The city quickly began to transition from small businesses into casinos, bars, and strip clubs. The change was abrupt—one second, Elise was staring at peaceful storefronts and the occasional tattoo parlor, and the next, she was surrounded by flashing neon lights and towering hotels.

The sign on an adult store displayed a woman wearing only a thong and a suggestive smile, its mannequins decked out in boas and corsets. The Wild Orchid's sign flaunted its topless dancers across the street from the city courthouse. The bus hung a right, and tall signs over what had once been a casino advertised an off-Broadway show and a car event, both of which had left over a year ago.

People crossed from sidewalk to sidewalk amongst slow traffic, ignoring the buses and cars as they lurched from a bar to a pawn shop to get money for one more pull on the slot machine. A woman with overdone curls and skin hanging limply from her bones almost got struck by the bus as it turned onto Center Street. She didn't notice. She wobbled on, disappearing into the maw of a casino and out of sight.

The bus stopped at the downtown transit center, tucked between a bowling stadium and yet another hotel-casino. Elise was the first to hop off.

The casino lights flashed in time with music piped over

sidewalk speakers. A man by the front door played the saxophone. He hesitated when Elise passed. She gave him a quick once-over, taking in the translucency of his skin, his long, brittle fingers and strangely-proportioned face. Nightmare. Probably second class. Hardly a threat.

She nodded at him as she passed. He didn't look worried, so maybe he thought she was a demon, too. As far as the underworld here knew, there were no local kopides. What was there to worry about?

Elise plowed through the casino, ignoring the glittering machines and their inebriated patrons. She passed the poker tables, the blackjack, the rows of machines in front of huge plasma TVs, and the diner in the back. She exited through an unmarked door to an alley.

Wedged between the casino and its attached hotel, the dark passage appeared to have no purpose except for gathering trash. A chain link fence blocked one end of the alley, and the other side was a rotten brick wall that most people wouldn't realize belonged to the prettier side of Craven's. Elise never went through the front door—too many people watched it.

Elise ducked around a Dumpster, kicking a case of empty beer cans out of the way. A set of cement stairs led down into shadow.

Only a single word on a small, rusted sign hinted at the door's purpose—*Blood*, it said, the metal so pocked and rusted it was almost unreadable.

She pushed it open and went inside.

Elise was never sure how long it took to get from the surface to the club—time took on a strange quality in the descent, warping and fading. Maybe she only walked for a few seconds; maybe she walked for hours. The black walls narrowed as she moved down the passage, guided by the pulsing thump of bass.

In time, Elise came upon the end of the hall. A neon sign blazed a single electric word above the door: BLOOD.

She crossed the threshold and left the human world behind her.

Music thrummed around her, shaking inside her chest and against her eardrums. The back door was on the top level of Eloquent Blood. Humans sat amongst half-demons known as the Gray, doing business and swapping spit as though they weren't different species. Many of the humans probably didn't even know who they were associating with—a few idiots stumbled upon the bar thinking it was an underground Goth club, and nobody was in a hurry to tell them differently. Idiots were great incubus food.

Yellow sulfur formed a fine layer on the floor. The thick stench of sweat and whiskey almost overpowered the brimstone. They tried to keep it clean in the club, but Elise was all too familiar with the stink of demons. She could have recognized it if they drenched the entire building in formaldehyde.

She glanced at the dance floor two stories down. A DJ spun a dance beat and the bodies below pulsed in time to the rhythm. Hips rolled, arms twisted, and now and then Elise would see a flash of pale skin as another dancer stripped off her shirt. It was hot enough in Blood without dancing. Throw in a fast beat and a racing pulse, and it was nearly intolerable.

She moved through the tight press of bodies on the spiral staircase as she would have waded through an ocean tide. Speakers on either side of the bar pumped out music so loud it drowned out even the conversations hollered inches from her ears. Elise peered up at the bartender through fog from the smoke machines to determine if it was someone she knew.

The blonde girl on the bar swayed side to side, her hands trailing up her hips and stomach. Her fingers traced the swell of her bare breasts. Her nipples were erect despite the warmth, and her skin was dark olive. She was one of the Gray bartenders Elise didn't know. Probably part-basandere, judging by the heavy iron chain around her waist.

Someone waved at her from behind the bar. Neuma's hair was liquid midnight, like each individual strand had been dipped in an inkwell. As she moved toward Elise, she faded slightly into the shadows behind her until only her white skin and bathrobe were visible. The half-succubus Gray hadn't yet dressed for the night, and she earned a few strange looks for it.

"What you doing here?" Neuma asked, leaning on the bar. "Business or pleasure?"

Elise had to yell to hear herself over the music. "Business. Can we talk in back?"

The bartender's welcoming grin slipped off her face. "Sure." Elise jumped over the bar and followed Neuma down a hall. The volume of the music faded the further they went. "How you doing, doll?"

"You know me. You also probably know why I'm here."

Neuma grimaced. "Money?"

"Money," Elise confirmed.

An entire wall of the dressing room they entered was dedicated to shelves of alcohol. The other wall was a line of messy vanities. Black light illuminated the room, darkening everything but Neuma's skin, which glowed violet in the shadows.

She gestured to the alcohol. "What you want today?"

"Information and a paycheck," Elise said, dropping her

jacket on the dressing table. "You can help me with the first one, but I'll need David Nicholas for the second. Where is he?"

"Shot of vodka it is." Neuma dragged a stool out of the closet and positioned it under the shelves. "I haven't seen you in a couple weeks—how's life being sugar and spice?"

"Not as profitable as I would like. I really need to talk to him, Neuma."

She snorted. "Yeah, good luck. He left an hour ago to 'restock,' so the fucker's probably higher than the moon by now."

Neuma stepped onto the stool, lifting onto her toes to reach for one of the higher shelves. Elise watched her pale calves and ankles flex under the hem of her bathrobe. She made a triumphant noise and dropped to the floor again, alcohol in hand.

Elise forced herself to look away from Neuma's legs. "What's he taking?"

"I think he's gotten into lethe, but he ain't going to admit it." She took out two shot glasses and opened the vodka. "I can't imagine how a sexy girl like you got stuck accounting when you could be doing fun shit, like touring with me and the other Blood girls. We're leaving for St. Louis on the twenty-third. You can still come."

"I'm not an employee," Elise said.

"Could be by the twenty-third."

"Believe it or not, I like my job."

Neuma shrugged and handed her a shot. "The offer's out there."

"I'll keep that in mind." Elise tossed back the vodka. The alcohol burned hot all the way from her throat to the pit of her stomach. "When do you think David Nicholas will be back?"

"Could be a few minutes, could be a few days. Depends on how good the trip is."

A few days. She couldn't wait that long to pay rent. Elise dropped the shot glass amongst a pile of leather straps on the counter. "Where's the shift manager?"

Neuma's full lips split into a grin. "You're looking at her, beautiful!"

"Congrats. Where did our least favorite witch go?"

"Moved off to live with some aeshma." Neuma took a swig right out of the vodka bottle. "I hope she gets put into slavery by something with a lot of boils and a fetish for shit-play."

"Speaking of slavery, there's a lot of humans here tonight. What's going on? I thought you guys banned humans below the casino level."

"New policy from on high. We gotta play nice. Too many people wandered in and disappeared, so we're not letting humans into private rooms anymore, neither. We're gonna lose business like this."

"Demon business, but not the humans," Elise said. "And it will keep the police out of your hair."

"Cops are easy to pay off." Neuma sighed. "I kind of wish the Night Hag would come out of hibernation. Then we'd have someone to deal with public crap. You know?"

Elise grimaced to think of it. Demonic overlords were seldom thrilled to find kopides hiding in their territories—even retired ones. "Since you're the manager now, I need news. Anything you can tell me."

"There ain't much to say," Neuma said. She started changing into her costume for the night. "Like I said, I've heard tell the big boss is stirring, but you know, people say she's going to wake up every six months or so."

"Where did you hear it this time?"

"David Nicholas. I think he's just stirring shit up so nobody will kill him and take the casino, but..." Neuma dropped the bathrobe. "You know how he is. He's not even keeping hours down here anymore. He's got an office on the ninth floor like he thinks he's some fucking big shot."

"Is that all?"

"There have been some bodies going missing around town, too," Neuma said, grabbing a pile of leather straps off the counter. "Not just grave robberies. It's the hospital too, and it ain't some ambitious thief. When we gossip about it this much, you know one of us has gotta be involved." She donned her costume piece by piece, buckling the shorts on the side and holding one of the straps over her breasts. "Mind hooking me up?"

Elise pulled the strap tight and slipped it through the buckle, but her fingers wouldn't work the way she expected. The proximity to Neuma's skin was distracting. "Why would a demon stock up on bodies?"

"Food? Hell if I know."

Grave robbing didn't sound like a wholesome activity, but Elise doubted it had anything to do with Lucinde's problem. "Have you heard about anything big, bad, and incorporeal in the area? I'm looking for something that might be possessing people."

"Don't think so, babe. If there was something that nasty around, we'd already know."

"Yeah. You're probably right. Look, I'm going to go, but thanks for the shot. I'll try David Nicholas again tomorrow night."

Neuma pouted, sticking out her lower lip. It was ruby-black as though she had painted her skin with fresh blood. "I'd love to see you on the bar with me tonight. We could have a lot of fun."

Elise couldn't seem to tear her gaze from those lips. "No," she said unconvincingly, "I don't think we could."

The door to the dressing room swung open. A man with an angular chin and a too-large nose stuck his head in. "Why aren't you on the bar, bitch?" His gaze turned to Elise. It felt as though a wet rat slithered up the vertebra of her spine. "Oh. *You* again."

"David Nicholas," she greeted.

The club's manager was a full-blooded nightmare—hundreds of years old, but ages past his heyday. David Nicholas made people dream of rotting alive. He had been extremely powerful in the Middle Ages, when everyone feared leprosy, but now his specialty was being obnoxious.

"What do you want?"

"I'll give you three guesses," Elise said. "Let's have a talk in your office."

His lip curled. Smoke trailed from his thin lips to the caverns of his nostrils. David Nicholas stabbed a finger at Neuma. "Bar. Now."

She gave him an ironic salute, and Elise followed him out of the room. When she shut the door to the dressing room, Neuma's draw lost strength, and every step away made it easier to keep walking.

David Nicholas led her up the stairs behind the changing room, taking long drags on his cigarette. Elise could almost see the smoke billowing down his esophagus.

They emerged on the ground floor of Craven's. The lights were dim and the slot machines glowed like oases in the desert. A cocktail waitress that could have been Neuma's sister hurried by in little more than a leather leotard with a tray of drinks on her shoulder.

He led her up a couple levels of escalators, past a handful of imps that weren't pretending to be human, and through a locked door marked MANAGER.

David Nicholas's office overlooked the casino floor. Tinted glass dimmed the tables until Elise could barely make out the dealers, although monitors on the walls gave her a clear view of the cards. They were also the only source of light in the room, which Elise considered a mercy —it meant she could only imagine how bad the mess in his office was by the smell. It reeked like the dorms from Elise's college days.

She had to step over a pile of rags to get through the door. Piles of books and papers formed columns to her shoulder. Some had tipped over. And that was all what she could make out in the darkness—there were too many vague, shadowy shapes that could have been any number of horrible things.

David Nicolas twisted his lips and spat into a shallow metal bowl filled with cigarette butts and black smears of ash. "Let's make this fast, bitch, I don't have all night. What'd I do to earn a personal visit from the big boss's accountant? You got a problem with our taxes or some shit? I don't want to hear about it. It's *your* job to fix it."

"Everything is as good as can be expected with your finances, except for one thing."

"What?"

She leaned over him, arms folded across her chest. "I'm not getting paid."

"Bullshit. We paid you."

"You paid my retainer a year ago, and nothing since," Elise said. "That's six months of outstanding fines. I've sent you three notices."

He rolled the cigarette between two of his fingers,

contemplating the glowing end. "Haven't seen anything. Maybe the Night Hag got them. Did you hear she's waking up?"

"She's not going to stir and you know it."

David Nicholas spread his hands wide in a helpless gesture. "Yeah, if that's what you want to think, but I can't pay anyone that much money without getting it approved. Rules are rules."

Elise set her jaw. "You want to do this fast? We can do it fast."

"Oh no. Don't hurt me," David Nicholas said in a tone of mock horror. "I'm so afraid of the accountant."

She drew her boot knife. "I need to get paid. I'm going to make that happen one way or another."

"You don't even know what to do with that."

She stabbed. It sank into David Nicholas's stomach as though he was made of putty rather than flesh, and she jerked the knife across his torso, tearing it out the side. Black smoke puffed from the wound.

He lurched out of his chair, spidery hands clutching the entry point. "Fuck! What the hell?"

"I can force you to insubstantiate, and I can make it hurt. Believe me, I know which buttons to push." She lifted the knife again, and he tripped over a pile of trash trying to backtrack. He hit the floor and pushed himself away from her with his heels. "Or you can pay."

"I don't need the Night Hag to wake up to ruin your fucking week," he hissed. "Some dark night, you're going to go to sleep, and I'll be waiting. And I'll be there the night after, and the night after, and every other night of your life until you die shitting yourself. You'll learn to fear sleep, and to fear me."

Elise gave a little laugh. "The first night I dream of you,

David Nicholas, I'll tip off Aquiel. He'd be happy to know where you're lurking these days, and I'd enjoy watching you get ripped apart."

He stared at her. She stared back. A challenge.

"You'll fear your dreams yet," he whispered. He spoke so quietly that Elise shouldn't have been able to hear him over the music, but she did. His voice was dead fingers scraping down her neck, and she couldn't help but shiver. She didn't show it.

"Money. Now. I take checks."

It looked like he had many colorful words trapped between the spikes of his teeth, but he swallowed them down.

Fifteen minutes later, she trotted down the stairs into Blood again, flicking the check against the fingers of her free hand. David Nicholas slunk behind her, his arms wrapped tight around his body. He wasn't going to fall apart yet—not if he could hold himself together long enough to feed. But Elise hadn't made it easy on him. His shirt was in tatters, and the flesh beneath it wasn't much better.

The amount on the check was more than what they owed her for six months of work. It would cover the next quarter, too—and two months of her office's rent. She tucked it down her belt along with her dagger.

"Pleasure doing business with you," Elise said over the thudding of music. David Nicholas's eyes flashed.

A scream.

Elise twisted, facing the direction from which the scream had come. *The dressing room.*

David Nicholas was already gone, jumping shadow to shadow to disappear from the stool and reappear at the end of the hall. He vanished around the corner in a swirl of tattered clothing.

Elise grabbed the doorknob to the dressing room and shook it. Locked.

Neuma screamed again, and the door rattled in its hinges as something heavy slammed against the other side.

She took a step back and unleashed a powerful kick next to the lock mechanism. The door shattered around the handle.

Elise kicked again. It slammed open.

Neuma was pressed against the counter, her back smashed into the now-shattered glass of the mirror. A gray creature with branded flesh crushed her, its stubby hands locked on her wrists as its slavering mouth lowered toward her chest.

"Hey!" Elise shouted.

The demon turned. Its bulging eyes were almost all black. Opens slashes across his face wept blood and pus, and saliva dripped from its mouth.

It focused on her, and its pupils dilated.

Elise drew back her fist and punched, throwing her whole body behind the blow. The demon's head snapped to the side. It toppled with a keening scream.

The half-succubus cried out as she got off the counter. Several shards of glass stuck in her back, and blood poured down her perfect spine.

The little demon clambered to its feet. Elise pushed the bartender behind her.

"What do you want?" Elise demanded. The demon's thin gray tongue darted out of its mouth to lick where its lips should have been.

It lunged at Elise.

She moved into its attack and it slammed into her

shoulder. They hit the ground, and she rolled with their momentum. Her entire body felt the impact. It was like getting hit by a raging bull.

The fiend recovered instantly. Elise wasn't quite so fast.

It came at her with a roar, and a flash of inspiration struck—the black lights, the vanity bulbs, the demon's huge pupils. Elise threw herself out of the demon's way, and it hit the wall behind her instead.

She launched across the room. Elise fumbled in the darkness behind the rack of costumes. She heard the sound of clawed feet against ground, and shut her eyes against the impact—then found the switch.

Click. The lights over the vanities blazed to life.

Her eyes watered from the sudden light, but it was nothing compared to the demon's reaction. It screamed and clawed at its eyes, stumbling toward Elise. A stray swipe of its claws slashed her arm. Pain flared, and she jerked back with a shout.

The demon plunged into the dark hallway.

"Wait here," Elise told Neuma.

She expected the demon to go make a break for the club —and the fresh meat the partiers could provide—but instead it went for a door she hadn't noticed before. Elise began to follow.

"No!" Neuma cried, grabbing Elise's arm. "Don't!"

"It's escaping—"

"You can't go in there!"

"Why? Where does that door lead?"

"It goes down to the Warrens," Neuma said. "You'd get eaten alive."

"Shit," Elise said.

"Shit," Neuma agreed, stepping back into the room. She twisted around to look at her back in the mirror. Some of the glass was still in her back, and the injuries streamed thin, watery blood.

Elise grabbed the bathrobe and moved to cover the wounds. "We need to get you to a witch right now."

"No. I'm fine. I have a charm to accelerate my healing to human speed. You know, for when I'm playing submissive." Neuma grabbed a shard of glass and jerked it out of her back with a sigh. "Jewelry box. Toe ring with a red stone."

Elise shifted through the gaudy bracelets and necklaces to find the ring. She passed it to Neuma, who leaned against the wall to slip it on her foot. The blood thickened and grew sluggish as she watched, slowing to an ooze.

"That's a new toy," Elise said.

"My girlfriend gave it to me. She likes playing rough." Neuma pulled another shard of glass out, and another, dropping them in the trash can.

"Why did that demon attack you?"

"I don't know. Don't even know what it was. Would you pick some of this out for me? I can't reach it all."

"I think that might have been a fiend," Elise said, ignoring the request. Neuma would have enjoyed it way too much. "They're lesser demons, but it takes a strong demon to control them."

"It looks like it dropped something," Neuma said, pointing at a crumpled scrap of paper on the floor. Elise smoothed it out on her thigh.

It was an Eloquent Blood staff photo printed off the internet, and the former manager was circled in pink highlighter. "You sure this was on the demon?" Neuma nodded, and Elise studied it more closely. Aside from the circle, there was nothing odd about it. "Maybe it wasn't after you. Maybe it was after that witch. Why would it have wanted the old manager?"

"I don't know. Dumb bitch could owe someone money. Where did you see one of those before, anyway? Those are hellborn, and I don't think you've been hanging out in Hell," Neuma asked.

No, she hadn't. Elise found herself recalling her fight against the death goddess again—the feel of her swords connecting with demon meat, watching the bodies hit the ground, the stink of their final, sulfurous breaths.

She had tried hard for so long to forget it that she wasn't sure if she was imagining it now, but she was almost certain that the demons had been fiends.

"Maybe I have," Elise muttered.

Part 3: The Clock

Mexico – May 2004

Two demons were discussing the end of the world over crispy fish tacos. They sat in a shady corner of the patio to conceal their strange faces, and spoke Latin to prevent humans from overhearing.

"Hernandez says someone's taken over the pyramid in the undercity." The first speaker looked like a man whose eyes had been wrongly attached at the temples. His name was Vustaillo. He was a nana-huatzin, and he made his living trafficking slaves for the drug cartels.

"Who cares? Let them have it." The second speaker was a woman named Izel. Sharp teeth filled her mouth in rows like a shark. "Nobody wants that dump of a den anyway."

"But they said she's a goddess."

Izel dug into her fish and let the grease dribble down her chin. "Such a goddess must not have godly brains if she wants anything in the undercity. She's an idiot and a fool. May she enjoy her blessed ignorance."

Those kinds of insults made her companion uncomfortable. He toyed with his beer. "You heard the ninth bell ring," he whispered. "The clock's been wound again."

"More suicidal humans fascinated with death. They won't accomplish anything."

A shadow fell across their table, abruptly ending the conversation. A dark-haired human took a chair from an adjacent table and sat down. He wore a white button-up shirt and slacks, like a tourist on vacation, but he had a bandage on his cheekbone and not an ounce of body fat. Vustaillo could smell the magic pouring off of him.

"Good morning," said the newcomer. "I couldn't help but overhear your conversation."

He was speaking Latin fluently.

Izel's eyes narrowed to slits. "Who are you?"

"My name is James. Forgive me for intruding, but I heard you mention the clock, and I hoped you could tell me where it's located."

"*Bistak*," she spat.

James arched an eyebrow. "And you too."

What kind of human understood insults in the demon tongue and spoke Latin with such ease? Not the kind of human Vustaillo wanted sitting at his table. Definitely not the kind of human that should be anywhere near a doomsday clock, either.

"You should move on," Vustaillo said.

"Come, now. I'll buy your drinks."

Izel's hand lashed out, latching onto his forearm. Pinpricks of red sprung up where her nails dug into his skin. Even though she hadn't touched him, Vustaillo flinched. Izel's touch was murder. Sometimes literally.

"He said that you should—"

Izel froze. A figure had appeared behind her and pressed a knife against her throat. A thin line of blood dripped down the blade.

The woman at Izel's back was made of hard angles, from her Aquiline nose to the jut of her wrist. In the sunshine, her hair was like flame, and she looked furious.

"Get this blade off me," Izel whispered, barely daring to move her lips.

The woman spoke. "Let go of my aspis."

The color vanished from Izel's face, and Vustaillo felt dizzy.

Women did not have aspides. Only a kopis could have an aspis—but there were no female kopides.

Except one. And she was known as the greatest.

Demons whispered about her. They said she had no name and that she was as tall as a gibborim. She had become the "greatest" by slaying angels, which was something most mortals would not dare to do, even if they could. Obviously, the first two things were not true, but if the third was, then Vustaillo feared he and Izel did not have long.

"I don't want to die," Vustaillo said, and he wasn't ashamed to be on the verge of tears.

It was James who replied. "Then you might want to tell your friend to let go of me."

Vustaillo begged for her to comply with his eyes. One at a time, Izel's fingers uncurled. She slid her hand back across the table.

The kopis's blade did not budge.

"Release me," Izel said.

A single word from James: "Elise."

She sheathed the knife and took position at his back. He lifted his arm to show it to her. The demon's hand had left a red imprint burned on his skin, but he was not seriously injured.

Vustaillo pushed his plate away. The sight of food

suddenly made him want to retch. "I'm sorry. For both of us. We didn't know."

"The clock," James said, voice mild.

"It's in the undercity—south of here, very far south. In Guatemala. The entrance is hidden. You would never find it."

"You might be surprised," he said, pushing aside the plates to clear space on the table. He spread a map in front of them. "Where should we go?"

The eyes of the demons met over the map. What would be more profitable—a truth or a lie?

Elise unfolded her arms and folded them again. Her biceps made Vustaillo suspect she could pop off his head with a pinky finger.

He pointed at the map. "There. I can't be more specific. I haven't seen the entrance myself."

"How close do you think that is?"

"I don't know." Vustaillo fidgeted under Elise's stare. She hadn't moved since almost slitting Izel's throat. "Within five miles."

"And how certain are you about that?" James asked.

"I said I've never been there, didn't I?"

He marked it with a pen, folded the map, and put it back in his pocket. "Are you going to eat that?"

Vustaillo couldn't think of a response. James ate the tacos, and he seemed to enjoy them despite the uncomfortable silence around the table. Music played at a restaurant down the road, the wind breezed through the trees, and the witch chewed loudly. He offered chips to Elise, and she shook her head.

"What else do you want?" Izel spat, fists clenched atop the table. She was trembling. "Our money? Our lives? You think you can threaten us without recourse because…

what? You're *famous*?"

"If you're offering, we could use a guide to the undercity."

Izel barked out a laugh, but Vustaillo perked up a little. "For how much?"

James stood, wiped his mouth with a napkin, and dropped it on the empty plate. He was a full head and shoulders taller than Elise. Definitely not bigger than a gibborim. "From what we've heard, everyone dies if this clock strikes twelve. Humans. Demons. Anyone on Earth when Hell crashes into us. It's in your best interests to help."

"For how much?" Vustaillo pressed.

Elise turned to leave. The message was clear: They would not pay. He may not have been a demon of much prestige, but he didn't work for free. Even the cartels wouldn't be so insulting.

With a roar, Izel shoved the table. It exploded in front of Vustaillo. He flung himself to the ground and screamed as margarita glasses shattered around him.

Izel leaped over the table, lunging for James's throat with clawed hands.

She stopped short with a gasp.

Something crimson spattered on the back of Vustaillo's hand. He looked up to see a silver blade jutting from Izel's back. The exchange had taken a half a moment—no more. The only sound had been Izel's shout.

Vustaillo's heart shattered when she sagged against the kopis. Elise lowered her to the ground.

Nobody sitting outside the restaurant reacted. They continued eating and chatting, completely oblivious. Izel had picked the most discrete table, after all. Her body cooled beside him.

Elise stepped back and sheathed her dagger again. James put the table back in its place, picked up the plates they had spilled, and glanced uneasily at a waiter watching from the doorway.

"Get your friend out of here," James said. Disgust curled his upper lip. And then they were gone again, as silently as they arrived.

There is no currency more valuable than information. When it pertains to the location of the greatest kopis and her aspis, such information is priceless—and dangerous.

News of Izel's death reached the overlord of Cancun by nightfall, then passed to the overlord of Chetumal. Whispers traveled on shadows, crossed continents with the ocean breeze, and found waiting ears before dawn.

Vustaillo had been murdered by first light.

The tenth bell chimed two weeks later.

June 2004

Elise killed fourteen demons on the day that the clock struck ten. She knew this for a fact because she counted the skulls while piling the bodies.

Once they were stacked together, James tore a page out of his Book of Shadows, flicked it at the pyre, and whispered a word of power. They ignited in an instant bonfire, flushing Elise with heat and scorching her eyebrows. The fire didn't touch the foliage around them. The misty drizzle couldn't slow it.

"You've improved." Elise didn't sound complimentary

so much as exhausted. Her hair was stuck to the back of her neck, and she wasn't sure if she was soaked in rain or sweat.

When the tenth hour chimed, the sky had split with fire and gateways opened, dumping demons on top of Elise and James. She killed anything that passed, but a lot of them had scattered. The villages were going to be a mess. And if the rest of the world was the same…

"Whomever is winding that clock isn't playing games." James took several large steps back before flicking another paper at the fire. The flames leaped fifty feet into the sky.

"At least we have this." Elise lifted a strip of skin between two fingers. She had skinned brands off one of the demons. If she could find the symbols in Hume's Almanac, they would be able to determine the demons' allegiance.

But it suddenly grew hot, and the skin blackened and crumpled around the edges. She gave a shout and dropped it. It was ash before it hit the ground.

"What did you do?" she asked, spinning on James.

His eyes were wide. "Nothing. That wasn't me." He clapped his hands, and the flames on the bodies vanished in a flash of smoke. There were no charred bodies where the fire had been—not even bone fragments.

"Shit," Elise said.

"Some greater demons clean up their minions to destroy evidence. This must be one of them." He groaned and rubbed a hand through his hair, leaving a streak of white ash. "Fantastic. At least that narrows it down to…oh, a few hundred demons."

Elise sheathed her swords, inspected herself for major injuries—nothing worse than a few bleeding claw marks—and started hiking back to the villages. James shadowed her. They had been combing the area Vustaillo noted on the map for days and hadn't found anything but mud, ants, and several rainstorms.

The village streets were empty of life when they arrived. There hadn't been many people in the first place, but the few who had stayed outdoors were dead now.

Elise and James turned a corner and startled a group of feasting demons. They were ugly things, like living grotesques hunched over half-eaten bodies with dirty fingernails and leathery skin. Elise had never seen the likes of them. She hoped she would never see them again.

She cut down the demons. They turned into ash a few minutes later.

"I got a couple of the symbols," James said. He had written down as many as he could before they ignited.

"Good. I have twenty seconds."

He looked at her. "Twenty seconds of what?"

"I timed the bells. There are twenty seconds between from the start of one to the start of the next."

"You timed them? While fighting?"

Elise shrugged.

"So that's four minutes," she said. "For twelve bells. Four minutes from the first chime until..." *The end of the world.* She didn't need to say it aloud. "I'll be back."

Elise headed to the post office, which was uninhabited by humans—living or dead. There was one package addressed to "Bruce Kent." She ripped open the box, took out the copy of Hume's Almanac sent by James's former coven, and threw the packaging in the trash.

She met up with James again, put Hume's Almanac in his backpack, and shouldered her own.

It was time to move on. There would be more victims, more demons, more battles to fight before they could find the clock.

"What happens with the eleventh bell?" Elise asked. "What happens with the *twelfth*?"

James shook his head.

"Let's get to the clock before we find out."

Elise went weeks without resting, but she couldn't keep moving forever. When she became so exhausted that she almost failed to avoid decapitation by a stray demon, James picked an abandoned condo in a village on the ocean and insisted they stop to sleep.

At first, she refused. But fatigue won out. For a few blessed hours, she slept.

He studied as she rested, working his way through Hume's Almanac with the drawings of the demons' brands. There had been a letter from the high priestess tucked in the back, but no note from Hannah. She had never written to him, not in five years, and her rebuke almost didn't sting this time.

When he got through the second section of the book without finding anything useful, he dropped it on the chair with a sigh, leaned back, and massaged his sore eyes. He needed reading glasses, but every time he bought a pair, they got broken in a fistfight or dropped down a canyon or eaten by monstrous demon larvae.

James went to the bedroom door. Curled up in the stolen bed, Elise looked almost childlike, if he ignored the injuries. Her face was relaxed and unguarded. She didn't twitch when he sat on the edge of the bed. How long had it been since she slept?

His heart ached as he watched a curl in front of her nose sway with every breath. The urge to protect her was ridiculous. There was nothing he could fend off that she couldn't. But he knew, watching her sleep, that he would do anything to defend her. Anything.

James retrieved a page from his Book of Shadows. He touched it to her skin and whispered a word of power. The cuts closed. The bruises on her face yellowed. She sighed without waking up.

He went back to reading Hume's Almanac as darkness fell. He was beginning to doze in his chair when the sky blossomed with light and the eleventh bell chimed.

James jerked upright. Elise was already standing in the doorway, a falchion in each hand. Her hair stuck up in the back where she had been laying on it.

"Let's go," she said.

Demons poured through the streets. Pillars of flame flashed through the sky with each chime. The bells reverberated through the earth, and James clung to a tree, barely staying on his feet.

Elise slashed and stabbed, as light in her hiking boots as she could have been in toe shoes. She was locked in adagio with slavering grotesques. *Ballon, aplomb, allongé*—James's former students would have been envious to see it, if not for the splattering blood.

People shrieked and fled. James wanted to tell them to go inside, to lock themselves where it was safe, but the sky fire and ravenous horde had driven them to mindless fear.

Children fell under the jaws of the demons. Not ten feet away, a man's head was bashed against rocks. Elise danced to her silent andante, slicing through flesh and bone. Her swords glistened in the rain.

She climbed on top of a stall. Demons moved to follow, but James flung a page at them. Before the rain could soak it, he shouted.

A silent explosion rocked the air, knocking the demons off their feet as though the hand of God had swatted them aside. The ones still standing turned on James.

"*Ayuda!*"

An old man with his face covered in blood ran down the street. He was followed by two of the grotesques, and he reached desperately for Elise. She grabbed his forearm and hauled him onto the stall. Then she leaped down, lashing out with both feet. Skulls cracked.

Magic poured from James, swelling and crashing with the flick of paper. He was a shining light in the gloom, his Book of Shadows like a brilliant star. He set fires and brought wind upon the demons.

There were too many. Dozens. Hundreds. The jungle seethed.

He flipped through his Book of Shadows, searching for a spell that could stop everything, to save the people ripped open by blunt teeth. But then the earth rocked with the eleventh bell and he was slammed against a wall. The Book flew from his arms.

A demon crashed into him. He saw a flash of bloody tongue a heartbeat before its heavy foot mashed into the side of his knee.

James heard a wet crunch. He hit the ground. The pain struck him a few seconds later.

He roared, gripping his leg. The demon fell on him, pressing more than two hundred pounds of weight upon his chest like the crush of a boulder. Its breath stank of acid.

"James!"

Teeth ripped into his sleeve. He shoved the demon off of him, but another took its place.

And then it shrieked, blood sprayed out of its severed neck, and disappeared. Elise stood over him where its face had been. He couldn't draw enough of a breath to thank her.

She sheathed one sword before lifting. He tried to put weight on his leg and cried out. "Lean on me," she said, pulling his arm over her shoulder.

"We can't go—those people—the Book—"

"I'll come back for it. Move!"

She dragged him from the village. Slowly, so slowly, they fought their way into the jungle, where the trees grew thick and the demons could not follow.

He slid to the ground with a groan.

"I think it's dislocated. My knee. I can't walk—can't feel my foot—"

Elise kneeled in front of him. His leg looked crooked through the slacks. She sliced open the pant leg, and her jaw tensed when she saw the unnatural twist of his knee cap. Seeing it made the pain worse.

"I'm going to relocate it," she said. "Try to relax."

"Maybe we should wait—"

But she had already put both hands on his leg and twisted.

When the sun rose, Elise sat in the common area of the village, wiping down her blades with a soft rag. It used to be someone's shirt, but they didn't need it anymore, and there was something immensely cathartic about cleaning blood off her falchions.

There were more bodies this time than after the tenth hour. Shopkeepers, farmers, laborers, friends and mothers and brothers. All dead. Losing so many lives was hardly a victory. It made her tense. Her neck felt like it might never unknot.

But cleaning her blades and gently oiling the metal—it was better than a professional massage, better than the comforting burn of whiskey, even better than her ex-boyfriend's ministrations. It made her feel a little less guilty to be sitting next to a child whose face had been torn off. Just a little.

Elise walked into an abandoned house. The doors had been left open, and rain made the carpet squish under her feet. She used the phone to call McIntyre.

"Fly to Guatemala. I need you here," she said.

His responding silence was long. "Elise…"

"Did you see what happened with the last bell?"

"How could I miss it? It was a massacre in the Warrens." He paused, and Elise thought she heard his girlfriend crying in the background. "You'd laugh if you saw how the news is trying to explain the deaths away. They're calling it a new outbreak of SARS. Those mundane bastards will make anything up to avoid seeing the truth."

"There won't be eyes to see if you don't help me," Elise said. "My aspis is out of commission. I need backup."

"And my aspis is pregnant."

Nausea flipped Elise's stomach. She gazed at the body on the couch. Flies were starting to cloud around it. "If you want Leticia to live to give birth, you need to help."

"Screw you," he said without real ire.

"You can be down here in twelve hours. We'll go get this together. It'll be the Grand Canyon all over again. Call some of your friends—I know you have a lot of them."

"And I'm the only one you have?"

That was probably meant to sting. "I have better things to do than make friends. Your priorities are fucked up."

This was an argument they had been through a dozen times. McIntyre switched tactics. "Would you leave James to save the world?"

Yes. That was the plan, after all.

"Just get down here," she said. She gave him the coordinates of the condominium. He said that he wrote them down. They hung up.

Elise found the Book of Shadows in a puddle of mud. Half of the pages were stuck together. She didn't need to be a witch to tell that they were ruined.

She stole a bottle of pills from an unoccupied pharmacy to soften the blow. James was covered in sweat and half-asleep when she returned to the condo on the beach. "Here," she said, folding two pills into his hand. "Sorry it took so long. Have you slept?"

"Barely."

He swallowed them while she looked at his knee. It had swollen to twice its normal size. She suspected there were torn ligaments and arterial damage—the kind of thing that would require surgery if he planned on walking again. "You'll get over this in no time," Elise lied.

He laughed. "Good thing I don't dance anymore."

She took an avocado from her jacket, sliced it lengthwise, and pried the pit out with her knife. He took half. "At least all the dead people mean we don't have to pay for food."

He stopped laughing.

By the time he ate the avocado and some plantains, James's color had improved, and he didn't look like he was in nearly as much pain. "We can't move you to a city for surgery," she said. "We don't have time."

"I know. But I think I can heal myself, with your help... and the Book of Shadows."

She handed the Book to him. His face fell.

"Is it enough?" she asked.

He flipped through the pages and gave a hard swallow. "It will have to be. I can do a ritual."

"Why? You've written spells more powerful than this. You could fix yourself in a half second." She took the Book of Shadows, flipping through it to one of the pages in the very back. James jerked it out of her hands.

"All my benign healing spells were destroyed."

"So use one that isn't benign."

"Do you see this?" He turned it to show her a page. It was completely obscured with ink. "This is all I have left. It would 'fix me,' but requires a small sacrifice."

"How small?"

"If I used you as the subject, it would also render you unconscious for a week."

She couldn't afford to be useless any more than he could. She considered the page. "I could get someone else. A survivor from a nearby village."

"This spell might kill a normal person."

"That's dark magic, James. Your aunt would be ashamed."

He snapped the Book shut. "As I said, we'll use a ritual."

James made a list of supplies, and she collected everything from the village of the dead. The bodies were in the same places she had left them. Nobody was coming back to dig graves.

When she returned with the stones he needed—pried from cheap jewelry at a tourist shop—and some herbs, James had created a circle of power out of pillow feathers on the bed. "What next?" she asked, eyeing his circle dubiously. He was a powerful witch, but she wasn't sure he was powerful enough to work with such a weak circle.

"I'm weak. Let me piggyback for strength."

Elise didn't hesitate to offer him a hand.

He took it, and his magic washed through her. It sent warmth cascading from the top of her skull to her toes. Her awareness of James's senses came to her one at a time—first, the smell of rain grew stronger, and then she felt his knee (which hurt as bad as she imagined), and then she glimpsed her face as though peering through his eyes. Her cheeks and eyes were hollow. She looked skeletal.

His emotions came upon her last. He was tired. Worried. Relieved to have painkillers. Happy to see Elise. Angry at all the devastation. Once the power securely fastened around them, it faded, but Elise was left unsettled. James *felt* too much.

He leaned back against the wall with a low chuckle. "I didn't realize I looked that bad." Of course, he had seen through her eyes at the same time she saw through his.

She rubbed her own aching knee. "You're fine."

Elise followed his diagrams to apply the stones and herbs to his leg. James activated several spells from his Book and left them on the bedside as they worked.

"Careful now," he said when she pulled out the bandages.

She closed her eyes to process the information coming silently from James. He showed her the motions to make, and she did.

When she was done, he eased back against the wall with a groan. "How long?" she asked.

"I'll be dancing again by tomorrow."

Elise could tell he was lying through the bond. It would

be days before he was in service again—and with a crippled Book of Shadows.

Her knee throbbed. James looked sympathetic. "I can lift the bond."

"No. You'll heal faster while piggybacked." She locked what was left of the Book in its case. "I called McIntyre again," she said, just to change the subject.

"Is he coming?"

"Yes."

"Good."

There was nothing else to say, after that.

Rain coursed down the eaves of the condo. Ocean rushed up the beach like it was going to devour them, and then receded after lapping at the wooden supports. It made the condo feel just this side of dangerous, even though James sat back on the bed. He kept Elise in the corner of his eye. She stood on the edge of the porch, and it made him nervous. He could easily imagine an errant wave rising to slap her off the balcony.

The spray blew back her hair as another crest swept toward their temporary condo. A thin layer of water sloshed over her feet. She reached out a hand so the rain drummed on her exposed fingertips, and a thrill raced through his stomach when he saw that her glove dangled from the other hand.

"Careful," James said.

She turned her hand over so the rain fell on her palm instead. "Who cares?" she muttered. "He can't get me if the world's going to end anyway."

"Let's not test the theory. Come in and close the door.

Our room is getting wet."

She pretended not to hear him. She did that a lot.

James traced the outline of a symbol onto tissue paper. He could feel the power vibrating in his wrists as he wrote it. He had filled almost the entire notebook with spells before it was damaged, one at a time. He could do it again.

His aunt had been the inventor of paper magic, but he was the innovator. There were things she taught him that nobody else knew—ways to store immense, unthinkable amounts of power; methods of copying spells without performing them again; how to distort a spell after binding it to the page—and the knowledge was so dangerous that he seldom used it.

The only person he trusted to have in the room while he worked was Elise, and she wasn't paying any attention to him. She was staring at the ocean and getting soaked.

He wrote the final curl of the symbol. The page glowed with their shared power before fading.

James carefully stood, using a tall stick as a crutch to stagger to the patio. The wind gusted around him. He braced himself on the railing. "Come inside," he said.

She trailed a finger along her palm. "Do you think He can see when one of my gloves is off?"

He didn't even like discussing the subject. James grabbed her arm and slid the glove back on. "You only get this contemplative when you're exhausted. And don't forget, I can feel what you're thinking." He tapped his temple.

Elise tucked her hands against her sides. "It doesn't matter. The twelfth hour is coming soon. I should be searching."

"You can't do anything in this downpour."

Another wave sluiced over the patio. She finally went

inside, helping James settle in bed again.

They sat in silence with nothing to entertain them but the thrum of magic as his knee knit itself together.

He tried to remember the last time they had sat together in comfortable silence for longer than a few minutes. James couldn't recall having ever done it before. They were always on the run. "This is nice," he said, surprising himself.

He was even more surprised when a smile spread across Elise's face. A real smile. "What if it was always like this?"

"What, if we were in a monsoon with a dislocated knee?"

"No," she said, gesturing between them. "Like…this. You and me. Not fighting. Not running."

James studied her for a long moment—damp hair stuck to her forehead, bruises on her jaw, bandages concealing her arm. "It can't ever be like this. We can't stop running."

"I know. But…what if we could?"

The question gave weight to the air between them. James was tired, and it wasn't just because of the healing. He was tired of having no home. He was tired of trying to stay a step ahead of the death that pursued them. In the past, he had imagined what would happen if he could stop, and it involved reconciling with Hannah and rejoining the coven, but James hadn't dwelled on those thoughts long. The fantasies hurt.

He tried to imagine stopping with Elise. Living a normal life. He couldn't fathom what that would be like.

"It would be nice to teach again," he said slowly. "I could start a dance company."

"I've always wanted to own a business."

"Really? I didn't know that."

She shrugged. It wasn't something they had ever

discussed. "Maybe I could be in your company. I could be a professional with enough practice. I think it would be... fun."

Those were the probably most words she had ever strung together that didn't have anything to do with dying.

"You should sleep," she said, tipping a couple more pills out of the bottle on the bedside. He swallowed them. "You'll heal faster."

She was right. His eyes fell closed, and he let himself relax as the painkillers kicked in. His breathing grew deep and even, keeping time with the ocean, and he thought he could almost hear Elise's heartbeat. He could certainly feel the magic knitting his knee, even as he dozed.

The fatigue of healing and magic was powerful. It sucked him under.

He wasn't sure how long he floated in the gray haze before he felt lips on his forehead. "Take care of yourself," Elise whispered. It alarmed him on some distant level, but he couldn't rouse himself enough to figure out why.

When James woke up, the active bond had been closed, and Elise was gone.

Elise gave McIntyre sixteen hours before calling him back. He was still in Las Vegas when he answered.

"I've sent two of my friends down to help you," he said. "This guy, Bryce, and a kid called Diego—he's already close. They're going to meet you at the condo. They should only be four hours away, max."

"You're a goddamn bastard, Lucas McIntyre."

He blew air out of his lips. "Maybe you'll have a family

someday. Maybe you'll understand then."

"Not a chance in hell," she said.

Bryce and Diego. Elise didn't know any kopides named Bryce and Diego, and she didn't *want* to know them. Whenever she ran across other hunters, like her, they were always a disappointment—too weak, too emotional, or too fixated on her gender. She had never met another kopis she couldn't hate, and that included her ex-boyfriend. She wouldn't go into a fight with anyone but James or McIntyre.

So Elise armed herself and went into the undercity.

The entrance was easy to locate. Demons left telltale marks to help each other find their dens: a stack of rocks, a symbol carved into a tree, a sign with demonic text written in graffiti on the back.

She found the trap door in the basement of a shop five miles away. It was dirty and smelled like a latrine, but the mark on the wall was unmistakable.

Elise descended the narrow steps. The air became still as the world above was blocked out, and soon, she only had her flashlight as a guide. When she finally reached the bottom, her legs were weak, her nerves were ragged, and one sword was drawn.

She took a deep breath and pushed through.

The undercity should have been a home away from home for the horrors that lived on Earth. It *should* have been teeming with life.

But it was motionless. The buildings were rotten from time and mildew, and faced the path with open doors. Empty.

Where were the demons?

Elise took a step forward and her foot connected with something soft. She knew without having to look that it was a body, and once she recognized the first, she saw the rest—lumpy shapes spread across the uneven ground of the cavern.

She kneeled to examine the body at her feet. It had the same marks as the corpses of the humans on the surface. Bones gnawed by dull teeth, missing flesh, shattered skull. The tolling of the bells had struck underground, too.

Stomach acid soured the back of her mouth as she slipped through the undercity, stepping around bodies and avoiding sinkholes. Something smelled like brimstone.

She strode through the city, focusing on the path. Elise didn't want to see the racks where they hung slaves for sale. She didn't want to see the demons—many of which were indistinguishable from humans—that lay in bloody piles.

It looked so similar to Dis. There were even skulls over the doorways. They grinned at her with missing teeth and dusty eye sockets.

Many of the homes had pens in front of them, too. In Dis, it was where they kept their more docile slaves. In this undercity, there were strange, grotesque skeletons instead —unholy things that looked like a mix of pig and human. Chills rolled down her spine. She refocused on the street.

So many dead. The air was thick with it.

Elise ducked out of one cavern into the next, following a short tunnel that had been carved by a stream. It let out into a murky pool.

Something scraped on the shore. She lifted her swords, gripping the hilts so tightly that her arms trembled.

A dark form on the ground moved, then groaned. A

survivor.

Elise made a wide circle around it, squinting through the dim red glow. It looked like a human, but no human had skin so papery-thin that the outlines of its bones were visible. Its eyes twitched open. They were completely black.

"*Tikest vo*," it whispered in a quavering voice. That was the demon language. James spoke it, but Elise didn't.

"Don't move," she said.

It gave another groan, and spoke again, this time in Latin. "Help me."

Cautiously, she sheathed one of the swords and kneeled at its side. The young nightmare was dying. Its skin faded in and out of Elise's vision. For a few seconds it looked like a skeleton with a tangle of innards; then it faded back.

Nightmares couldn't be killed by physical means—it could suffer for centuries without disappearing.

"I need to find the clock," she said.

A pale hand reached for her. She jerked back. "It hurts," said the nightmare. "Help me. Please."

Elise set her jaw. "Do you know where it is?" After a moment, it nodded. "I need to find it."

The skin faded. The nightmare shivered. "This path goes down," it said. "Down. Beyond the Temple of Yatam—a stair. Down, down, down."

"Is that where the chamber is?"

Its skeletal hand touched her arm. Elise's skin crawled. "The door is behind the statue." Its black eyes begged. "Please."

She didn't have her exorcism charms, but the blade of her sword was carved with some of the same symbols. She slid the falchion between two of its ribs. "*Crux sacra sit mihi lux. Non draco sit mihi dux. Vade retro, Satana, nunquam suade mihi vana. Sunt mala quae libas. Ispe venena bibas."* The sword glowed briefly. The demon's eyes fell closed. "Return to the Hell in which you belong. Begone."

Its hand slipped off her arm, and a moment later, the body was gone. She stood over the place it had rested and stared at the empty ground. Killing demons was usually satisfying, but this time, she felt nothing.

"Be at peace," Elise said to the empty chamber, sheathing her sword. She was surprised to mean it.

There was only one other path leading down from the cavern. Elise took it. It sloped into darkness, away from the red glow of the undercity, and she followed it down, down, down.

It took her an hour to reach the Temple of Yatam. The path opened into a quiet chamber with smooth walls. A stream spilled down the rocks to her right in a frothy mist, illuminated by the flickering glow of blue flame.

The only thing that made the room look like a temple were nine columns surrounding a faceless statue. It stared at her without eyes. Elise edged around it. As the nightmare said, there was a stair behind the statue, spiraling deeper into the ground. The air grew warmer and warmer as she descended.

Distantly, through the earth, Elise could hear the clock. Every swing of its pendulum gently rocked everything around her. Rock groaned. Dust showered from the roof of the stairwell. The stairs felt like they swayed from side to side—the slightest motion that made the entire world vibrate.

Tick...tock... The clock echoed through the air.

At first, she didn't realize she heard it with her ears. But then she came upon a doorway and stumbled through, and she saw it.

The clock stood at the end of a very long chamber with sloping walls that rose high above her in the shape of four-sided pyramid. Elise wouldn't have been able to reach its face if she stood on James's shoulders. The mechanisms inside its body were made of glistening white stone.

The dagger-shaped pendulum rocked in time with every beat. It pulsed through her and made it hard to breathe. The hands on the face crept toward the place the twelve should have been—and all six were going to align simultaneously.

Dusty skeletons lay on platforms around the edges of the room. Scraps of red cloth hung from the bones, although time had eaten most of the robes away. They trembled with every *tick* and *tock* of the swinging pendulum.

Elise made her way through the room, stepping around metal grates that blasted hot air. She peered into one as she passed. It glowed red faintly, as though there were fires miles below.

She had to climb onto another platform to reach the body of the clock. It was almost too loud to approach. Elise drew her left-hand sword as she peered into the workings of the clock. Something throbbed in the depths of its cogs —a heart.

Why hadn't the hour struck yet?

She didn't wait to find out. There had to be attendants somewhere close.

Make it fast.

Bracing herself, Elise seized the handle on the cage of its body and swung it open.

A distant *thud* rocked the pyramid. The platform pitched beneath her feet. An invisible hand smashed into her chest, shoving her away from the clock.

She soared through the air and struck the opposite wall. The sword clattered out of her hand. Elise collapsed onto a grate and the metal seared her skin.

The *tick tock* was even louder than before. The beating heart thrummed. And when she rolled over, her face came up against a pair of bare feet. Her gaze traveled up bare legs.

The woman wore a necklace of skulls. Her dark hair was tangled with teeth, her dagger was carved of stone, and her hips were draped in folds of leather. The silhouettes of demons framed her—dozens of them. The stink of brimstone was strong.

"What a surprise," said the goddess in perfect Latin.

Elise leaped for her sword.

Something connected with her head from behind. It cracked her skull and rattled her brain.

A flash of white light—and then darkness.

Elise could see the sky.

Her eyes opened to slivers. There was a window above her—an open square too small for a human to slip through. The sky was a churning mass of violet and crimson.

No, wait. That wasn't a sky at all. It was smoke from the fires beneath the clock.

Elise was still inside the pyramid. But she was in a separate room, with the same jagged gray stone and hazy air. Her eyes and throat burned with it.

She had been chained to the wall. Her hip burned, and she shifted her legs out from under her, stretching out to see a mess of blood smearing her shirt. When had she been injured?

"That came from my children. They wanted a taste."

Elise twisted around, trying to see the speaker, but the goddess stood beyond her field of vision. Her motion was limited by the shackles. "Who are you?"

The response came right behind her ear. "I am the cold kiss of death," she whispered, "and you can never defeat me."

Elise's stomach churned. "Let me go."

"No. You chose to come. Now you must live with that choice—and die for it."

"I'll kill you," she said. It wasn't a threat. Just a statement of fact.

"Maybe. Alive or dead, I will come back for you." The flames outside flared, turning the smoke from purple to orange before fading back to red. A blast of heat filled the room.

Somewhere in the pyramid, people were screaming. Human voices. Elise wasn't the only one trapped.

The goddess stepped in front of her, blocking her view of the window. In one hand, she held a staff of sharpened human bone; in the other, a stone knife carved with symbols. The whites of her eyes were consumed with the endless darkness of space.

"I didn't expect anyone to find me," she said, "much less the greatest kopis. I've heard of you."

Elise responded by twisting her wrists in the shackles. They rubbed against the skin of her right wrist, and she realized one of her gloves had been removed. She clenched her fist.

The goddess must have seen what was on her palm. She must have known what it meant. And she wouldn't have been there if she didn't need Elise alive.

"You're missing something for the clock—something that's keeping you from tearing apart Hell and Earth. It's a sacrifice, isn't it?"

"Astute," the goddess said.

Elise shifted, and her chains rattled. It wasn't hard to be astute when she was tied up like a pig waiting for the spit.

The woman kneeled in front of her. She smiled.

Then she buried the point of the knife in Elise's shoulder.

Pain flamed down her skin. She grit her teeth and took deep breaths, refusing to cry out. It only hurt worse when the goddess pulled the knife free.

"You can't think this will do any good," Elise said, her voice barely shaking. "You can't kill me yet. Not like this. Not without screwing up your apocalyptic plans."

Her laugh was deep and throaty. From anyone else, it would have been pleasant to hear.

"Who says I plan to use you?"

The goddess dragged the knife down her chest, drawing a line of pain along her skin in crimson ink. Elise's blood swelled and dripped in a line down her ribs.

I won't scream. I won't scream.

Her resolve lasted for almost an hour. The goddess lasted much longer.

Part 4: The Walking Dead

Chapter 4

Reno – May 2009

The afternoon arrived bright and sunny despite the steel-gray clouds lingering overhead. The sun should have warmed the air, but the light only succeeded in washing the colors out of the already-barren landscape. Beads of rain quivered underneath the letters on the street sign, *Westfield*.

Anthony Morales slowed his Jeep to a stop in front of Motion and Dance and glanced at the clock on his dashboard. Three-fifteen. Betty hadn't asked him to pick her up until four (or, as the text had said "get me or die!"), but Elise handled the finances for the coven, and she always went in on the esbats.

There was movement beyond the glass doors. It was probably Elise.

He examined his reflection in the visor mirror, trying to order his brown curls by running his fingers through his hair. Anthony only succeeded in messing it up further. He scrubbed at an oil mark on his cheek. It was the best he could do for his appearance—he couldn't make himself into Don Juan with a little spit and an attempt at a suave smirk.

He tried out the smile on himself, but it quickly faded. Smirk or not, Elise was way out of his league. She usually made him feel like nothing but Betty's kid cousin.

A man Anthony recognized as James, the high priest of Betty's coven, emerged from behind the building. He propped the open front door and went inside. All Anthony knew about the high priest came from his cousin, who liked to use adjectives like "dreamy" for him and said he was the most important person in the world to Elise.

"What kind of guy is a *witch*, anyway?" Anthony muttered to himself, climbing out of the Jeep.

Subsiding into half-coherent insults, he slammed the driver's side door and headed up the sidewalk to the front doors. He heard voices and hung back to listen, easing in sideways to see who was talking.

James and Elise were in the midst of an animated conversation. Her posture was straight, shoulders back, chin lifted, like she was ready to fight.

"You were the one who wanted me to investigate, and I did. You see this?"

"I'm sorry."

"This is serious, James, real serious, and I don't want to be involved. I don't want *you* involved."

"What will the Ramirezes do? Someone has to help them, and if—"

She cut him off. "I'm not going over this again."

All the tension drained from James's shoulders, and he leaned forward to press his lips to her forehead. She closed her eyes. He whispered something into her hair, but it was too quiet for Anthony to make out.

A swell of jealousy rose in his chest, and he bumped the door with his foot. The entrance bell jingled.

James's straightened. He glanced at Anthony without expression. "We'll talk more about this later."

Elise's mouth stretched into thin line. "Fine." James left, and she sighed, rolling her right shoulder to loosen it.

Anthony opened his mouth to speak, but words failed him—Elise always managed to render him nonverbal. Today, she wore a shirt that was swooped low in the front to reveal a lot of cleavage that he had to struggle not to look at. She was wearing gloves again—she always wore gloves—and cutoff shorts.

He cleared his throat and tried to find his voice. "Hi, Elise." He shouldn't stare at her legs, either. Really.

She sat down at the reception desk, dragging a squat filing cabinet to her side. "What are you doing here? Did you feel like taking up ballet all of a sudden?"

"No," he said. "I'm picking up Betty."

"The coven's not done for another half hour."

"I guess I lost track of the time."

The corner of Elise's mouth twitched. "That's fine. You can hang out with me while we wait for the witches to finish. They're boring when they're meditating."

"Awesome," Anthony said, and he tried not to sound *too* enthusiastic about it. He took the second chair and moved over.

The door between the entryway and the dance hall was open and James's voice echoed through the studio. "How did that meditation make you feel? Ann?"

"I felt in tune with the Earth," she responded. "It was relaxing. Finals have been crazy."

Others made assenting noises. Elise made a face at Anthony, and he grinned.

"You feel like working? There's a lot of paperwork to go through," she said. "I need to find where James stashed last year's registrations that came through the workforce education program. They have to be here. He's organized, but in the most obscure way possible."

"I would love to help," he said, and Elise turned the filing cabinet to face him.

Anthony absorbed himself in his search, trying to forget how tedious he found paperwork. She focused on her laptop, fingers ticking away at the keyboard, and Anthony shuffled through the folders. Elise's bare legs occupied the corner of his vision.

The seconds dragged. She hadn't been joking about James's bizarre methods of organization—everything was neatly tagged and labeled, but with indecipherable codes. He had no idea what "G-3B" had to do with receipts for cleaning supplies, or why the thick folder full of yellow-tabbed sheet music was marked "T6" (or why it was between the receipts and what looked like coven inventory lists), but it meant that Anthony had to read everything to figure out what it was.

He distracted himself from his chore by scooting his chair back enough to peek through the door to the next room. An assortment of women and men rested comfortably on cushions around a small altar. Smoke rose from a censer between them.

Anthony's cousin sat beside James, her blonde hair pulled into loose pigtails. She listened raptly to the high priest, nodding along with everything he said.

"As we discussed last week, Marisa's family is facing some troubles right now," James said. "An exorcist determined that Lucinde may be possessed. I believe we should partake in a cleansing ritual."

Elise began typing with renewed vigor. "Do you hear this?" he whispered.

"I don't listen to their crazy witch nonsense."

"Who's the exorcist?" Ann asked.

"She prefers to preserve her anonymity," James said.

"It would be so interesting to talk to her for my thesis. It's on the supernatural and old-world religion in modern times."

"I can pass along questions for you." His tone left no room for argument. "What do you all think of my proposal?"

"An exorcist," Anthony murmured. "It's like they think they're in a movie or something."

Elise typed harder.

"Do you mean actual demons, or the kind of demons we regard as goddesses, like Lilith?" asked a man whose voice Anthony didn't recognize.

"The two aren't mutually exclusive," James explained. "This one may be little more than an angry spirit, though. As such, it can be cleansed and cast out with ritual and positive energy."

"I don't think we should get into it," Ann said. "Demons are risky business."

Elise sighed and stretched in her chair, drawing Anthony's attention away from the conversations in the other room.

"It's hot in here," she said, slipping off her sweater.

He had to look. Her tanned skin was flecked with freckles, creating alluring trails that dipped down into the neckline of her shirt and out along her shoulders. He would happily explore those paths with his fingers and lips, if he could just get the balls to make a move.

And then the sweater dropped enough for him to see the gashes—three deep, parallel slices on her arm. That was what James had apologized for. Had he hurt her?

"What happened to your arm?" he asked.

"What? Oh. I got attacked by a bush when I was out running last night." She pulled her sweater back on. "It's nothing."

"I thought you said you felt hot."

"I changed my mind. I'm going to close this door, okay?" She shut it, and the coven's conversation became an inaudible mumble.

He struggled to think of something right to say. He had a hard time imagining James, who was a witch (of all the stupid things) and a dancer (even stupider) managing to injure Elise. But if he had, Anthony couldn't let it slide. He just wasn't sure he could take James in a fight.

Suppressing the wild and ridiculous urge to challenge James to a duel, Anthony held up a folder. "I think I found the registration forms."

She gave it a quick scan. "That's it. Great." Elise immediately turned her attention back to the computer. "Thanks for the help."

"Yeah, no problem," he said, and then he took a deep breath. "Maybe you'd like to hang out tonight. There's this band performing at the Knitting Factory. I know you listen to Black Death, and this band is supposed to be a lot like their early work."

"Yeah? What time?"

"Doors open at eight...but we could get dinner, if you like. Before the show."

Elise's eyes narrowed. "Are you asking me on a date?"

He gave her his attempt at a suave smile.

"Yes?"

The time until she responded dragged on. It couldn't have been longer than a moment or two, but the sudden racing of Anthony's heart made it feel like hours, and

Elise's expression was unreadable.

She didn't smile at his suggestion, but she didn't laugh at him, either, which had to be a good sign.

"Yeah," Elise said. "That sounds good."

Relief washed through his body. The next second, it was replaced with nervousness. "Cool," Anthony said, jamming his fists in his pockets. "Cool. Since I'm just in the duplex next to yours, we could go together. That way, only one of us has to drive. With the price of gas and parking and stuff."

"Oh yeah. Gas is a huge concern from here to downtown," she said. "I have things to do tonight, so I don't have time for dinner, but I can meet you for the concert."

"Then it's a date," he said.

Elise nodded, turned back to her laptop, and started typing again.

Why did he feel even more nervous now than before he had asked her out?

The door between the rooms opened, and the coven emerged. James exited first, accompanied by a leggy strawberry-blond.

"We'll need more information on Lucinde before we decide to do a cleansing," the woman said. "I don't feel comfortable performing a ritual unless we've ruled out a health problem."

"What do you suggest?"

"Lucinde has had extended hospital stays, so her medical records should be there," Stephanie said. "I could look at them."

James cast a glance at Elise. "We should discuss this somewhere quieter. Come upstairs."

Ann trailed behind the last of the coven. Her ratty

brown hair was pulled into a ponytail at the nape of her neck. She hauled a heavy backpack over her shoulder and wandered over, waving at Elise.

"Hi guys," she snuffled, digging through her pockets and coming up with a packet of tissues.

He gave a weak wave. Through Betty's chronic inability to dislike people, she had managed to collect some bizarre friends over the years—Elise included—but Ann might have been the weirdest. She was an undergraduate at the university where Betty worked on her thesis. They met at the library while researching obscure blood diseases, which led to Ann joining the coven, and now she was Betty's latest pet project.

"Weird stuff, huh?" Ann asked Elise.

She didn't look up. "Yes."

"What do you think about this whole thing with Marisa's daughter?"

"I don't think much about it at all."

"Just seems too bad, you know?" Ann stepped closer to allow Morrighan to pass, and Elise rolled her chair a few inches back. "Poor kid. Still going to the gym tonight?"

Anthony stole a look at Elise. She had finally given her attention to Ann. He had no idea what her expression meant, but if Elise ever looked at him like that, he would have run in the opposite direction. "Yes."

"Guess I'll see you there. Bye!" She lurched out of the studio. The heavy backpack on her shoulder gave her a lopsided walk.

A squealing golden blur struck Anthony in the side, and he staggered.

"You came!" Betty exclaimed, squeezing her cousin tight. Anthony made a gurgling noise.

Elise's cold look dissolved. "Did you leave any espresso

at the Starbucks you violated?"

"I only had two triple fraps this morning," she said, and then she gave Anthony another squeeze. Betty was not a small girl—she was equal to Anthony in both height and weight, and he had to struggle to breathe.

"Why does Ann know we're going to the gym tonight?" Elise asked.

Betty released Anthony. "Ooh. I invited her to come along. That's okay, right?"

"The gym is a public place."

"Yeah, but I invited her to come, you know, work out with us. She looks like she could use some exercise, and I know she's got to be lonely going to college so far from her parents, so *please* tell me you were nice to her."

Elise chose not to respond, turning back to the computer instead.

"She was…polite," Anthony said. Betty rolled her eyes.

"Elise! Did you *have* to scare her?"

"I said she was polite," he protested.

"Yeah, but I know my roommate better than that. Look, if it's a problem, you can skip the gym tonight and I'll just hang out with Ann. Okay?"

"I don't mind," Elise said, although it sounded like she did mind very, very much. "I have to take these papers back to my office before we can work out. I'm going to go."

"Yeah, yeah. I should change clothes anyway. I'm not exactly exercise-appropriate right now." Betty pointed at her breasts, which were very prominently displayed in what was probably a continuing attempt to get James to look at them. "Ready, cuz?"

"Sure," Anthony said reluctantly. "Let's go."

"Cool," Betty said. "See you later, Elise!" She dragged

him away by the elbow. "Come on, I want time to shower, too."

Anthony sighed. "I don't see why you want to shower *before* you go get sweaty."

"One day I'll explain the concept of 'looking sexy for hot guys at the gym' to you," she said, ruffling his hair affectionately. "I heard you making plans with my foxy best friend. What are you guys doing tonight?"

"What? Nothing," Anthony said, reaching in to unlock Betty's door.

She shot Anthony a sly look. "Don't give me that. I heard you flirting with Elise."

His cheeks heated. Oh God. Now Betty was never going to let him forget it. "I was helping her find some papers, and we talked a little. That's all. We were talking."

"Shopping amongst the cougars, huh? I thought I'd raised you better than that."

"You're sick, Betty."

"What were you talking about?"

She was staring at him, and Anthony had to say *something*. He thought of the gashes on Elise's arms, and her long legs, and James confronting Elise about her injuries. He thought of her smile and the Knitting Factory, and secretive high priests with exorcists on-call.

But he only shrugged.

"Just the usual stuff," Anthony said.

A half an hour later, Elise hadn't left for the office. She was still staring at the same cell on the spreadsheet with her fingers poised over the number pad.

Anthony had asked her on a date. It was…well, weird.

Elise had only dated one guy before—another kopis, back when she was eighteen. He turned out to be a total waste of oxygen, but Elise's life had been too dangerous to share with anyone anyway. A normal guy like Anthony wouldn't have stood a chance.

Things had changed since then, but she still hadn't been on a date in years. Sex was nothing but a distant memory. Elise wasn't sure if she was excited, confused, terrified, or all of the above.

James wandered back inside the entryway, Stephanie at his side.

"Thank you for your help," he said.

"It's for Lucinde," the doctor said firmly, twisting a key off her key ring. Her fingers lingered on his when she passed it over.

"I'll return this to you tonight."

"I look forward to seeing you." She strode out of the room, three-inch heels ringing out against the wooden floor. Stephanie smelled like she bathed in Victoria's Secret perfume, and the scent mingled poorly with the odor of incense.

"The doctor has a great bedside manner," Elise remarked.

"We're going to retrieve Lucinde's hospital records tonight. Stephanie wants to be certain that there isn't some other problem we need to address before taking care of the metaphysical end of things, but she can't walk out with Lucinde's records for no reason."

"She's a better candidate for it than we are."

"She also has a meeting with the board scheduled. It's more convenient if we take them."

"That's called stealing, James," Elise said. "She could get a slap on the wrist for taking them. We'll get arrested."

James pinched the bridge of his nose and sighed. "We have the key to the records room, which is usually unattended at night, so we won't get caught if we're quick about it. You don't have to come."

She gathered the papers on the desk. "This is a bad idea."

"Fine, then I'll—"

"I'm not going to let you do it alone. I'll come along." Elise hugged the folder to her chest, taking a deep breath and letting it out slowly. "Look...you know I don't care about stealing, but we can't take long. I have plans."

"Plans?"

"Yeah. I'm about to go to the gym, and then I have a date."

James took a few seconds to respond.

"A date. I'm glad to hear it."

Elise's eyes narrowed. "You're not mad? You hated my last boyfriend."

"You were eighteen and he was an idiot. You should have fun." He checked his watch. "When do you want to go over to the hospital? I was thinking seven."

"That's fine."

James left to clean up the altar in the other room. "If he's so certain dating Anthony is okay, then why aren't I?" Elise asked the empty entryway. Unsurprisingly, it didn't respond.

She stopped by the bank to deposit David Nicholas's check before going to the gym. It made her feel warm to look on his signature and recall his expression as he slashed it underneath that large number, and Elise couldn't wait to turn those warm feelings into her half of rent for the month.

"This check is bad," the teller announced.

Elise had been drifting in a daydream of being able to pay off her credit card, but this announcement brought her back to reality as quickly as a blow from a hammer.

"What?"

"This check is bad," he repeated slowly, one word at a time. "There's a twelve dollar fine for attempting to cash a bad check. If you go down to the office of the—"

"How the hell is it *bad*?"

He typed at his terminal, looking bored. "This account number belongs to our bank, but it's been closed for a year. No money. Bad check. Twelve dollar fine. Understand?"

Elise made two mental notes: Firstly, that she should use a credit union instead of a bank apparently staffed by pure evil, and secondly, that David Nicholas was going to die.

The teller shredded the check as Elise watched, and her heart dropped into her stomach.

"Have a nice day," he said with a big smile.

Chapter 5

Elise and James pulled into the parking lot in front of the hospital as the sun dropped behind the mountains, setting the sky aflame. A wet chill lowered the temperature several degrees. She shivered and shrunk into her coat.

"Nice summer we have coming along," she muttered.

James locked the car. "Let's get inside."

They passed through the hospital doors and all sound died. It felt as though the volume on life had been turned down low in the empty halls.

James glanced down at his watch. "Stephanie said the records room is empty during shift turnover. If we head down now, we should have enough time to get in and out before someone comes down."

"What happens if we get caught?"

He smiled mirthlessly. "We get arrested."

Her forehead throbbed with the first signs of a headache. She shut her eyes and pressed the heel of her palm against her temple. "That doctor of yours better help us out if we get in trouble. It's her fault we're here in the first place."

"But it isn't her fault Augustin Ramirez refused to cooperate with us," James said. A sharp pain lanced through Elise's skull, and she gave a small gasp. "Are you all right?"

"I don't know what's wrong. I feel strange. Almost as though…"

Almost as though there was something that didn't belong in a hospital.

She let out a slow breath and stretched out her senses, probing the strange presence.

"Elise?" James asked when she was silent for too long.

"It's a demon," she said. "Faint. Weak."

"An actual demon, or one of the Gray?"

She tilted her head to the side as if trying to catch the faint strains of a distant song. It made her ache from crown to jaw. "Hellborn."

"What's it doing in a Catholic hospital?"

"I would love to find out." Elise punched the down button.

The elevator began to lower, and Elise's sense of the hellborn grew stronger by every inch they dropped. She covered her eyes with the heels of her palms, pressing gently, as though she could squeeze the uncomfortable itch out of her skull.

The doors opened on the basement level, and James consulted a map Stephanie had scribbled on the dance studio's stationary.

"The medical records office is over here," James said, peering through a door with a window. "There should be a fax machine inside."

"Okay," Elise said. "Watch the hall."

She slipped into the records room. It was a long room filled with shelves, and at the far end stood a desk and plastic chair.

It clearly wasn't designed to be comfortable for human

occupation: the walls were concrete and water-stained, and the carpet was hardly in better condition. The only lights were harsh and unsteady, flickering on when Elise flipped the light switch.

She went along the side of the room, searching for the records that began with R. She found them quickly, but locating Lucinde's records in particular was much more difficult. There were so many folders all over the place—she couldn't imagine how the hospital hadn't moved to digital records yet.

She thumbed through the names. Rand. Randall. Ramirez. *Success.*

Elise skimmed Lucinde's records as she began feeding them through. She continued to skim the second part of the stack, which contained duplicate records from Lucinde's general practitioner. Chicken pox, a case of the flu, referrals to several cardiologists over the years. Elise didn't see anything about psychoses.

Each sheet of paper seemed to take forever to feed through the machine, and slow inch by slow inch she grew more nervous. She strained to detect any noise from the hallway, half-certain she would hear James failing to ward off a nurse outside. With David Nicholas's bounced check, she definitely couldn't afford an attorney.

The fax kicked out the rest of the papers and beeped. She put them back in the folder.

A pulsing noise throbbed between Elise's ears. The pit of her stomach dropped, and a familiar nausea crept through Elise's body. She slid the folder into place and headed for the door, holding her stomach.

And then the pulse *burst.*

She staggered, slamming against the wall. Her dinnertime snack of yogurt and granola rose into her throat. She took slow, shallow breaths, trying to hold off the urge to vomit—and failed. The sour tang of bile flooded her mouth.

There was something in the hospital, and James was alone outside.

She spat into the trash can, wiped her mouth with the back of her hand, and threw open the door.

James was not waiting for Elise outside.

For a second, all she could do was stare at the naked man standing where her aspis should have been. He wasn't breathing. In fact, he didn't look like he was alive at all. A toe tag dragged on the ground beside him.

She would have been sure he was a corpse, except that he was standing, and staring, and drooling. Corpses couldn't drool.

Someone whispered behind Elise. *"Take care of her."*

She spun, but the hall behind her stretched empty. A light flickered several feet down.

A heavy weight slammed into Elise's side, and all the breath rushed out of her body. She struck the floor an instant later. Pain exploded in her shoulder.

Elise squirmed out from under his body, freeing her legs so that her foot could lash out. The kick landed in his face. He reeled, unable to get his balance. Another kick, and he collapsed.

His shoulders twitched, and a shudder ran through his body. His mouth flopped open, and his tongue rolled out, covered in thick green mucous.

"Elise," he said from the floor. His mouth didn't move to articulate the words, and the voice was garbled and echoing. He almost sounded...feminine. "I wish you hadn't become involved."

She stared. *"What?"*

The hallway lights flickered once, and went out completely.

Elise backtracked and hit the wall. She blinked rapidly, trying to make out shapes in the darkness, but the only light came from around the corner, and it wasn't enough.

Something moved, slipping across the floor, scraping on the linoleum.

She spun, trying to face the source of the noise. It moved behind her, and she raised her fists. "Who's there?" Elise said, trying to sound calm. Adrenaline sang through her veins.

More noises. Almost like...claws.

To her right.

She twisted, but not quickly enough. Pain flamed across her torso.

She cried out, clutching her stomach. Elise could almost see bulbous eyes sparkle in the darkness, but it darted away before she could focus.

She threw herself at the motion and barreled into something living.

They rolled. Elise punched blindly and was rewarded with the shriek of something inhuman, something terrible. Another fiend. She threw her body weight to roll it over, grabbing at what she hoped was its neck and pressing against the linoleum.

"Who do you work for?" she demanded.

It choked.

Something struck the back of Elise's head. A gong chimed in her skull, shooting pain down her spine, and she fell.

The fiend scrabbled away. It sounded like the footsteps moved all around her, up and down, inside her skull.

The noise faded. She floated in a sea of her own pulse,

trying to feel her limbs. Her fingers twitched, and then her toes. *Thank God.*

Where had they gone?

"Elise?"

Lights flared on. Elise moaned, covering her eyes. The pressure in her head had suddenly disappeared, and despite the pain in every inch of her body, she felt better. The fiends—and the body—were gone.

"James," she groaned. "Help me up." He knelt by her side and lifted her into a sitting position.

"Are you okay?" he asked, touching her arms, her forehead, her shoulders, her neck. When his fingers brushed the back of her head, she flinched.

"Yeah," Elise groaned. "But...don't touch that again. Where did you go?"

"A nurse passed and I had to ask her where the bathroom was to allay suspicion," he said. "I doubled back as soon as I could. How bad are you hurt?"

"I could be a hell of a lot worse." She parted her jacket to check out her stomach. "Oh, damn. I liked this shirt." It was torn into bloody shreds.

"We need to get you upstairs. What happened?" he asked, helping Elise stand.

"That thing I was feeling earlier," she said. "It was a fiend. And something else, too."

"A fiend?"

She stumbled when she tried to stand. James caught her. "They're these little gargoyle-looking demon things." Elise touched her fingers to the back of her head. They came away clean. "I don't think they like me."

"At least we're in the right place for horrible injuries."

"I'm fine," she said. "All I need is a shot of whiskey and an aspirin."

"I want Stephanie to check you out," he said. Elise groaned. "Head injuries are dangerous things. We'll want that looked at." She didn't respond, so he went on. "You're saying a lesser hellborn was just wandering the hospital?"

"Not quite." They got into the elevator, and she leaned against the wall. Even that small motion made her ache. "The fiend was with someone. I don't know who. He was dead."

James stared. "…Dead."

"Yeah." The elevator chimed and began to move. "There was a toe tag on his foot and his skin was blue. He looked like he'd been dead for a couple days."

"So the fiend was dragging him."

"No."

"How was it moving him, then?"

"You're not getting what I'm saying," Elise said. "He attacked me. He was animate, but…unconscious."

"A zombie," James said.

"I guess. Damn, my head hurts."

"Hold still. We're nearly there."

They got off at the ground level, and James guided Elise toward the nurse's station. He interrupted a passing candy striper. "Excuse me, but do you know where Dr. Whyte is at the moment?"

"She just went that way." The girl pointed.

Just around the corner, Stephanie spoke to a pair of men in suits clutching attaché cases. She took one look at the blood on Elise's shirt and excused herself, ushering James and Elise into an empty room.

"What happened?" the doctor asked, snapping on a pair of blue latex gloves.

"I got in a fight. Something—someone—hit me in the back of the head."

Stephanie nodded. "Sit."

Elise perched herself on the bed, and Stephanie drew a chair up to her side. The doctor thumbed open Elise's eyelids. She had a second to register Stephanie's badge—Dr. Whyte, with so many degrees after her name they almost didn't fit—before a bright light blinded her.

"What year is it?"

"Two thousand nine."

"Hold still. What's your full name?"

"Elise Christine Kavanagh."

Stephanie shone the light in her other eye. "Good. Move your arms. Good. And your legs." She grabbed a blood pressure cuff off the wall and gestured for Elise to remove her coat. "Hold still for a minute."

"Is she okay?" James asked, hovering nearby as Stephanie worked.

After a handful of quiet seconds, the doctor took the stethoscope out of her ears again and removed the cuff. "If someone was trying to hurt you badly, they failed. Here, have a couple of these." Stephanie pulled a bottle of extra-strength headache medicine out of her pocket. "For the next few days, you need to watch out for headaches, sudden fatigue, difficulties with speech or sight. If you experience any of these symptoms, call an ambulance. What happened to your abdomen?"

"Fight with a rabid badger," she said curtly. "Do you have time to look at it or not?"

"I could be spending this time making friends with the directors." Stephanie pressed a thermometer to Elise's forehead. "You're surprisingly healthy for fighting badgers. Take off your shirt and lay back." She grit her teeth and lifted her shirt over her head. The skin below her strapless bra was torn and bloody. Purple bruises were rapidly rising on her torso. "When did you get in this fight?"

"Just a few minutes ago."

"Interesting. This looks hours old." Stephanie probed Elise's stomach with her fingers. "Did you two get what we need?"

"Yes," James said, slipping the key into her jacket pocket. "Thank you."

"How did it look?"

"You're the professional. You'll have to decide," Elise said. "Ouch. Is this necessary?"

"Does it hurt more when I press down or when I release?"

"When you press down."

"Lucky for you, all this blood isn't a sign of internal damage." She examined the scratches on Elise's arm from the night before. "Are you a frequent visitor to my emergency room?"

"No, I usually treat my own wounds," she said, pulling her arm away from Stephanie.

"Well, in *that* case..." She worked quickly—and not gently. Stephanie wrapped bandages around Elise's torso to hold the sterile pads in place. "You two better get out of here. I'll review Lucinde's files later. Do you think you can get the coven together again tomorrow?"

"I'll do what I can," James said. "You have my phone number if you'd like to come over and look at the files, Stephanie."

"Come on," Elise interrupted, hopping off the table as she buttoned her jacket over the bandages, "let's get out of here. I have a concert to attend."

Chapter 6

Elise woke up tangled in blood-stained sheets.

Her first panicked thought was that she had been attacked overnight. She found the dagger under her pillow and gripped it like a teddy bear, staring around for signs of danger.

When nothing jumped out, she finally remembered her visit to the hospital. Dancing at the concert afterward must have been too much for her new wounds, and judging by the condition of her bed, she had been thrashing in her sleep, too.

She peeled back her bandages to examine the injuries. The bruises were already yellowing. Healing faster than the average person meant she would be back to normal by the end of the weekend as long as she took care of herself, but dancing had ripped open her scabs. Her skin was slick with blood.

"Shit," she muttered.

Elise showered in scalding-hot water, bracing her hands against the wall and letting her head hang between her shoulders. The water coursing down her skin stung her injuries.

Her nightmares were getting vivid again. She used to dream about the dead every night, and it was all returning because of James and his goddamn hero complex. Two fights with fiends were more than enough to get the memories flowing.

But she hadn't been dreaming of death last night. Instead, she had been remembering the day she woke up in the Russian wilderness with James standing over her like an angel.

She toweled off and rewrapped her injuries. Normally, she would have jogged to Motion and Dance for breakfast with James, but she needed to heal. Instead, she started a pot of coffee for Betty and hopped in her car to drive over.

There were already four other cars in the parking lot when she arrived. Elise's eyes narrowed. Motion and Dance didn't have any morning classes on the weekend.

James's apartment was filled with the smell of pancakes and an entire coven's worth of witches.

Elise stood in the doorway, staring at everyone intruding on their weekend breakfast. Ann and Morrighan chatted on the couch while Stephanie stared down a griddle covered in batter and sausages as though she had never cooked breakfast in her life.

The doctor was wearing the same clothes as the night before. She must have spent the night.

Elise felt numb as she shucked her jacket. So James and Stephanie were together. How long had that been happening?

"You made it!" Ann said brightly. She was eating a piece of toast smothered in jelly. A spot of butter dotted her chin.

"What are you all doing here?"

"We're going to visit the Ramirezes today to purify their house," Morrighan said. "We're getting ready. Are you coming?"

Elise fought to suppress her irritation. "No."

"Why not?" Stephanie asked.

She stared back in silent challenge.

James must have heard the door shut, because he peered out of his bedroom at the end of the hall. He had a phone pressed to his ear. "Elise," he called. "Could you please come here?"

She stepped into his bedroom. "You didn't tell me we were going to have company," Elise muttered. His private space was just as tidy as the rest of his house. He had even arranged Stephanie's shoes next to his own in the closet. "Who's on the phone?"

"It's McIntyre. He wants to speak to you."

Surprise melted away her anger in an instant. "McIntyre? Seriously?" She took the phone. "This is Elise."

"Hey there," he responded. Lucas McIntyre's voice flooded her with memories—mostly bad ones.

"What's do you need?" Elise asked. James hovered over her shoulder to listen to their conversation.

"The semi-centennial summit is coming," McIntyre said. "It's in our state. I thought you would want to know."

Every fifty years, the major world powers met to form treaties and settle disputes—the best of the kopides, the greatest demons, and the most powerful angels. Her father had been on the planning board before he left.

"You're right. I do want to know. But I'm still retired."

"Still?"

"It's supposed to be permanent."

"I just never thought you, of all people, could lay down the sword for long." He chuckled. "I thought if you did give up those things, it would be to upgrade to guns."

"The summit is your problem, not mine."

"Sure, but they've taken over Silver Wells. There's also going be a lot of traffic through the state for the next few months. The travel licenses between Hell and Earth have been sold out and demons are starting to move in."

Elise and James exchanged glances. "Do you have a list of the summit participants?"

"My friend on the board gave me one. I can email it to you. Long story short, there might be some folk who recognize you. If you want to stay out of trouble, you better be careful."

Elise massaged her temple. "Great. Thanks."

"Leticia wants to talk to you. Here you go."

She talked with McIntyre's wife for a few minutes. Leticia chatted about Dana, their first child, and the names they were planning for the second one, due around Thanksgiving.

When she couldn't tolerate any more family gossip, Elise said, "I'm going to get going. Tell Lucas thanks."

"We're thrilled to help," Leticia said. "You haven't visited us in years. Promise you'll come down soon so we can catch up?"

"Of course. Talk to you later." Elise handed James the phone. "I'll visit them as soon as Hell throws us a pizza party. Did you call McIntyre, or did he call you?"

"He called me. He doesn't have your number anymore."

"That's not an accident. I don't want anything to do with this. And you should have told me you were going to have the witches over during breakfast." She barely refrained from remarking on Stephanie's shoes.

James frowned. "I hoped you would come with us today."

"Nobody else needs to know that I'm a kopis and exorcist. The Ramirezes are bad enough."

He sighed, running a hand through his hair. "Elise…"

"I'm going to the office to do some work."

"Are you angry about Stephanie?" he asked. She left the room without responding, but he followed. "Won't you at least eat something before you go?"

Elise grabbed a piece of bacon off a plate on the counter and bit off the end. The witches were all standing in the living room now, and they pretended not to notice that James and Elise were obviously arguing.

"Feel free to call me when you finish if you're not too busy fucking around," she said, tearing her sweater off the hook by the door.

She slammed the door shut behind her.

Chapter 7

Even though it was drizzling again, Augustin Ramirez was waiting outside when James and arrived with the coven. The umbrella on his deck's dining set was folded down. Raindrops rippled in a tall glass of amber liquor.

He lifted his head from his hands when they approached. "What took you so long?" he asked.

Stephanie didn't bother hiding her severe frown. "We needed to confirm your daughter's health condition, since you wouldn't cooperate with us. Where is she now?"

Augustin waved vaguely at the front door of the house.

"Can we go in?" James asked.

The lawyer nodded and let his head drop on his folded arms. Ann was the first through the door, hurrying inside as though she was allergic to rain. Morrighan followed, holding her bag of supplies over her head as a makeshift umbrella.

James hesitated by Augustin. "Has anything changed?"

"Why can't you people just leave us alone?" Augustin asked without looking up. "We were fine two weeks ago. Lucinde had a ballet recital. She was fine."

It was hard to get angry when he looked so pathetic.

"Hopefully we can leave you alone very soon, Mr. Ramirez," James said. "This shouldn't take long. Would you please come inside with us? The weather is only going to get worse."

Augustin didn't move.

James went inside to find the other three witches clustered near the front door, huddled together for support. He couldn't blame them—the house had been miserable when he first visited, but it had gotten worse. The air was freezing. It smelled stale. Every window was closed and the lights were turned off.

And they could hear screaming.

All of them turned to look at the stairs. Something heavy was banged against the floor, and each thud made the wall photos bounce and rattle. One had already fallen off its nail and shattered on the steps.

That noise didn't sound like it came out of the lungs of a little girl. It didn't sound like it came from a human at all.

"I'm going to check on Lucinde," Stephanie said, but she didn't go for the stairs. Instead, she slid back until she could grab James's hand with clammy fingers.

A slip of paper on the mantle caught his eye. It was Elise's business card. James slipped it into his pocket, hoping nobody would notice, but Ann was watching.

"Where's Marisa?" she asked.

"She's most likely upstairs with her daughter." James took a deep breath and straightened his back. "Right. Let's get this done. Morrighan and Ann, bring out the smudges. I'll find somewhere to cast the circle."

His orders were enough to get everyone moving. They broke apart. Stephanie crept upstairs while Morrighan began removing things from her duffle bag. "Think we can open the windows and stuff?" she asked. "Everything in here now is doused with negative energy. It's horrible."

"Hold onto that thought. We should speak to Marisa first," he said.

Stephanie reappeared on the landing almost as soon as she left. "James?"

He joined her upstairs. The air felt heavier in the hallway, like James was moving through thick, murky water. He had to struggle to breathe.

"What's wrong?"

Stephanie pointed. He peered down the dark hall to see a shadowy form huddled against Lucinde's door. Marisa.

James knelt beside her. Her eyes were puffy and her nail polish had been chipped off until there were only a few flakes left. She hugged her knees to her chest. "It's getting worse," she whispered. He could barely hear her over the screaming and pounding.

"We're going to cleanse your house of all these negative energies and drive out whatever is hurting your daughter." He didn't speak with any conviction. He wished that Elise would have come.

When James moved to stand, she grabbed his arm, holding him in place. "You don't understand. It's not supposed to get worse. She's supposed to get better."

"Yes, I know, but—"

Marisa's chin quivered. "She's going to die."

"Nobody is going to die. We're going to open the curtains and windows. All right?"

"No! You can't do that! You'll hurt her, and she's already…" Her chest hitched. "She's already in so much pain. This isn't supposed to happen. She's supposed to get *better*."

James didn't realize Stephanie was standing behind him until she spoke. "I should check on your daughter."

Marisa shook her head. "She's out of control."

"I'm used to difficult patients."

He cut off Stephanie with a slash of his hand. "This isn't the time. Will you help us with the ritual, Marisa?"

She shook her head. A line of white rimmed her lips.

When they returned to Ann and Morrighan, they were parting the curtains and throwing open the windows. They had already positioned censers in every doorway. The smell of white sage drifted through the air. Lucinde screamed louder.

James did a quick search of the rooms downstairs and decided to cast the circle in the kitchen, where a ring of salt would be the easiest to clean up. It was also positioned directly beneath Lucinde's room.

He and Stephanie lit candles, laid out stones on each of the cardinal directions, and called the other witches into the kitchen without closing the circle. He handed each of them photocopies of the ritual. "You three should stay down here within the protection of the circle," he said. "Focus on the incantation."

"What are you going to do?" Stephanie asked.

"I'm going upstairs."

Ann paled. "Is that a good idea?"

He didn't think it was, but James smiled and nodded anyway. "Of course. You can begin the ritual as soon as I'm gone."

Stephanie sealed the circle behind him. The three women began chanting together. James could have spoken it along with them without glancing at the Book of Shadows—he had written the ritual himself, and they had used it before to great success.

Of course, they had never had to cleanse anything as horrible as Lucinde before, either.

With every step he took toward the locked bedroom, James became more and more certain that the ritual would be ineffective. The idea of using traditional magic against whatever had seized the house seemed ridiculous. It was like waving a cardboard sword at a dragon.

Marisa had vanished from the hallway upstairs. A cold fist clenched in his chest.

And Lucinde suddenly fell silent.

He froze for a moment, heart pounding. He strained to hear something within her room—a hint of motion, or a whimper. But there was nothing.

Her door was unlocked. He pushed it open.

His eyes adjusted slowly to the darkness. The portable swamp cooler was on its side. Something dark was on the white bed sheets—something wet.

And the little girl was crouched in the center of it.

She grinned. Her teeth were stained red.

"Lucinde?" James asked. He wasn't speaking to Augustin Ramirez's daughter. He dropped his voice, hand tight on the doorknob. "What are you?"

"I am the cold kiss of Death," she rasped. "And you're next, James Faulkner."

She leaped off the bed with a shriek, hands extended.

He jumped back and slammed the door shut. Her body thumped into the other side. The wood groaned and the entire house shuddered from the impact.

Downstairs, the witches weren't chanting anymore.

"I told you, she's going to die," Marisa whispered. James spun to see her wavering in her doorway. He thought her hands looked bloody, too, but the vision cleared when he blinked. She was clean.

Lucinde was screaming again.

"What happened?" Stephanie asked when he came

downstairs. All the candles had gone out, but there was no other indication anything had changed.

"Pack up. We can't do anything," James said grimly.

"What are you going to do?" Ann asked as Morrighan grabbed a broom and began to sweep up the salt. James didn't know how to respond.

Elise was wrong. Lucinde was definitely possessed.

Augustin didn't look up when they left the front door. Stephanie was dragging her feet, reluctant to leave without checking on Lucinde, but James kept a firm grip on her arm so she couldn't go back. He had seen possessions leap between people before.

"I'm going to return with reinforcements," James told Augustin while the other witches loaded the car. "I'm sorry."

The lawyer stood silently, went inside, and locked the door. By the time they pulled away, all the windows and curtains were shut again.

Chapter 8

The parking lot outside Elise's office was empty when she arrived, so she didn't have to hide the stack of unusual books she carried into her office: The Infernal Lexicon and Hume's Almanac, both of which were large, leather-bound texts that could hardly pass as light reading.

She shut her office door with a hip bump and settled in to reread the list McIntyre had sent her. Elise recognized many of the demons without looking them up; her father had drilled her on many of them as a child. The shedu had no interest in the dead, nor did Aquiel and his kin, and she marked them off. Those too weak to command fiends were also immediately crossed out. She halved the list in minutes.

Even after her eliminations, hundreds remained. It could take days to check them all.

Considering the alternative was following James around while he tried to relive his glorious youth of saving people, she decided she would much rather have the tedium. Elise started a pot of coffee, found a notebook, and began to work.

For hours, she searched. Elise immersed herself in the

lore of Hell as shadows crept across her office floor, filling and refilling her mug. She covered an entire notebook page with writing. Then another. And another. Outside, the clouds moved in, and the sun inched toward the mountains. By the time she started on her third pot of coffee, her handwriting looked more like a series of tiny, angry slashes than language.

After a while, her attention wandered. Demons were boring. Elise had recently downloaded a book on ethereal lore, so she started researching the names of the angelic attendants instead. A single angel could match a thousand demons in power, but their snobbish attitudes meant they seldom lowered themselves to visiting the earthen planes.

Ethereal mythology was much more interesting than that of their infernal counterparts. A couple big names were going to the summit. Gabriel himself would make an appearance.

She read his section in her book, then scanned up to the Metaraon—the voice of God. There was an engraving of his face, unmerciful and cold. It gave her chills.

Elise had read his chapter before. He hired architects to construct seven angelic cities on Earth. There weren't any left—the angels abandoned them in centuries past. But there were supposed to be ruins left in some places.

In fact, they said angelic ruins were buried deep below the Sierra Nevada Mountains. Elise stared at the Metaraon's face and drummed a pen against her desk.

The ruins should have prevented most demons from possessing anyone nearby. It wouldn't be any minor lord stealing bodies and attacking Lucinde. Whatever it was had to be huge.

Her door opened, and Elise's hand dropped to a hidden dagger. The visitor came in back-first, but she recognized his broad shoulders and dirty shoes.

"Knock, knock," Anthony said. He cradled two large coffees and a brown bag to his chest, and he set them on the edge of her desk with a smile. "What are you doing?"

"Anthony," Elise said, flipping over her notebook and sliding it on top of the Infernal Lexicon. "Hey. I'm just doing some work."

A smile played at the corners of his lips. His hair was extra tousled, his t-shirt wrinkled, and there was an oily hand print on his jeans. "Secret work?"

"No." She didn't try to sound convincing, but he didn't seem to care.

"Betty told me you were working on the weekend," Anthony said, offering one of the coffees to her. "I thought you might need some energy...but I can see that's not really a problem." Dirty mugs were scattered around her office, and a new pot was percolating on her filing cabinet.

Elise took a deep sniff of the latte. "This is much better than what I've been having. Thanks."

"I got you a muffin, too," he said in a hopeful tone.

"Great," she said, sliding her books and notes into a desk drawer. Anthony leaned around to read the spines, but Elise shut it too fast. "What are you up to?"

"I just got off work and was on my way to meet Betty, but I thought I'd visit you first. Are you busy?"

Elise stood. Her back ached. The clock told her she had been hunched over her desk for over eight hours. Her injuries from the night before had stiffened.

She checked her cell phone, which had been on silent. Seven missed calls from James. Great.

"No, I'm not busy." She put her phone back in her pocket. "Don't let me get in the way of meeting Betty. I know she goes nuts if you're late at all."

"Let me walk you to your car."

"I'm right outside the door."

"Well...me too." Anthony ducked his head, peeking at her through his bangs. "Did you have fun last night?"

It took Elise a moment to realize what he was talking about. She had almost forgotten about their date. "Oh, yeah. The band was really good."

"I never saw you like that before."

"Like what?"

He flashed a grin. "You know...having fun."

"Did I embarrass myself?"

"No, of course not. It's nice." Elise arched an eyebrow at him, and he hurried to add, "I mean, you're always so serious. It's like some black cloud is following you around."

"A black cloud," she echoed—and then, surprisingly, she laughed. "I guess that's a fair description."

Elise locked the office door and headed down the hall. Anthony's hand stuck out at his side, and she got the impression he wanted her to take it. She pretended she didn't notice.

His Jeep was beside Elise's car just outside the building doors. "Thanks for walking me," she said. Elise moved to get into the driver's seat, but Anthony stopped her, grabbing onto the door.

"Maybe you want to hang out with me tonight?" he said. A pink flush had risen on his cheeks. "I mean, if you're done for the day, I just have to see Betty for a few minutes. We could go down for a walk by the river or something."

Elise studied him, head tilted to the side. Was she that intimidating, or was he just a nervous person? "You can just ask me on a date, you know."

"Oh. Okay. So, do you…?"

"Yes," Elise said. And then, to save him from the stuttering, she added, "Nine o'clock."

"Nine. Awesome."

She tried to get into the car, but he didn't let go of her door. He stepped in close, shadowing her from the sun, and she had to tilt her head back to look at him.

"Anthony, I don't—"

He bent down and kissed her. Elise stiffened. He tasted like coffee and chewing gum—totally benign—but she felt cornered, and a voice in the back of her mind screamed for escape.

Anthony straightened. "Are you okay?"

She touched her mouth. "Yeah." Her fingertips were tingling. Elise hadn't been kissed in years.

It wasn't that bad. Not really.

She leaned up to kiss him again.

His hand on her arm was heavy, and his breathing deepened as he leaned into her. She felt something stirring inside of her that she hadn't felt in a long time, and the foreign sensation made her knees shake.

The sound of the eaves dripping on the pavement and the cars rushing down the street suddenly seemed too loud, like a hundred eyes were watching and waiting for her to drop her guard.

Elise pushed on his chest—not hard, but enough to get his attention. He blinked at her like he was coming out of a sleepy haze. "What?"

She ducked into the driver's seat and slammed the door, leaving Anthony standing awkwardly next to it.

"I had a great time at the concert," she said, rolling down her window as her engine grumbled to life. Anthony looked bereft. His cheeks were flushed. "I'll see you again tonight, okay?"

She left before he could say another word.

Elise entered the studio to the sound of someone playing the piano. She set her folders on the reception desk and peeked around the corner.

James played piano in the blue light of the storm. The windows at the opposite end of the room were cracked, and a soft breeze smelling of wet sage drifted through. His brow was lowered over his eyes, and his mouth had taken on that distinct slant that said he was concentrating.

"'Marriage d'Amour.' Toussaint, right?" Elise said when his song trailed off, and he looked up, surprised.

"You haven't answered my calls."

"I've been busy." Sitting on the bench beside him, she spread her fingers over the keys. Elise pressed, and the piano responded with a warm *ting*. She struck another key, and another, in no particular order. "How was the visit with the Ramirezes?"

"It didn't do any good. Lucinde is getting worse." James selected a note an octave lower than the last one she hit, and his fingers followed hers up the piano. "You were wrong—she's definitely possessed. But you knew that, didn't you?" He struck the deepest note on the piano, and it vibrated through her hand. "Do you have any potential culprits?"

"I narrowed the list down." She dropped her hands, letting the last note ring through the silent air. "Do you think it's true?"

"Yes," James said, "I do think she's possessed, which is why you should have—"

"Not that. Do you think there are really ethereal ruins beneath the Warrens?"

He considered the question as he tapped out the beginning to "Für Elise." James loved to play that song for her, even more so because she found it irritatingly cute. "It's a distinct possibility." He pulled the cover over the keys. "We should see the Ramirezes as soon as possible. Lucinde must be exorcised."

"Fine. Call Father Night down from Washington. He can do it."

"I already tried to call him, and he's busy for the next week. You're the only person in the area who has ever performed a successful exorcism."

"I've got plans with Anthony later. I can't do it."

James folded his arms. "And that's more urgent than this family's problem? What happened to your priorities?"

"We retired," she reminded him. "We're in hiding. Doesn't *everyone* need help? There's probably a half dozen possessed people throughout the country who need exorcisms right now, and I'm not knocking on their doors, either. I said I'm done being a hero. I meant it."

She slid off of the end of the bench and moved to leave.

James spoke before she reached the door. "Does the phrase, 'I am the cold kiss of Death,' mean anything to you?"

Elise stopped and turned around slowly. "Where did you hear that?"

"Lucinde. Why? Is it familiar?"

"You remember…the last time we fought?" She didn't have to say, *the time we saved the world*.

"It would be impossible to forget."

"She said that to me while she was…" Elise trailed off. She touched the scar on her breast. James hadn't been there

119

when the goddess said that, nor had she told him anything about her long hours under the knife. "Are you sure that's what Lucinde said?"

"Positive." James frowned. "And then she told me I would be next. She knew my name."

"Next for what?" she asked.

"I don't know."

I am the cold kiss of Death...

"But we killed her," she whispered.

"Since that night, I've wondered if that woman was demon-possessed, rather than the deity she claimed to be. Killing a human might not have killed the responsible demon at all. Maybe it has returned."

They shared a long, silent look.

If the thing that tortured her really was back...now *that* might be something worth fighting about.

James opened his mouth to speak again, but Elise's phone interrupted him by ringing.

She answered it. "Hello?" The only response was a buzz and white noise. Elise moved closer to the windows. "Who is this?"

The call crackled. "—Ramirez, we need—help—"

"I can't understand you," she said, moving out into the entryway. James hung a few steps behind her. "Is this Marisa?"

"Lucinde—something's wrong—"

Static hissed, and then the line went dead.

"Hello?" Elise said. "Hello?" She sighed and snapped her phone shut. "Great. This place must have the worst reception in the city limits."

"Who was that?" James asked.

"It *sounded* like Marisa Ramirez," Elise said. "I think something's up with Lucinde." She tried to call the number again, but after several rings, nobody picked up.

Elise shut her phone again.

"No answer?" James asked.

"No answer," she confirmed. "I think we need to get over there sooner rather than later."

James rang the bell by the Ramirez house's front door. Rain drizzled off the drain pipe, splattering against the concrete porch behind them. A church tower rose beyond the roof of their house, the cross at its peak stretching toward the navy sky. Elise shifted uncomfortably at his side, cold and wet and extremely unhappy as minutes passed without answer.

He pressed the doorbell again, and the bells of the church tower tolled in response.

James peered at one of the windows by the door, but the curtains drawn to prevent even the faintest sliver of light from making it through. "Are you sure they're here?"

As if on cue, Augustin Ramirez opened the door. His face was haggard and gray.

"You came back. Thank God. Get in, quick." He locked the deadbolt as soon as they were inside, pushing the curtains aside to glance furtively at the street before closing it up again.

James's nose wrinkled. Something stunk of feces, urine, and blood, like a dirty litter box used by a dozen sick animals. But the Ramirezes didn't have cats. They didn't have any animals at all. It hadn't smelled earlier in the afternoon.

"You have to see her," Augustin said, trying to push Elise toward the kitchen door. "You have to exorcise her.

You have to—you have to do that magic stuff again."

"What's wrong with Lucinde, Mr. Ramirez?" James asked. "Where is Marisa?"

"She's downstairs, in the basement," Augustin said. His hands were moving restlessly, as though he wanted to try to grab Elise again, or throw the door open and leave, or just do *something*.

"Take us to Lucinde," Elise said, outwardly unruffled despite Augustin's panic. But James could tell she was straining at the presence of a strong demon. Not for the first time, James was grateful that he couldn't feel what Elise could feel.

"The kitchen," Augustin said. "The door to the basement."

He pointed to the door and just stood there, the scion of a gateway he wouldn't enter. Elise pushed the kitchen door open and went inside, James following closely.

"What's his problem?" she muttered. "He's regressed to the behavior of a militant five-year-old."

"I don't know. I imagine we'll have to see for ourselves," he said, letting the door swing shut behind him. "Somehow, I don't think it will be pretty or pleasant."

Elise pressed the heel of her hand to her temple. "You've got that right."

The foul scent was more pungent in the kitchen, and it grew stronger as they approached the basement door beside the pantry. The basement door had a large panel of frosted glass, but they couldn't see beyond it—Augustin and Marisa had hung a black blanket over the back by stuffing the top into the small space between the door and its frame.

A woman screamed in the basement.

Elise flung open the door and ran into the darkness

below. James hesitated in the doorway.

With the door open, the pressurizing air between the kitchen and the basement blew the stench of piss and blood into James's face. He gagged, covering his nose with his sleeve. The screaming had grown much clearer. He could almost make out words.

Even with the door open, the light did little to penetrate the darkness below. He made his way down the steep stairs, keeping a hand on the railing and the other over his face. The sounds of a scuffle echoed up the stairway.

The screams intensified, and then cut off. Something heavy struck the other side of the wall.

"Elise?" James called, quickening his pace. "Marisa?"

His eyes adjusted to the darkness, and he could make out a short hallway, a door set in the unfinished wall. The walls were only partially insulated, and James could hear the shrieks inside all too clearly.

Marisa stood on the other side of the door, sobbing over a stuffed rabbit. The stench was the worst down here, and he could instantly see why—feces were smeared on the unpainted wall, although it wasn't entirely excrement; some of it also appeared to be fresh blood, brownish black in the dim lighting provided by lone bulb.

Elise struggled with a growling blur. Claws lashed at her face, and she ducked, catching its wrist and twisting it behind its body. She put a foot on its bare back and pressed it to the ground, unwinding a rope she had coiled around her arm. It occurred to James that the beast was clothed, and he wondered why something like that would bother to dress itself.

It took James a full second to grasp that the beast with which Elise fought wasn't a demon—it was Lucinde.

She knelt on the girl's back, tangling the rope around

Lucinde's body. Elise swiftly tied it off, securing it to a pipe jutting out of the wall. Lucinde kicked and thrashed. She looked more like a wildcat trying to escape than a human child.

Elise grabbed a piece of dirty cloth that had been laying nearby and stuck it in Lucinde's screaming mouth.

The little girl paused, as though to gather her strength, and then strained against the ropes anew. She shrieked and wailed, chewing at the gag and slipping a black tongue around the cloth. Elise backed off, letting the light fall on Lucinde's face. A symbol burned on Lucinde's forehead like her skull had been branded.

"How did this happen?" Elise demanded.

Marisa wept, smothering her face with her hands. "My baby...my little girl..."

As she sobbed louder, Lucinde screamed louder as well, throwing her head back. Her neck strained, and purple veins bulged from her throat. The gag did little to muffle the sound.

Elise grabbed Marisa's shoulders. "I can't help your daughter unless you talk to me. Did you see someone come in here? Did somebody, or something, come into your house?"

Marisa shook her head, and she kept shaking it, her entire body trembling. Her cheeks ran with tears and her chokehold tightened on the stuffed animal until it looked like it might burst at the seams.

"For the love of..." James swept out of the room, but Lucinde's screams followed him up the stairs and echoed against the walls of the basement.

Augustin stood at the door upstairs, leaning heavily on the counter. He had calmed in the minutes since James had gone downstairs, but not without help; he clutched a large glass of alcohol in one hand and a bottle in the other. It was cold inside the house, but Augustin was drenched in sweat. Damp patches stained his shirt at the chest and arm pits.

"When did she get like this?" James asked. "Your wife is incoherent."

Augustin gazed into the amber fluid in his glass, swirling the ice in circles. He was silent for a time, but his mouth moved as though he chewed the words he considered speaking.

"She had grown quieter. We thought she was improving after your ritual...*thing*. I even went into work for a couple hours. Marisa stayed home with...with Lucinde."

He took a long drink and wiped his mouth. His eyes were watery and red.

"She stopped moving. She stopped breathing. We thought she had fallen asleep, and we were glad. I mean, she hadn't slept in days. All she would do is crouch in her bedroom like some goddamn animal and scratch at the walls and eat flies. She was eating *flies*, for fuck's sake. She was catching them and smashing them and eating them and we were so happy when she fell asleep." He drew in a shuddering breath. "When we *thought* she fell asleep."

"What happened?"

"She wasn't asleep." Augustin laughed, and it turned into a sob. "She wasn't asleep. My God, she stopped breathing. Her skin had been hot for weeks and all of a sudden she was cold." His eyes met James's, and the pain in them was so harsh, so raw, that he had to fight not to look away.

"Are you saying she...?"

"My daughter *died*, Mr. Faulkner. I don't have to be a doctor to know that." He laughed again. "My daughter died. My little girl…" Augustin spun suddenly and hurled the glass into the sink. It shattered, shards of thunder crashing into stainless steel.

Augustin moved toward the sink, raising his arm as though he was going to smash the bottle too. He stopped short, breathing hard.

"God!" he cried, burying his face in his hand. He smacked the bottle against the counter, and the bottom cracked. Alcohol bled across the marble and dripped onto the floor. "But she didn't stay dead. She didn't stay. We were sitting by her, getting ready to call the hospital, resigning ourselves to what we had known was coming for —since—ever since she was born."

"But she wasn't dead," James prompted.

"Oh, she was dead, all right," Augustin said. "But she woke up, and all of a sudden she was worse than before. She got that shit on her forehead and she was screaming words I don't understand, and she ripped off her bed post trying to escape when we tied her down. We had to move her to the basement to keep her from getting outside. She's an animal. She's not human anymore."

Elise came up from the basement, a few shades paler than when she had gone down. She shut the door, and the screams became nearly inaudible again.

"James, we have to talk," she said.

He nodded. "You're right." He faced Augustin. "Elise and I need to discuss the…options."

"You won't leave," Augustin said. "You're not just going to disappear."

"We'll be right outside. We just need to talk."

"Okay," he said. "Okay."

He watched them go with frightened eyes, as though he didn't quite believe them. For being a powerful lawyer, he suddenly seemed very, very small. And that scared James more than Lucinde's screams ever could.

They stood under the shelter of the eaves, just beyond the light of the house. The neighborhood was completely silent and every house was dark. It was as though everybody had spontaneously gone out of town. Not a single car passed. The silence felt unnaturally heavy.

Elise glared at James. Her pale face glowed in the light that peeked through the curtains.

"I'm not going to do it."

"There's a little girl in there that will die if we don't help her," James said.

"I could die, too. Hell, so could you. Do you think the life of some kid is worth more than yours? We've seen possessions leap between bodies before."

"It only happened once. You can control it."

"Once was more than enough."

James stared at her. It was like he was speaking to a stranger.

It felt so long ago since they had traveled the world together to fight evil. The two of them against the world— that was how it had always been. They had rightfully earned a reputation for being amongst the best of the kopides and aspides.

A chasm had since opened between them since then—a chasm formed of people like Betty, Stephanie, and Anthony.

For some reason, James suddenly remembered the day he found her in the wilderness surrounded by bodies. Elise claimed she couldn't remember whether she killed them or not. He had only asked once, afraid she would tell him the truth. James didn't want to know anymore.

"You wouldn't have turned the Ramirezes away five

years ago," he said.

"Five years is a long time." Elise stuffed her hands into her pockets. "I think the demon is after witches. Marisa's a strong witch, and Lucinde's showing signs of having a similar gift. Those fiends were also after a witch at Eloquent Blood. If what Lucinde said is right, you're next, and you're probably the most powerful witch in the entire country."

"Is that why you don't want to be involved? Because you're concerned I'll be hurt?"

Her eyes flashed. "Don't say that like it's some small thing. Of course I'm worried about you. What the hell do you expect?"

"I can take care of myself, Elise."

"Are you sure? I don't think they want the witch alive. Lucinde feels like the body at the hospital did." She touched her temples. "I think she died. That's what changed today."

James's fists clenched. He stared at the gray sky and the pouring rain.

When he spoke, his voice was low and tense. "You have to do it. You can't leave them like this."

"But it's that death demon again. I know it."

"I know it, too." James reached out and took her hand. Elise's gloves were damp. "Please. If you won't do it for them, then do it for me."

She glared at him. "Sometimes you're a real bastard, James Faulkner. You know that?"

Elise went inside before he could think of a response.

They stood before Augustin and Marisa, dripping rainwater and mud onto the kitchen floor. Marisa had stopped crying. She stared at nothing, but Augustin focused on James and Elise, his eyes ringed with dark bruises.

"I'll do it," Elise said. "I'll exorcise her."

"And God help us all," James murmured.

Chapter 9

James half expected Elise to vanish completely when she left. When she returned forty-five minutes later equipped with an MP3 recorder and her golden chain of charms, relief overwhelmed him.

A grimace stretched across her lips when she walked through the door, but by the time Augustin and Marisa turned to greet the woman they viewed as their last potential savior, she blanked her expression.

"I've got everything I need," she said.

"We're almost done as well," James said, gesturing to the paperwork he had been going over with Augustin. "We only need your signature."

"What's that?"

"A contract assuring that you're relieved of liability in the event of any ritual-related accidents," Augustin said. His face was purplish and dripping with sweat. He had discarded the pretenses of drinking from a glass and clutched a half-empty bottle of whiskey now, which Marisa had been sharing for the last fifteen minutes. "James insisted upon it. He seemed concerned the we would—we might press charges if Lucinde was accidentally hurt."

"We wouldn't," Marisa added quickly.

"Where do I sign?"

James scratched an X in the blank signature box and pushed the paper to her. She didn't read it before scrawling her signature across the bottom line. Elise dropped the pen and Augustin took the paper.

"Good," he said. "Good. So…what now?"

"We'll go downstairs and exorcise your daughter," Elise said. "You might prefer to stay up here."

Augustin nodded immediately. Just as immediately, Marisa shook her head. "I want to be with my daughter."

"It won't be easy," Elise said.

"I won't leave her. I won't."

"Suit yourself." She managed to make it sound like a death sentence.

They passed through the blanket-covered doorway. James caught a glimpse of Augustin staring at the contract on the table, the whiskey bottle pressed to his forehead, and then the door closed.

The darkness in the basement was palpable, as though they waded through warm water. James felt along the wall by the landing and found a light switch. He flicked it, but nothing happened, and he swallowed a lump in his throat. "I need to speak to Elise before we do this. Can you wait up here, Marisa?"

"Yes," she said, and she waited on the top landing as Elise and James went to the bottom.

Light shone from the cracks around the door to the room where Lucinde was held. James could barely make out the carpet underfoot, striped red and purple and stained with water or something worse. He could see that Elise's brow was pinched in the half-light.

"If you want to emotionally blackmail me again, so help me God, you better wait until—"

"No," he interrupted. "I was thinking—piggyback?"

She let out a breath, shoulders sagging. "Piggyback. Good idea. I haven't done an exorcism in a while, and... well, I'm not sure I'm strong enough anymore. I could hurt her."

"Or yourself."

"I'm not worried about that," she said.

"And that worries *me*."

Elise almost smiled. "Just do it."

He reached within himself, searching for the wellspring of power that flowed from the earth beneath his feet. He caught it and wove it within himself, tighter and tighter until it felt like it might burst out his skin.

James brushed his fingers down her cheek as he released his power. It cascaded through both of them, warming him from the inside out. At the same time, he could feel it warm Elise. He felt the churning sickness in her stomach from being so close to the demonic power of the possessed child, and the ache in her muscles from the earlier struggle.

And then the power coalesced around James's midsection, like a chain tying him to Elise. It was a secure, comforting feeling. Elise's sickness abated, and James's nerves settled.

For one instant, he shared in her emotions as clearly as though they were his own. She was angry, but some part of her did want to save the child—very badly, in fact. She regretted snapping at James. But her fear trumped all. She was terrified of fighting that thing again.

James's stomach dropped out, and it was as though they both free-fell from a great height. Her eyes shocked open, and she staggered backward, breaking the physical connection between them. But the chain didn't break. They were connected.

Neither of them was willing to look at the other. "I'm sorry," James said. "I don't want to fight that demon again, either."

"I'm sorry, too." And he knew she meant it, because he could feel it. "You can come down now," Elise called, her voice resonating with power. Marisa joined them.

"What now?" she asked.

"Now we perform an exorcism." Elise pushed the door open, and they filed in, one after another.

Lucinde huddled in the corner, her entire body trembling. Scratching echoed through the basement, and there were fingernail fragments lodged in the plaster. Marisa whimpered.

Elise turned on the MP3 recorder.

"My name is Elise Kavanagh. I am exorcising a demon from Lucinde Ramirez at the behest of her parents, Augustin and Marisa Ramirez. It's the ninth of May, two-thousand nine, at twenty-one hundred hours." Elise set the recorder by the door.

Lucinde glared at them over her shoulder, revealing a face that had only grown less human with the passing time. Swollen blood vessels rimmed the edges of her red-tinged eyes.

The girl's upper lip curled, baring even white teeth. Her gaze flicked from Elise to Marisa, resting briefly on James before focusing on the kopis once more.

Her pupils dilated, and her irises were completely devoured. A low, soft breath escaped her mouth, almost like a snake's hiss. The note carried demonic power and the stink of sulfur, and the mark on her forehead flared with power.

James felt Elise gather their joined strength around herself, and he fed into it. It built until the air trembled and her very skin seemed to be trying to shiver off her body, and still they kept gathering it, clashing against the energy of the demon. James felt their strength press against Lucinde, and she pushed back. Elise shuddered under the pressure.

Lucinde shifted forward, digging her bloody hands into the floor. Too late, he realized that the ropes Elise had used to bind the girl earlier were piled in the corner. She was free.

"Watch out!" he called.

Lucinde launched from the corner of the room. What was left of her fingernails slashed through the air.

Elise jumped to the side, throwing out an arm to block her. She brushed Elise aside and kept going, striking Marisa instead.

The mother screamed, and down they went.

Blood splattered to the floor. Lucinde growled. Her teeth sunk deep into the flesh of Marisa's arm, and she worried at it as a dog might gnaw on a bone. Marisa collapsed to her knees, trying to wrench her arm free of her daughter's mouth. "No, *bambina!*"

Elise clamped her hand around the girl's jaw and dug her fingernails into her skin, but Lucinde's bite only tightened. James leapt in, wrapping his arms around Marisa's waist. He tried to drag her away, but even with the strength of two sets of adult legs, they couldn't separate mother from daughter. Elise clutched a fistful of Lucinde's hair and yanked.

"Let go." Lucinde growled, and Elise jerked harder. "I said, let go!"

Lucinde released the arm. Marisa collapsed into James,

cradling her bloody arm to her stomach.

The girl shot between Elise's legs. Elise turned, but Lucinde was too fast. She clambered up a half-complete shelf toward the narrow window at the ground level. She wiggled through the opening, bare feet kicking behind her.

Elise grabbed for an ankle, but missed.

"Shit!" she swore when the feet disappeared, jumping up to grab the ledge herself.

James was only just behind Marisa in running out the door, up the stairs, and into the kitchen. Augustin blinked wetly at them as they passed. "What…?"

Marisa hit the back door without opening it, stumbling over her own feet. She sagged, favoring her bleeding arm, and the skin began to boil. James caught her, lowering her slowly to the ground. Outside, Elise struggled with the girl in the muddy back yard.

James tried to block out the sensations Elise felt and concentrated on Marisa's bite, pressing his hand to the wound. "Does it sting?" he asked.

"It feels like acid!"

He reached into his pocket and withdrew a scrap of paper. His connection to Elise made summoning his magic easy, but all too quickly it began to draw off his partner. She wavered, and Lucinde took the opportunity to squirm out from under Elise and bolt for the fence.

James concentrated on healing Marisa's arm, flicking the healing magic into the air around her. She whimpered. The skin twitched and writhed, but it was no longer bubbling. It settled, red and raw but clean.

"Wait here!"

He joined Elise in the back yard as she tackled Lucinde, smashing both of them into the fence. It shuddered with the force of the impact.

Elise was completely covered in mud, from her knees to her gloves and jacket. Her hands slipped on Lucinde, and the girl darted for a pile of landscaping boulders at the opposite corner.

James moved to cut her off. She froze, then tried to dart in the other direction.

Elise was already there, uncoiling the extra rope in her fists. She was flushed, panting, and exhilarated, her excitement washing through James. Her chain of charms jingled at her belt, and the crosses seemed to glow. Lucinde glanced between Elise, and then to James again, and back. The rain struck her skin and sizzled, evaporating instantly. Her entire body steamed.

"We should get her inside before the neighbors call the police," he said, and Elise nodded.

Blood-caked fingernails flashed at Elise's face. She threw herself out of the way, grabbing the girl's wrist. Lucinde snatched the charms at Elise's belt. The belt loops popped, and she flung them aside. The charms sank into a puddle of mud.

James dove for Lucinde. She darted aside, but he managed to catch her arm. Her flesh was so hot it nearly burned his hand. He jerked her around, and she kicked him—hard—in the shin.

He growled, hefting Lucinde under his arm. She snapped at his arms with her teeth. He clamped a hand over her mouth.

Elise knelt in the mud, searching for her charms.

"I can't find them!"

"Forget it. Door," he grunted. Elise threw it open, and he rushed through.

Marisa and Augustin waited on the other side. The stuffed rabbit had reappeared, and she gave a ragged sob when she saw James and Elise come back inside with her daughter in tow.

"Out of the way!" she ordered. Lucinde kicked hard, nearly squirming out from under James's arms.

"Get her feet," he said.

Elise took her by the ankles, bracing them as James dragged her down the stairs.

Marisa squeezed around them and shut the basement window before they dropped Lucinde again. The girl scrabbled over to the corner, curled into a tight ball, and screeched pathetically at James.

Fumbling at the back of her neck, Elise took off her cross necklace and pressed it to Lucinde's cheek. Her voice hardened, deepening with power as she summoned up the memory of the oft-recited rituals from ancient books to do her first exorcism in years.

"I exorcise you, impious demon," she recited, and James could envision the same old pages Elise was remembering with perfect clarity. Lucinde's face screwed up with pain. "In vain do you boast of this deed. I command you to restore her as proof you no longer have any rule over her soul. I abjure—"

Lucinde swung. "Elise!" James yelled.

Her fist connected. Elise's back smacked into a wall, and Lucinde lunged.

Elise braced herself and took the impact, translating the momentum into a throw. Lucinde slid, but regained her footing immediately.

Elise scooped her rope from the floor, holding it in the joint of her elbow to keep her hands free. She grabbed the girl by her collar and slammed her into the wall. The drywall cracked.

"No—!" Marisa cried, throwing out a hand.

James caught her arm. "Stay out of it. Trust me. She isn't feeling any of this."

"I *abjure* you," Elise went on, voice rising as she shoved the cross into Lucinde's face again, "stripping you of the arms with which you fight. I revoke the powers by which —" the girl clawed at Elise's wrist, trying to pry her off, "—this creature became bound to your service."

Her back arched, even with Elise's hands holding her flat to the wall. Lucinde's nails dug into her sleeve.

Elise pushed the girl to the floor, pinning her arms to the dirty linoleum with her knees. She flung her head from side to side, but even with all the strength the demon provided, Elise had size on her side.

"This creature is restored, rejecting your influence, granted divine mercy for defense against your assaults!"

Lucinde began to scream, high and loud. Something pulsed underneath the surface of her skin where Elise held the cross.

She focused all the energy she possessed on that point, building it up between them. Heat rippled across James's skin. Elise seized upon the darkness within Lucinde.

"*Crux sacra sit mihi lux,*" Elise said, and the power poured out through her words. "*Non draco sit mihi dux. Vade retro, Satana—*"

The power of the demon boiled through the air like hot oil, simultaneously slimy and as dry as a desert wind. Her screaming reached a pitch, and Elise released the cross so she could cover her mouth with her gloved hand.

The girl bit down, but her teeth got nothing but glove. Even muffled against her hand, James could hear screaming. It didn't come from her throat.

"*Nunquam suade mihi vana,*" Elise continued. The stench of sulfur was almost choking. "*Sunt mala quae libas. Ipse venena bibas!"*

A silent clap of thunder roared inside Elise and James. Lucinde wrenched her head to the side, out from underneath Elise's hand. "Mother!" she shrieked in a hundred voices. "Sorrow!"

She roared once more, wordless and agonized, thrashing beneath Elise.

Lucinde gasped, and then slumped. Her eyes closed, her mouth hung open, and she stopped moving.

Elise released the child, and Lucinde didn't move. She lay limply between Elise's legs, unconscious but breathing. The black symbol rapidly faded. Her veins sank into her skin once more.

"*Madre de dios*," Marisa whispered.

James followed her gaze. She was watching the same place as Elise—not at the girl, but at the ceiling. A dark shadow manifested above the room. A smell like burnt ozone and charred hair, traced faintly with the iron tang of blood, permeated the entire basement.

Elise dropped her necklace into the pocket of her jacket, staring into the depths of the demon's form.

"Servant," she said in a low, strong voice. "Return to the Hell in which you belong and never return. Be gone."

The demon dissolved. The pressure eased.

Elise pressed her fingers to Lucinde's throat. James could feel the pulsing of her heartbeat in his own fingertips, steady and strong.

She was alive.

"Lucinde," Marisa cried, pulling her arm free from James and scrambling over to her daughter. "Is she okay? What did you do to her?"

"She's fine, Marisa," Elise said. "You might both want to get checked out by a doctor, though. I'm sure Stephanie would be happy to pay a visit once she gets off her shift."

Marisa smoothed her hand over Lucinde's cheek. "Baby...baby, please wake up..."

The girl's eyes opened. The whites were no longer yellow and veined. Lucinde had to swallow twice before she could speak. "Mama?"

"Oh, *bambina*." Marisa choked on a sob and collapsed over her daughter, raining kisses all over her face and arms and tummy. She spoke rapidly in Spanish, too quickly for James to understand, but he got the gist of it. "My baby, *querida, mi corazon...*"

James rested his hand on Elise's shoulder and lifted the magical binding between them. Her feelings disappeared from him in a rush. More than the physical sense of being tired, though, he felt drained spiritually—he couldn't have lit a candle if he wanted to, with or without paper magic.

He didn't need to read Elise's mind to see she felt the same. "I almost forgot what that was like," she said.

"Yes, but perhaps now we should..." he said, gesturing toward the door.

"Wait," Marisa interrupted, scooping Lucinde into her arms. Blood seeped through the makeshift bandage on her arm. "*Gracias*, thank you so much. She's okay again. You really did it. It wasn't..." Lucinde looked dazed, as though she wasn't quite sure what was going on. It was a pleasant departure from the screaming. "That was nothing like the movies."

"Life usually isn't," Elise said.

"How can we ever repay you?"

"Don't worry about it."

The temperature in the kitchen was much warmer than the basement. Augustin stood when they entered.

"Is she...?"

James pulled Elise aside from the doorway, letting Marisa enter the kitchen. He froze, going completely expressionless.

She blinked several times, squinting against the fluorescent lamps, and buried her face in her mother's shoulder. Marisa stroked Lucinde's hair, murmuring to her softly, but her eyes were all for Augustin. For the first time, James glimpsed real love between them.

And Augustin crumbled. He collapsed against the table as though he could no longer stand.

"Thank *God*."

Marisa brought Lucinde to him, and they cried, relieved and happy and still sort of drunk off the whiskey. The kitchen felt so much brighter without the weight of the possession heavy over the entire house.

"Call us if you need anything else," Elise said, but the Ramirezes weren't listening.

"Let's go," James said.

They left the kitchen, and even though all the lights inside were off and the curtains drawn, it felt nowhere near as dark as it had been when they had first arrived. James found his jacket, and Elise took a moment to go to the thermostat, flicking off the air conditioner before cutting around the side of the house to find her charms in the back yard. They met again in the front.

The rain hadn't let up. They got in the car, and James fished an old towel out of the backseat, drying off his hair. He offered it to her when he was done, but she gazed thoughtfully out the window and didn't see.

"How do you feel?" he asked.

"Good," Elise said. "I feel...good. Are you okay? I saw you healing Marisa, but you didn't take it from me."

"I'm fine, but I certainly won't be doing any more magic

for a few days."

"What do you think about what Lucinde said?"

"'Sorrows,'" James repeated, and she nodded.

"What did it mean?"

"She said 'mother' as well, and I don't think she was calling Marisa. I believe it's a name." He removed a city map from the glove compartment and scanned it briefly. He pointed at a green oval on the north end of the paper. "See here—Our Mother of Sorrows, right by the university."

"Why would a demon yell the name of a cemetery?"

"A lesser demon, such as the one that possessed Lucinde, is merely an appendage of its master rather than an individual entity," he said. He started the car. "So as it is exorcised…"

"It goes back to its master and sees or thinks exactly what its master sees or thinks," Elise said. "I'm going to the cemetery."

He stopped at the red light. "*You're* going?"

"Listen, James…" She paused to collect her thoughts. When she spoke, her voice was soft. "You're right. I have to take care of this. This bitch—the death goddess—almost skinned me, and she owes me her blood. But I'd feel a lot better if you weren't around for it."

"You're completely unprepared."

"I don't have time for preparation. I have to get her now. Who knows where she'll be tomorrow?"

"You realize this is likely to be a trap," he said.

She nodded.

He gave a low, thoughtful hum, drumming his fingers on the steering wheel. The light turned green and James lurched into the intersection, making a fast illegal left turn. Elise gripped the side of the door, staring at him. "James,

Motion and Dance is the other way," she said.

"We're not going to the studio," he said. "We're going to Our Mother of Sorrows."

Chapter 10

Elise and James sped toward the cemetery in silence. The windshield wipers whisked a quick rhythm back and forth, clearing sheets of water off the glass with every swipe. The air blowing through the vents was cool, like the air outside, smelling sweetly of petrichor and sage.

The white monolith of the cemetery's church rose out of the darkness. He parked in the circular driveway before the building, and Elise hit the radio button, silencing the oldies station in the middle of a Led Zeppelin song.

"It's really close to UNR," she remarked. A stone angel loomed in the dark distance.

"There are several graveyards around here," he said. "When old west towns such as this were founded, they always put the cemeteries at the tops of hills to keep the bodies—and their smell—out of the way."

She studied the faces of the apartment buildings on the ridge overlooking Our Mother of Sorrows. "Guess they didn't plan on people building homes out here. At least your neighbors would be quiet."

"Even your living ones, apparently," he said, taking the keys out of the ignition.

James was right: most of the apartments and houses surrounding the cemetery were dark. Even though it was almost the weekend, and there should have been parties in the college neighborhood, the blocks surrounding Our Mother of Sorrows were strangely silent.

"The dead aren't getting any deader," she said. "Let's go."

They climbed out of the car into the rainy night. She wandered toward the church, and James retrieved a flashlight from the trunk before joining her.

A small graveyard splayed in front of them. The newer headstones to the front were in neat lines, arranged in narrow rows that left no room for walking without treading upon someone's final resting place. A single path led to a hill where the older graves stood. A lonely stone angel, illuminated by flood lights around its base, glowed like a star in the drizzly night.

James stepped on the grass. Energy swept over him, and he froze.

Elise caught his expression. "What's wrong?"

"Someone's been working magic here. The entire cemetery's inside a circle of power."

"That's not unusual. People cast spells in graveyards all the time." Elise kept walking. "Come on, hurry up. We don't want to get caught trespassing. Do cemeteries have security details?"

"Considering the gaping holes in their fence, I'm going to say no."

Elise and James moved between the graves, feet slurping in and out of the mud with each step. Grass was not native to the desert, so it didn't take root in the hard soil properly and melted into sludge at the slightest hint of rain.

James shone his flashlight on every marker they passed. "Mario Perez," Elise remarked. "I had that guy for class when I was a freshman."

"I remember that," he said, wiping rainwater off his face. "Stroke, wasn't it?"

"Yeah." She pulled out her cell phone, glanced at the screen, and pulled a face.

"What's the matter?"

"Forget it," Elise said, shoving it back in her pocket. "Let's find this demon bastard and get the job done."

They gave a quick search of the graves. In such a small cemetery, there wasn't much looking to do.

"You must have misinterpreted Lucinde," she said. "There's nothing here. It would be pretty obvious if a major demon was around."

He swept the flashlight side to side in fruitless searching. "It doesn't seem—"

"Wait. Is that an open grave by the statue?"

They weaved through the tombstones to the next row. The flashlight died when they stepped up to the very edge of the plot, and James bashed the flashlight repeatedly against his thigh.

"It's definitely open," she said. "Too bad we can't see it."

"I know," James said, looking down into the LEDs and jiggling the batteries. "From what I can tell, though, it almost looks new." The flashlight blared on, burning his retinas for an instant, and then turned off again. "Damn!"

"How can you tell that it's new?"

He gestured toward the sky, blinking green shapes out of his vision. "It's been raining for quite some time. The soil erodes rapidly. This grave, although messy, hasn't been washed out."

"Isn't that Amber Hackman's grave over there?" Elise said. "I heard something about her on the news recently. Her body went missing."

Their gazes met.

"You wouldn't remember when Amber Hackman died, but it was quite the event for the witch community worldwide," James said. "She's best known for her work as ambassador for the U.N., but she also fought to obtain asylum for witches in superstitious villages. Her work saved many lives."

"This grave is…" She squinted. "Grace Finch, beloved grandmother. I would bet anything she was a witch, too."

"How many bodies does this demon have?"

"At least three, probably more. All witches."

He let out a slow breath. "This isn't good."

"Is there something down there?"

She moved closer to the grave. The only warning James had when she fell was a surprised shriek, and suddenly, Elise wasn't standing in front of him anymore.

"Elise!" he yelled, stepping forward.

Loose earth crumbled under his feet, and he jumped back, landing on his backside. The light flashed once, and stayed dead.

James scrambled to his knees, moving carefully to the rim of the grave. "Elise?"

He could just make out her pale skin as she tilted her face up toward him. "My fault. Erosion. At least I had a soft landing. Can I get any light?"

"The flashlight won't work," he said, opening it to reseat the batteries and fiddle with the connectors.

"I think there's a pair of security guards down here," Elise said. A beat, and she added, "They're dead."

James closed the battery door and the bulb came back on. He beamed it down into the grave. Elise shielded her eyes, back pressed into the muddy wall.

The bodies looked like mud-covered sacks, half-concealed by a sheet flung over their legs. He could make out the *Securitas* logo on the breast pocket of the man on the right. His stomach pitched.

"Shine the light over that way," she said.

James obeyed, watching as Elise knelt in the space beside the bodies. She felt the throat of the closest guard and hovered her hand over his mouth. When she began wiping mud away from their throats to bare bloody gashes, James looked up at the sky.

Gray clouds, highlighted with shades of blue and purple, shifted slowly across the heavens. The moon wasn't even visible through the cover. Casino lights to the south turned the clouds green and orange and a dozen other unnatural shades of the rainbow.

"Someone slit their throats with a sharp knife. The wounds are pretty clean," she said from below. James took deep, shallow breaths, grateful that the rain kept the smell of death from reaching him.

"We should get you out of there. We need to...I don't know, report this or something."

"Report it? Are you crazy?" She dug her hands into the wall of mud, trying to haul herself up with the side of the grave. The soil slipped under her fingers. She lost her footing, stumbled back on the bodies, and one of the guards squelched deeper into the mud. "Uh, help?"

James offered a hand to her. She took his wrist, and he hauled her out of the hole. Elise crawled a few feet away from the grave before trying to wipe mud off her arms. "Are you all right?"

Elise cast a grimace at the grave. "Better than some people. We can't report this. Once the police are here, we'll never get the opportunity to find out what happened."

"But..."

"Business first. Then we tip off the law." She scooped the flashlight off the ground. "You never would have had a problem with this five years ago."

He glanced down into the shadowy depths of the grave and quickly averted his gaze once more. "You said it yourself. Five years is a long time."

Her head snapped up. "What was that?"

James scanned the cemetery with his eyes as Elise did the same at his back, but he heard it before he saw it—slow, shuffling, squelching. Footsteps.

"Perhaps it's the next shift," he muttered.

"Or maybe it's a zombie," Elise said.

She pointed, and James followed her finger to the street beyond the fence.

A figure slid into the light. His shoes were visible first, and then his shoulders illuminated. His hanging head shadowed his face and chest. The man was clad in a poorly-fitting gray suit, torn and splattered with mud. There was no shirt under the jacket, baring a sunken chest covered in raised veins and swimming black marks that were darker than shadow.

His head lifted. Light spilled onto his nose and angular jaw, which were gripped with veins. A single sigil was emblazoned between his eyebrows. James didn't need to look closely to know it was the same mark Lucinde had borne not too long before.

"You again," Elise murmured.

The possessed corpse shambled forward. His eyes didn't quite focus on either of them.

Elise and James backed toward the gate.

A twig snapped.

James spun. A woman lurched toward them from the darkness at the other end of the cemetery, her straggly hair caked in dirt. She, too, was clad in clothes that didn't suit her—a plain frock and a pair of cheap sandals. The dress was several sizes too big, and it hung off her shoulder, exposing a sagging breast.

Black tears streaked her cheeks. The other possessed one was close enough for James to see the swollen blood vessels in his eyes as well, and he realized that the woman's eyes had burst.

James edged over until he was shoulder to shoulder with his kopis. "This is your area of expertise. What do we do?"

"Kill them." She held a long, curved knife in one hand. James hadn't seen her draw it.

The woman sped up, and the man angled to cut off their exit. It took him a moment to realize Elise wasn't following him toward the fence.

"If they're here, their master won't be far," she said.

"You're suggesting we fight."

Elise was never given a chance to respond.

The man pitched toward her. She ducked away from his clumsy hands, delivering a kick squarely in the middle of the back. He tumbled into the mud.

"James—look out!"

He spun, but it was too late. A pair of hands dug into his shoulders, and the earth rushed to meet his face.

There was a smack, a crack, and the female was suddenly on the ground with him. A small sound came from her throat, more instinctive than a protest of pain.

James gasped and tried to squirm away, but the mud sucked him down, making it hard to move. Elise's foot came down on the woman's face once. The possessed one caught her ankle. She stumbled out of the grip.

The possessed woman clawed at his ankles when James

scrambled to his feet. Elise kicked her in the side of the head, even harder this time. It was accompanied by an even louder *crack*, and her skull caved in like a rotten egg that had been smashed against the asphalt.

The older man lurched forward, grabbing James's neck in both hands. He was slow, but too strong to stop.

James struggled to pry the hands away. "Elise," he groaned. "Help—please—"

The female grabbed Elise, dragging her to the ground. "I'm a little busy right now," she said.

He heaved with all his strength, peeling the arms away inch by inch. He could feel his pulse throbbing in his temple. The man, however, showed no signs of exertion. The possessed one pushed steadily on, its half-focused eyes fixed squarely on James's throat.

Out of the corner of his eye, he saw Elise grab a felled branch the size of his arm. She swung her makeshift club like a bat, and it hissed through the air, smashing into the woman's face.

James leaned back and pushed his knee between himself and the zombie, trying to kick him off.

The cold fingers tightened around his neck, the heels of his palms pressed into his esophagus, and the world grew darker—

Then a familiar blade came down on the servant's elbow, slicing across the inner joint. Blood gurgled sluggishly from the cut.

Elise cut again, and suddenly, all the pressure was gone from the right side of James's throat. The servant's hand fell limply to his side, and James wrenched away from him with a gasp. Fresh oxygen rushed into his lungs, and he coughed as the graveyard swam around him.

The man turned on Elise, groping for her with the arm

that still worked. She flung him to the ground. "Hold him," she ordered, and James approached cautiously.

"Is he…?"

"I slapped him with the pendant of St. Benedict," Elise said, taking the necklace of charms from her pocket. It jingled in the night. "I stuffed it in his mouth. He won't be able to get orders from his master until he manages to spit it out."

James put his foot on the servant's chest just in case. "You still carry extra medallions?" he asked.

"I just started again. It seemed like a good idea."

"A very good idea," he agreed, watching as Elise hauled the dead woman to her feet. The rain made her bloody face run with red tears.

"Where is your master?" she demanded. The body twisted and writhed, fighting to break free with a whining shriek. "I know you can speak. One of your demonic friends spoke through a girl tonight, so talk!"

Motion caught James's eye. A small, leathery body emerged from behind a tombstone, perching on the top. Its bulbous eyeballs shone dimly in the light, yellow and bulging and focusing directly on him.

Another scaled the fence. He turned, and his gaze fell on another as it crept out from the shadows of the building adjacent to the cemetery.

"I told you to talk!" Elise said. She slapped the corpse across the face as James edged closer. Decomposing brain, like cottage cheese, crumbled out of the crack in her skull.

"Elise…"

Yet another gray demon crept out from behind the tree. This close, he could see the blood encrusting its nails and the droop of its lower lip as it salivated with hunger.

"What, James?" she asked without taking her focus off

the struggling woman.

"I think we're about to have bigger problems."

Her face darkened in increments as she counted each demon. "Fiends. I *hate* those guys."

James swallowed. "We fight?"

"No. We don't stand a chance against three." The possessed woman suddenly stopped fighting and went limp in Elise's arms as though all her strings had been cut.

"What the hell...?" James wondered.

"The master must have realized the servants weren't doing anything," she said, dropping the body. "Run!"

She didn't need to tell him twice.

Elise leapt over the fallen body of the possessed woman, snatching at James's hand and dragging him along with her.

Their feet made sucking noises with every step, but James could hardly hear it over the pounding of his heart. He felt cold, awash with adrenaline. His gaze narrowed, focusing on the door to the cemetery's attached office, until all he could see was the door half-lit in the darkness of stormy night.

He hit the doors before Elise did, throwing them open. The lock was punched out—someone else had been there first.

"Get inside!" he bellowed.

They jumped in and slammed the double doors shut. Elise threw herself against it, bracing her back against the place in between the handles. The bodies crashed into the other side.

James dropped the flashlight to help, but she shook her head.

"Find something to hold the doors!"

He searched the room. There were potted plants, but

none heavy enough to hold the door. He grabbed the edge of check-in desk and pulled experimentally, but it was bolted to the floor. James flung open the door labeled "janitor."

Another heavy *thud*, and Elise grunted.

"Soon would be good," she growled.

James snatched a steel-handled mop from the closet. "Push," he said, trying to fit the mop through the handles. "I can't wedge it in like this."

Elise lost her footing, and the door opened partway. A hand pushed through the opening.

She grabbed it and twisted. Something snapped. The fingers went slack.

Her weight still wasn't enough to close the door.

James threw himself into it. It smashed shut on inhuman fingers, and something on the other side gave a cry, jerking them out of the way.

The doors closed. He wedged the mop's pole through the door handles.

She stepped back. The corpses slammed into the doors, and the hinges groaned, but the mop held.

He sighed and leaned against the wall.

"Don't stop yet. Keep moving," she said, grabbing his collar. She burst through the hall to the office, shutting the sliding doors behind them.

James scanned the office. The stormy half-light of night outside filtered through slatted blinds, casting faint barred shadows across a cheap desk and filing cabinet. The brown shag carpet broke off at the head of a tiled hallway, and another door stood closed nearby with a sign that said "lab." A map of the building hung on the wall, with the fire exit routes marked in red.

The banging grew more distant, and more insistent.

They jogged down the tiled hallway. Another set of doors stood at the very end.

"We might be able to get out and make a break for the car before they realize we've gone," Elise said.

"I'm not sure—"

Shuffling.

They turned, falling silent as they faced the source of the noise.

Fiends crouched at the end of the hall. It wasn't the small handful they had seen in the graveyard beyond the office walls—there were more, many more, perhaps a dozen. They shifted in the darkness, crawling over each other and halfway up the walls.

A pair scuttled forward and up, digging their claws into the stucco to scramble over James's head. He ducked, but they didn't stop. Instead, they dropped on the other side—between Elise and James and the exit.

On both sides, the demons waited, staring at them with luminescent eyes.

Elise gripped James's wrist. She didn't say what she was thinking, but he suspected it involved several expletives. He felt much the same. James shifted so his hand squeezed hers, and he hoped it was comforting.

The fiends growled softly. His heart raced, and adrenaline turned his blood to antifreeze.

Her body tensed. She was preparing to run.

The office door beside them slammed open.

James saw a flash of yellow claws and leathery skin. Small hands wrapped around his leg, and he jerked free, kicking it in the face. The little demon keened, reeling backward, but in its place came another.

Elise's knife flashed, glinting through the air like a blade of moonlight. She cut, ducking low and slicing along arms, across faces, pulling away from strikes. She moved smoothly, quickly, a dance of fist and blade. He fought to get free, trying to break from the increasing crowd of fiends as they clambered to grab him.

And then the demons from the end of the hall leapt into the fray, and James was swarmed. He elbowed a face, pushed another away. The tide of small bodies pulled him toward the conference room, and inexorably away from the slashing blade that was Elise.

She reached for James. "Elise!" he shouted, throwing his hand toward hers.

Their fingers brushed. The fiends yanked. James lost his footing, and he fell, caught by clawed hands a heartbeat before hitting the ground.

"James!"

He tried to grab the doorframe, but the fiends released him before he could orient himself. His face hit the stripping at the bottom of the door. Elise's sneakers moved —rising to strike a leathery body, pushing against the ground, fighting to get closer to James.

Then they jerked, dragging him down the floor. The carpet burned the side of his face.

"No!" Elise cried, struggling against the restraining arms of the fiends, pushing and hitting and scratching and doing no good whatsoever.

The door slammed shut.

The fiends wrenched James to his knees. He had an instant to see tiled floors, a drain, metal tables, and then the fiends pulled again. Nails dug into his arms. James didn't have to count the fiends to know there were too many to fight.

One of the demons clawed its way up his slacks until it stretched tall, almost up to his chest. Its fingers ran over his cheeks, his jaw, his nose.

The other demons jerked on his legs. James lost balance and his knees struck the carpet. The fiends made slurping, hungry noises deep in their throats, staring at him like a slab of meat.

Claws slid down his neck, catching on the hem of his shirt with a ripping sound. His chest was suddenly cold. His shirt had been torn open in one long line down the center, baring his chest and stomach.

He felt the sharp press of teeth against his hip and gave a shout.

"What are you doing?"

The other door opened. His heart leapt when he saw a feminine figure enter—but it wasn't Elise. The newcomer was swathed in a long jacket and a formless skirt. The fact he couldn't make out her face, or even her body type, didn't disturb James so much as the feeling of sheer *power* that poured off of her.

It wasn't the normal power that James got from other witches, like those in his coven. This feeling was unmistakably *evil*.

The witch drew a knife from behind her back.

"Oh," James said.

She touched the blade to his skin, and after that, all he could do was scream.

"No!"

Elise threw herself against the door. Locked.

Something scuffled behind her, and she spun, dagger raised for a blow. But the fiends had dispersed—gone from the hall as quickly as they had arrived in the first place.

They had what they wanted, and it wasn't Elise.

The air shifted, and motion from a fiend she had killed caught her eye. Blood dribbled sluggishly out of the slit on its neck. And then…something changed.

In her biology for non-majors college class, Elise had watched a time lapse video of a decaying rabbit. Its skin had rippled and exploded with maggots, the flesh disappearing as tiny fragments were carried off by numerous insects. The decay of the fiend was similar—one moment, it was whole and complete, and the next, its skin crumpled and peeled and flaked off, baring bone that burned away as well.

She watched, stunned, as invisible flame spread from the brands down its back and devoured the entire body, leaving nothing but dust.

Only very strong master demons could destroy its minions after they died.

And it had her aspis.

He screamed on the other side of the wall.

"James!" she yelled. She shook the doorknob again, harder. "James!"

She took a step back and threw all her strength into a single kick. Her blow landed beside the doorknob. *Crack.*

His screaming grew strangled. She kicked again.

The door was made of heavy oak. It barely shook.

"Shit," she muttered. The room number, mounted on a gold placard beside the door, said *6B*. If there was a 6B, there must have been a 6A.

She left James's screams and scanned the map on the wall, trying to make sense of it in the dark. Finding the red dot marking her position, she traced the hall around the building.

6A. There was another door in the opposite hall.

Elise ran. Her feet pounded against linoleum, each step a clap of thunder.

James's screams suddenly silenced.

She skid around the corner and almost lost her balance, catching herself on a door. 6A. Elise tried the doorknob, and it turned smoothly.

She threw the door open, ready for a fight—but she was met by an empty room.

The embalming room was dark and windowless. Every surface was tiled or clean steel, from the table affixed to the wall to the sinks and ceiling. A sign read, "Danger: Formaldehyde Irritant and Potential Cancer Hazard. Authorized Personnel Only." A row of locked refrigerators for bodies lined the wall, and a pump sat on a desk next to the table with liters and gallons measured on the side of its barrel.

Elise picked her way through the shattered debris of the embalming fluids. The scent made her gag. She covered her mouth to keep from vomiting as she rounded the table.

Her breath caught in her throat. "James…"

He was slumped in the corner, limbs twisted like a ragdoll. James's shirt was torn open to reveal his torso. Elise didn't need much light to recognize the black smears staining his chest: blood.

She felt his neck for a pulse. His throat pulsed in a slow, weak rhythm under her fingers.

"Thank God," she murmured, pushing his shirt aside to examine the wounds.

Someone had begun to skin a patch of James's stomach over his solar plexus, but it wasn't a random, messy job. The looping lines were deliberate and strangely neat. The knife must have been incredibly sharp.

Elise recognized that knife work. She still had the scar

on her chest. "Oh, James," she said, brushing his bangs out of his closed eyes.

Something moved.

Her gaze snapped over. A shape snuck out from behind the door Elise had left open.

Launching to her feet, she barreled into the intruder. The person screamed in a woman's voice. She gripped a short stone staff, dirty with blood and mud, and there was a pentacle charm on her bracelet.

It was a human—not a demon at all.

"Help!" she cried before Elise could smother her mouth.

She slammed the woman's hand into the wall until she cried out. Her fingers lost their grip, and the stone hit the floor.

Hands buried themselves in Elise's jacket and ripped her away.

She sprawled to the ground, catching a brief glimpse of a fiend as it pushed at the witch's legs. The jacket flared behind her as they ran from the room. Elise scrambled to the doorway in time to see the exit swing shut behind them.

Elise hesitated, casting a glance at James. She couldn't chase them without leaving her partner behind.

"Damn it!" she swore. James made a sound of pain, and Elise dropped to her knees at his side. "We need to get you out of here before someone shows up." His eyes half-opened at her voice, and she gave him a tight smile. "Come on. I'll help you up."

She lifted him carefully under the arms. He gave a weak attempt at getting his feet under him...and then went slack.

He was unconscious.

Chapter 11

The door to James's bedroom banged open.

Elise rushed through the doorway with James draped over her shoulders. She tried to roll him onto the bed gently, but he slipped and hit the mattress hard. He made a small pain noise in his sleepy delirium.

"Sorry," she said. James didn't react to her apology.

She cut his shirt open along the sleeves and tugged it out from underneath him, chucking it in the trash. The bandages she had packed over his wound in the car had already soaked through with blood.

Elise searched through James's desk drawers for gauze and bandages, returning once she located them amongst a secret stash of Milk Duds. Blood welled up in the cuts as soon as they were bared to the air as though he had been sliced open anew.

She had suffered enough wounds to know that a little cutting shouldn't have knocked James out, nor should it have bled so much. Poison, or magic? Either was trouble.

Summoning first aid experience from the musty corners of her memory, Elise bandaged him carefully. Her gaze wandered to the phone on the bedside table as she worked. She couldn't call Stephanie. Even though the doctor would be all too happy to nurse James back to health, she would have questions Elise didn't want to answer.

But she couldn't give him the help he needed herself.

Muttering a terse prayer, she called Stephanie on James's cell phone. "James," the doctor breathed on the other end. "It's about time you called me."

"This is Elise."

"Oh. Really. What are you doing calling from his number at this time of night?"

"He's hurt. He might be poisoned."

"Poisoned?" Stephanie's voice sharpened. "Why are you wasting your time calling me? Hang up and call the poison control center, he needs—"

"We can't call anyone, go to the hospital, or attract any attention," Elise snapped. "He needs you. Are you going to come help him or what?"

"What are you doing, you stupid bitch? Call an ambulance! I'll meet you at the emergency room."

She counted slowly to ten, and then said, "Stephanie. I'm not messing around."

"What happened?"

Elise glanced at her prone partner. His face was ashen gray. "James is unconscious but breathing fine. He's bleeding from a shallow wound on his chest. I would guess that he's stable for the moment."

She cursed. "You did this to him, didn't you?"

"Now isn't the time for blame."

The doctor gave a disgusted sigh. "You're going to have to call someone else anyway. I was volunteered to take the directors to Sacramento International, so I'm still at least two hours away. If you care about him at all, you'll get proper medical attention."

"We have to wait for you." A grimace, and she added, "Please." She choked out the last word with no small amount of pain, but it made Stephanie pause. There was silence for a long moment. When the doctor spoke again, the venom had left her tone.

"If he dies…"

"I would care a hell of a lot more than you do. James needs to be looked at, and I can't do it myself."

"Make sure the wound is clean and well-wrapped. Two hours. Less if I rush."

"Then rush."

Elise hung up and sat back. She hoped she was right in trusting Stephanie. But…who would have known that Elise and James would exorcise Lucinde and get the "Sorrows" message?

The people in the coven might. They were the only ones who knew James was connected with an exorcist. But if Elise couldn't trust the other witches, she could be in even worse trouble than she suspected.

Elise studied James's room. What if Ann or Morrighan had left some kind of trap? She scanned the dark walls, watching closely for a telltale glimmer of eyes staring back.

James's bedroom was too small for anyone to hide in it. The walls were lined with bookshelves, and not an inch of space was wasted. His bed rested atop several archivist boxes, each lovingly packed with texts that were too valuable to see the light of day. His headboard was stacked with shelving, too. The only free space was in front of the window where his altar stood. A statuette of the Goddess leaned against the right side of the window frame, mirrored by the Horned God to the left.

Elise sank into the worn chair at his desk and swiveled

around so she could see James. A yawn caught in her throat.

Ignoring her body's demands for sleep, she withdrew the short stone staff from her jacket pocket. It felt heavier than it should have been at only twelve inches long, as though it was lead instead of rock. Elise rubbed her thumb on the surface, scrubbing away some of the dirt to reveal demonic runes.

The stone was cool under her hand, sucking her body heat deep into its core. The staff felt unmistakably alive.

And evil.

Elise cleared off space on James's desk, which was covered in notebooks with his precise handwriting and illustrations of sigils. Some of it was for the annual almanac his coven published, but some of it looked like fresh spellwork. Several were weighted down with crystals, collecting their energy for later use. She set the stone staff somewhere it didn't touch anything else.

James made a small noise again. His skin shone with sweat, and pain twisted his face into a grimace.

"Are you awake?" she whispered, sitting beside him.

He didn't move.

She let out a long, slow breath, letting her hand fall to his chest above the bandage. Sweat soaked through the material, and dots of blood were seeping through as well.

His eyes fluttered open. "Elise," he whispered. "Are you all right?"

"You're the one that got carved up by a big bad witch. Don't waste your strength worrying about me." He moved like he was going to sit up, but she held him down. It wasn't as much of a struggle as it should have been. "I'm here. Nothing will get you." He mumbled softly. "Nothing will get you," Elise said again, mostly as an affirmation to herself.

She sunk down lower on the bed beside him, rested her cheek against his upper arm, and laid her hand over his heart. The beat was slow. He sounded so...weak.

Elise could hear her own heart in her chest, beating strong. She wanted his heart to beat like hers. She wished so hard for a moment she almost convinced herself she could keep him alive on willpower alone.

He stroked her hair weakly. "It's okay," he said, and it was such a lie that she had to smile.

"You're right," she said. "It's okay."

His hand slipped over hers when she sat up. "Stay."

"James..."

"Stay, Elise," he repeated, more strongly this time.

She didn't want to argue with him. The weight of her fatigue was too convincing. Whether or not Elise had time to take a nap, she was failing her battle against sleep. And why not? Stephanie was still two hours away.

Elise kicked her shoes off the side of the bed and rested beside James.

The air was heavy and still, but she didn't dare open a window to let it cool. His heart thumped its steady pace under her hand, and his shallow breaths marked out a rhythm like water rushing up the sand before sucking into the ocean again.

Or like wind blowing in the trees, sweeping through the branches.

Her muscles were leaden. Her eyes couldn't open.

The walls of the room collapsed slowly inward. Moss spread beneath her cheek as vines of ivy slithered up James's bookshelves. Leaves spread between the pages of the books.

Thunder rolled. Papers dripped onto the desk one by

one and drizzled onto the floor.

Ivory fingers reached out to turn off the lamp, leaving the only light an occasional flash of lightning in the bellies of the red clouds. Rain began to tumble down the walls like a sticky-sweet waterfall.

Elise's parents stood beside the desk, waiting for her arrival as the second hands on the clock rushed toward twelve. She was running late. Somehow, she had gotten caught in the storm and lost her way.

She twisted and turned in search of a path. They were waiting. She couldn't keep them waiting.

A cool hand smoothed over her cheek, light as the kiss of the breeze. Forgiving. Her parents smiled down at her, calm but unseeing. Her mother's left eye socket was empty, and it rained within her skull.

The sky poured down, and Elise sat, her pale skin bared to the elements.

"Crux sacra sit mihi lux, non draco sit mihi dux..."

"Let the holy cross be my light, let the serpent not lead me astray."

"Vade retro, Satana..."

"Step back, Satan."

What do you think that means, Elise? A gentle smile. But who smiled? Where were the eyes belonging to those lips?

"Nunquam suade mihi vana..."

"What you offer me is evil..."

But what is evil?

The question wasn't part of the exorcism ritual. And neither was the second part—*what is goodness?* She had no answers for either. *"Sunt mala quae libas..."*

Such a sweet smile.

"Ipse venena bibas..."

"Drink the poison yourself..."

Fluid dripped from the corner of that mouth. There were hands, but they didn't wipe the poison away. It was dark burgundy, the crimson of wine...or blood.

One more time, Elise. From the top.

"*Crux sacra sit mihi lux, non draco sit mihi dux. Vade retro, Satana, nunquam suade mihi vana. Sunt mala quae libas, ipse venena bibas.*"

Very good. Again.

The branches scraped her vulnerable body.

"*Crux sacra sit mihi lux...*"

The ground disappeared. Elise fell, and fell...

The yawning blackness devoured her whole.

And fell...

Drink the poison yourself...

"I am the cold kiss of Death," the goddess whispered into her ear, "and you can never defeat me."

Elise's arms were bound to the stone wall behind her. Her face was bloody but set in a determined glare. Mud packed the open wound on her hip. A red cloak she didn't remember wearing pooled around her body. The death goddess—had she any other name?—stood high above her, swathed in shadow and holding a staff of sharpened human bone.

"Alive or dead, I will come back for you," the goddess murmured.

"You can't think this will do any good," Elise spat. The sky outside, visible through a small window near the ceiling, was black, blue, purple, and scarlet. Blood and pus bubbled from her wound. "You can't kill me yet. Not without screwing up your apocalyptic plans."

She laughed. Deep, throaty, bubbling like Elise's blood. "Who says I plan to use you?"

In her other hand, she clutched a stone dagger that sang

with power. It was covered in symbols, some more familiar than others.

Her blood bulged in her veins. *Ipse venena bibas...*

The witch had clutched a stone, too.

James.

The sky faded to orange and back to red.

He ran through the jungle searching for Elise. The branches scraped at him, though the trees never moved, but still he searched. She watched him from her prison with the goddess, and she almost wished he wouldn't find her as much as she longed for him to save her.

The death goddess drew intricate designs in Elise's skin with vivid crimson ink.

Her breast rose and fell with breath. Her heartbeat fluttered.

The witch. The stone staff. Death.

Who says I plan to use you?

Her eyes flew open, and she *saw*.

Sleep ripped away from Elise. Consciousness slammed into her body. She gasped, flinching against the blow that never came—and then realized she heard the familiar sound of cars rushing by on the street outside.

Elise sat up. Nothing inside the room made noise but James's erratic breathing. He had pushed the sheets off to bare his body to the waist even though the room was only sixty degrees. She pressed her hand to his back. His temperature almost scorched her palm.

He made a small noise and moved into her touch, rolling over without waking up. His eyelids were dark, almost bruised.

"James," she said softly.

She searched for her cell phone in the darkness. Only an hour and a half had passed.

Elise slipped out of bed to search the closet for spare clothes. She located clean jeans and a shirt by touch, identifying it as her Black Death concert top by the hole near the hem.

When she finished changing, she returned to James. She checked his temperature with a hand to his forehead, and he was even hotter than he had been before. Sleep had done neither of them any good. James hadn't improved, and Elise had lost time.

Someone knocked at the door. She looked out the window to confirm that Stephanie's car was in the lot before meeting her at the door. The doctor's normally neat coif was frazzled.

"Thanks for coming," Elise said as Stephanie pushed past her into the house.

"Is he in bed?"

Elise nodded, and the doctor blew into his bedroom.

She sat beside him on the mattress and opened her bag. Elise waited in the doorway while Stephanie gave James a short and clinical examination. After a few minutes, the doctor took off her gloves.

"Can you take care of him here?" Elise asked.

"It doesn't look too bad," Stephanie said. "He doesn't seem to have lost enough blood to be struggling, and there hasn't been enough time for infection to set in." The doctor leveled a stern look at Elise. "He needs to be taken to a hospital."

"Will he die if he remains untreated for a few hours?"

"I can't be sure."

"I need you to stay and monitor him," Elise said. "I have to find the person that did this. Once they're out of the picture, you can send him to any hospital you want."

"Don't you think you should call the police?" Stephanie

asked, following Elise out of the room. "Whoever attacked him is deranged."

"The police won't be able to help. You have to stay."

She folded her arms. "It goes against every good practice I know."

"Great," Elise said. "Now listen close. I'm going to lock all the doors and windows before I leave. Don't open any of them until I come back. James has set up wards around the apartment, so he'll be safe as long as they're shut. Don't let anyone in, don't call an ambulance, don't call the police. If you want James to make it to the hospital at all, you have to keep quiet."

Stephanie nodded reluctantly. "I'll take care of him."

"Thanks," Elise said. "Don't let him die."

She disappeared into the night.

The casino was full at three in the morning. Tricks of light and shadow made the room an endless plane of slot machines, where the drunk and down-on-their-luck hunched before digital screens. Listless, addicted gamblers fidgeted nearby as they watched for the next game to make them lucky.

Day, night. Neither mattered. Neither existed.

Money passed from player to casino attendant and became chips, and the chips went from hand to table, then to the dealer, and back to the attendants. The artificial clattering, jingling, singing sounds of slots and video poker paying out or begging to be played filled the air with discordant chorus.

The air was thick, and not with cigarette smoke. What it masked was impossible to ignore—an eternal depression, a feeling of being trapped. The feel of people imprisoning themselves in a place where the odds were low and wishing for a row of lucky sevens to change their ruined lives.

Elise moved quickly across the floor, watching each table as she passed. Cards whispered across the velvet—ten of spades, three of hearts, suicide king—and were taken into hands with nails yellow from tobacco.

She didn't enjoy the casinos here. She had been to Vegas and little back-alley stands in Eastern Europe where the dice were all hand-carved, and either was better. At least there was fun and good company to be had elsewhere.

It didn't take long for Elise to spot who she was looking for. David Nicholas never slept, and seldom worked, so he made up for decades of spare time with a platinum gambling card at every casino and a reserved spot at the Texas Hold-'Em table. He was a ghost beside two swarthy tourists with purple rings under their eyes. He cupped a stack of dwindling chips in one hand.

"Check," he said, tapping his cards on the table. He glanced up as Elise approached, his hand half-raised as though he expected a cocktail waitress. Then he realized who it actually was, and his face fell. "Shit."

Elise hauled him out of his chair and dragged him to the back door, flinging him into the alley behind the casino. The nightmare splashed into a puddle of rainwater and trash. He stared up at her with an expression like that of a rabbit spotting a hawk.

Jerking him up by the collar, she slammed him into the wall. "Tell me what you know," she snarled, pushing her dagger against the nightmare's stomach.

"Hang on, wait, whoa," David Nicholas said, holding his hands up. "All I know is I was winning a hand of hold-'em and you interrupted my streak. What do you think you're doing?"

"I've been inspired to take a break from accounting. If you cooperate, I can cut my vacation short. Understand?"

"I've got no idea what you're talking about."

"You're the one who told me something was coming when I visited Craven's," she said. "I'm starting to suspect you might have been onto something. I'm here to chat about it." Elise jerked on his collar again. He gurgled. "Chat, David Nicholas."

She dropped him back into the trash. Rats scurried away. "Don't think I got to chat about anything with you," he said. "It isn't profitable to play with humans...unless you want to try to make it that way, if you're catching my meaning."

She studied the blade of her knife, testing the edge against her thumb. "Tell you what. You tell me what you were talking about at the club, and I'll make it profitable by not stabbing you...again. I'm looking for a demon that can resurrect people."

He slipped a pack of cigarettes out of his sleeve and tapped one into his hand. He lit it, but didn't take a puff, contemplating the glowing end as he rolled it between his first finger and thumb.

"Demons can't resurrect people on their own."

"Yeah, but something is doing it anyway. Does the name *le Main de Morte* ring a bell?"

"The what *de* what?"

"The Hand of Death. That's what I said, the Hand of Death."

He sneered. "Death's Hand," David Nicholas murmured. "Old bastard."

"You know it, then."

"Know of it, yeah. It's hellborn. There was lots of talk about Death's Hand a few years ago. It was some big fad to talk about it, like, ooh, it's going to kill us dead, it's going to destroy Earth." David Nicholas took a drag. "Didn't happen, as you see. I wasn't worried about it. I never worry about that kind of thing."

"So it can resurrect people," Elise pressed.

"It can *reanimate*. Huge difference," he said, leaning one elbow on an orange crate. "Move corpses. You know, like a puppet."

"A little girl died," she said. "This Death's Hand thing possessed her. I performed an exorcism, and when he was gone, she was alive again."

"Treaty of Dis says demons can't perform resurrections. Only humans can do it, and not many of them at that. Just those special witches—you know, necromancers." He dropped his cigarette on the top of a nearby crate and ground it in with his fingers. His other hand was already moving to bring a second to his lips. "So can I go back to my game now?"

"No. What were you trying to warn me about?"

David Nicholas spread his hands wide. "What am I supposed to say? I got four hundred and sixty-three years of knowledge rattling around inside my skull. I could warn you about things that would give the Night Hag nightmares." His black eyes grew shadowed. "You got a necromancer on your hands, and you're in bigger trouble than anyone would be able to help you with."

"Tell me why."

"Death's Hand reanimates, right? Useful trick. You work your slaves to death, then bring 'em back and do it all over again." He shrugged, and it looked like his bony shoulders could almost pierce his jacket. "If it got a necromancer, though, it could resurrect, too. All Death's Hand's got to do is reanimate a freshly dead necromancer to create a bond with it, and—"

"I thought you said it couldn't come to Earth," Elise interrupted. "There are no necromancers in Hell. There aren't even any necromancers on Earth, come to think of it. Not in years."

"It can't actually come up. With a dark object, yeah, it can *appear* up here. But with the help of a necromancer, Death's Hand would have a heck of a lot easier time finding a witch to become a vessel."

Elise slipped her hand into her pocket, wrapping her hand around the stone she had taken from the witch. It vibrated ever so slightly as though it knew they were talking about it. "What do you mean, a vessel?"

"Someone to possess. A strong enough witch with the right power could become the body of Death's Hand. Like an ascension, you know, but without the centuries of building up its power first. 'Course, once Death's Hand has a body, it won't need a pet necromancer any more. It'll destroy him and keep the bits it wants, like everything else it reanimates."

"Destroy him," she echoed. "Do you mean…"

"Death's Hand destroys its legions once they're used up. Clean-up, you know. Real easy and nice. It won't need the necromancer to keep the power after awhile. Hypothetically, of course. That would violate the Treaty of Dis and bring down all kinds of hellfire, and nobody's stupid enough to do that."

"Good. Thanks." Elise turned to leave.

"*Vedae som matis*," he said. He said the words with a strange accent, almost choking on them, as though they were spoken in the throat rather than the mouth.

"What?"

"*Vedae som matis*. It's the demon language, and that's what they call it down there. Thought you might be interested."

"What does *vedae som matis* mean?"

"Hand of Death."

Shocking. Elise stuck her knife back in her belt. "Thanks for the information."

"This is twice now you've made me had a bad day, cabbage," David Nicholas called after her as she headed down the alley. "First one was free. Second one's going to cost you."

"Send a bill to my office," she snapped. "The check bounced, by the way. I'm going to get that money from you in blood if I have to."

"Go ahead and try," he said. His eyes glowed.

Elise mulled over the information he had given her as she navigated the alleys behind the casino. *Vedae som matis*. Death's Hand. Reanimation, not resurrection. That would explain why it had possessed Lucinde. She must not have been strong enough to become the vessel of Death's Hand. James had enough power, but Death's Hand needed a dead witch.

She wrapped her hand around the stone in her pocket, as though it might give her answers. The sense of demonic energy had grown in intensity, ringing throughout Elise's senses.

Had the staff begun radiating more energy, or was it something...else?

Elise picked up the pace again and stretched out her senses. Yes, there were definitely demons around, and it wasn't hard to guess what would be tracking her.

Fiends. And they were close.

She gripped her knife. Elise hurried down the sidewalk toward the parking garage. Dancing casino lights lit her path, casting flickering shadows on the street before her, turning the night into a tired carnival of once-great businesses harping their unwanted wares.

A chill crept up her spine, and the demonic sensations intensified.

Motion blurred at the corner of Elise's vision.

She spun, cutting the dagger through the night air. A huge fist grabbed her before she could even see the attached face—the corpse from the hospital again—and slammed her hand into the wall. Concrete scraped her exposed fingers. Pain shocked up her arm. Her fingers lost their grip on the dagger, and it clattered to the concrete.

The possessed one twisted her around, jerking her into his body and wrapping a steel-clad arm around her. He threw himself backward into the shadow of a building, taking Elise with him.

She lost her footing, and the servant forced her against a wall. His hot hand clamped over her nose and mouth, cutting off her breath. The rag in his hand smelled faintly sweet, and slightly alcoholic. Elise had never smelled anything like it before, but she'd seen enough movies to recognize chloroform.

She held her breath, but her throat burned with the taste of chemicals, and it was too late.

Chapter 12

Betty took the coffee pot out of the machine, grabbed a cozy, and set both on the table in front of Anthony. "Drink," she said.

Anthony slumped forward on her table and dropped his chin on his folded arms. He wore a button-down shirt and clean jeans, and there wasn't a spot of oil anywhere on his body. He was well-dressed for the crack of dawn. "I don't want it."

"Cheer up," she said. "Caffeine's a mood booster."

"I hate coffee."

She dropped into the chair beside him, moved the vase so it wasn't between them, and poured herself a cup. "Of course you like coffee. Everyone likes coffee. It's just a matter of how much sugar and creamer you need." She punctuated her statement by emptying the cream bottle into her half-full mug and sprinkling sugar atop it, stirring with a swizzle stick topped by a hula dancer. "Did you even change out of your clothes after last night?"

"No. I slept like this," he said. "I just don't get it. If she didn't want to go on another date with me, why would she agree to go out in the first place?"

"Isn't that just another delightful part of the enigma that is Elise?"

"It's fucked up, that's what it is." He glanced at the coffee pot. "What kind is that?"

"Komodo blend," she said, wafting the cup in the air. "Also known as percolated heaven. Sound good yet?"

"No."

Betty took a large slurp of the coffee and set it down again. "I'm going to give it to you straight, baby cousin of mine: Elise would not be afraid of refusing dates. If she thought your first date sucked, she would get that look that says in her not-so-sneaky way that if you speak to her again she'll break your nose. That's about as subtle as she gets. Agreeing to a date and then ditching you—that isn't her *modus operandi*."

He grunted. "I guess."

"Do you know how many boyfriends she's had in the time I've known her?"

"I don't think I want to know."

"None," Betty said. "Not one. And do you know how many guys have asked her out?" Anthony shook his head. "None. She scares everyone off. I think she was impressed that you asked her at all."

"Well, I'm not scared of some girl," Anthony said.

She smacked him. "Don't be an ass. Elise is terrifying."

"Fine, whatever, she's terrifying. I still really like her." He scoffed. "I *did* like her."

"Cut her some slack."

"She ditched me without a phone call. Her only text said that she got caught up doing something with James," Anthony said.

"Then that's probably true."

He leaned against the back of the chair, cupping his

hands behind his neck. He rolled his thoughts around for a moment before speaking. "Do you think Elise and James…?"

She took a long, slow drink of her coffee, setting it down with a satisfied sigh. "No."

"But—"

"*No*. That dance studio is a monastery. I promise."

"Then she just doesn't like me," he concluded stubbornly. Betty ignored him. "I'm not going to wait around for her to notice me and I'm not going to give her another chance."

"Sure," she said. "Did I remember to mention that she joined that pole dance class at that rival studio? They're doing an exhibition next week and she's going to be dancing in a bikini. Gyrating. Sweaty."

His eyes lit up. "Really? When?"

"I'm lying, Elise didn't join the class. She doesn't even know where her hips are." Betty laughed. "'Giving up on her.' You're so full of shit."

He couldn't help but laugh too. "You're nuts, Betty. You know—" Anthony suddenly went rigid. His eyes widened. "Wait. Did you hear that?"

The window exploded.

Glass showered into the kitchen. Betty shrieked, throwing herself under the table, and Anthony followed, sliding to the floor for cover.

Something heavy—not large, but insanely *dense*— crashed through the broken window. It rolled on the glass shards, knocking the appliances from the counters to the floor, and hit the linoleum with the *thud* of a cannonball hitting concrete.

It stopped moving for an instant. Only an instant. It was gray, hulking, covered in twisted red scars. Eyes like soft balls stuck out on either side of its head.

And it was screaming.

Its eyelids flashed open and then shut again. It clawed at its own face, its screech the mix of a sob and a wail, and Betty slapped her hands over her ears to block out the noise. Blood trailed from the corners of its eyes and the gash of its mouth.

Icy terror smashed into Anthony's chest, and for an instant, he couldn't breathe.

His focus narrowed on the monster. *Fight.*

He knocked the table over, putting it between himself and the monster. It smashed into the tabletop. Wood squealed against the floor, and Betty cried out.

"Move," Anthony said, "move! Hide!"

It barreled into the table again and then fell back, still tearing at its eyes and screaming. Betty hurried to her feet, and he pushed her toward the hallway. She knocked over one of the chairs in her haste.

The monster rushed her, a blur of shrieking rage and agony.

Anthony threw himself into its side, knocking them both down. Its three-fingered hands clamped onto his arms like a steel vice.

He was airborne. The wall became huge in his vision.

Pain rang through his body, and his face hit the floor.

It went for Betty again. Anthony pushed himself to all fours and shook his head to clear his vision. His cousin threw herself into the closet and tried to pull it shut, but it had gotten a hand in the way and she was screaming and Anthony couldn't revel in his pain. He had to focus.

"Where's your dad's shotgun?" he yelled.

Betty's panicked eyes met his. "My bedroom closet—it's not loaded—"

He slid into the kitchen, scooping up the first sharp thing he saw. The monster tore open the closet door and reached for Betty.

"Hey," Anthony said, "hey! Over here!"

He flung the knife at the monster, missing by at least two feet. It turned its bulging eyes on him. Eyelids cracked, he could just make out a sliver of massive pupil staring at him. Betty jerked her foot into the closet and shut the door.

Its jaw dropped wide and it roared, shrill and berserk. Sputum slapped against its chin.

Anthony made a break for the bedroom. The monster dodged into his path. He leapt over its head, dashing for the bedroom, and slammed the door. The lock clicked.

It crashed into the door with a wail.

Anthony paused for an instant, sucking in a hard breath of air, watching Betty's door. The monster hit again, but it held.

He went to the closet and began to search.

Tío Jacob didn't like the idea of his little girl living alone without protection, even with her cousin next door, so he had gifted her with a combat assault shotgun as a housewarming gift. At the time, Betty had teased her dad for being so paranoid, but it didn't seem nearly so paranoid now.

Anthony found the gun, unzipping the sleeve to withdraw it. The monster smashed into the other side of the door. It began to buckle.

He tore through Betty's shelves, knocking her collection of records to the floor and shuffling through a pile of stuffed animals to find where she kept the ammo. A stack of boxes were clustered in the back corner of her closet, dusty and unopened since the day Anthony had given them to her. He had bought her two kinds of rounds: one for target shooting, and double ought for making sure a live target would never get up again.

He grabbed the double ought.

Another hit. The door splintered.

Anthony slammed his shoulder into the crack to keep it from breaking entirely. His hands shook as he tried to get a round out of the box. He dropped it. Ammunition spilled across the carpet.

Swearing, he dropped to the floor and held the door shut with a foot, back pressed against the foot of Betty's bed. He slid open the loading port on the bottom of the shotgun.

Anthony counted out the shells he could reach as he loaded it—no time to panic—and pumped once. The chamber wasn't full, but if he needed more rounds to kill that thing, he probably wouldn't live to do it anyway. He kept the number of rounds hovering in his head—five— and let go of the door.

He had only an instant to get on one knee, shotgun braced against his shoulder, before the monster broke through. It rushed at him on all fours, its nails tearing into the carpet.

He angled down and squeezed the trigger.

BLAM.

The recoil knocked the butt of the shotgun into the pad of his shoulder and he rocked backward. The monster's arm disappeared in a spray of blood and pellets smacked into the floor.

He pumped the action and an empty casing went flying. *Four.*

It screamed a terrible scream that made his eardrums throb, rearing back on its stubby legs. Anthony braced properly this time and squeezed the trigger again.

BLAM.

Suddenly, the monster didn't have a face.

Three rounds.

With no flesh, Anthony could see all too well the pellets that had buried into its skull. There was blood everywhere, tassels of skin, the dribbling remnants of its left eyeball. Some of the pellets had implanted in the drywall behind its head and Anthony's ears were ringing.

It raised onto its remaining forearm and dragged its carcass toward him.

He stood, pointing the muzzle of the shotgun straight down at its head, and pulled the trigger once more.

BLAM.

The monster flattened without the back of its skull.

Two.

Was it dead? Anthony didn't care to find out. He pumped again.

BLAM. Pump. The casing hit the carpet. *BLAM.*

Empty.

Anthony lifted the shotgun and tapped the remnants of the monster with the toe of his shoe. Its mangled body didn't react. It occurred to him, distantly, that his only pair of nice jeans were soaked in blood and that he couldn't hear anymore.

But the monster was dead. *Very* dead.

"You can come out, Betty," he called. He wasn't sure if he actually yelled or not—he couldn't hear his own voice.

The closet door at the end of the hall opened and Betty crept out. Her mouth moved, and he knew she was speaking, but all he heard was a sound like a vibrating tuning fork.

She stood in the doorway, gaping at the body, and her mouth kept on moving. Judging by her expression, he was glad he didn't have to listen to her.

The quality of the air in the room changed, and the remnants of the monster dissolved into the carpet.

Anthony leapt forward and tried to grab what used to be a finger—for what, he wasn't sure—but it crumbled in his hand. Even the blood and chunks of intestine on his pants evaporated into puffs of smoke, leaving him as clean as he had been before the fight.

The entire thing was gone in seconds, and only the mess of shotgun damage proved there had ever been a fight.

Betty was agape. "Oh…my…god. What just happened?" It sounded as though she was whispering.

"I have no idea," Anthony said. Biggest understatement of his life.

"Dad is going to be pissed when I tell him what happened to his carpet." She stared at the floor—the empty shell casings, the chewed-up shag, and the pile of ash that had once been a body. Then she looked up at her cousin, the shotgun balanced between his hands, and a grin broke across her face. "That was *so* cool!" She punched his arm. "You're practically G.I.-fucking-Joe!"

He dropped the shotgun and collapsed on the end of her bed. Anthony's hands wouldn't stop shaking. "Fuck."

"Oh man, I think that might have been the most incredible experience of my life!"

Anthony worked his jaw around, trying to clear out his ears. His hearing had almost entirely returned, and the ringing was replaced by…silence.

"Why is it so quiet?"

Betty stopped quivering with delight to look at him. "Huh?"

"Where are the sirens?"

"There aren't any."

"That thing was loud. If someone had phoned in a disturbance, we'd have at least one car by now."

Betty peered through her window to the silent street beyond. "I don't know. There's nobody outside, so maybe no one's home—or the cops could be called away on something else."

"Or something big is going on," Anthony said. "I think someone just tried to kill us."

"Kill us? With a deformed monkey? Why?"

Anthony used Betty's bed post to haul himself into a standing position. "Something weird was happening with the coven. James said there were—I don't know, demons or something. He called in an exorcist to help him. Didn't he say that she was a friend?"

Betty nodded. "Yeah, but that was about Marisa's kid." A light clicked on behind her eyes. "Oh. *Oh*. But that's impossible, I would know if…"

"Elise is the exorcist," he finished. "She's been injured. She's not talking about why."

"Aren't priests the only ones who can do that stuff?" Betty asked, starting to pace. She didn't let Anthony respond before continuing. "Okay, let's say something is happening—maybe Elise is an exorcist or maybe she isn't. It already attacked Marisa's family. It attacked us. For all we know, it could have attacked Elise and James last night. Maybe that's why she ditched you." She gasped. "Maybe it's after our coven!"

"That's kind of a leap." He laughed. "This is ridiculous."

Betty rested her hands on his shoulders. "Anthony, not to sound patronizing, but you just killed a gargoyle on my carpet."

"Good point."

She left the room, searching through the rubble that had

been her kitchen. "We need to find out if anyone else has been attacked. Help me find my cell phone?"

Anthony nodded. "Yeah, sure. Who's left?"

"Those two witches that live up at the lake," Betty said. "Windsong and her husband, Phoenix. Then there's Morrighan, but she left to visit her grandparents in Virginia this morning. Stephanie lives in the area, but I don't have her number. The only person in town is Ann."

He plucked Betty's pink phone from the spilled coffee pot. "Found it." Betty hurried to remove the battery, but it was too late—something inside the phone fizzled. She sighed.

"Okay, we'll just have to use the neighbor's house phone to call everyone."

"Ann lives just up the hill from the university. I'll go check on her. Want to come?"

She surveyed the damage around her. "No. I should patch the window and clean up all that glass."

"Call her and tell her I'm on my way. Whatever's going on…it's serious. Do you think you could get a hold of Elise too?"

"I'll make sure she's okay," Betty said. She grabbed the shotgun from the bedroom and gave it to him, as well as a new box of shells. "I'll make sure everyone's okay. Call me when you find Ann—we should get together and figure out what's going on. She's smart. She'll know."

"Okay," he said, dropping the ammo into his pocket. "Watch yourself."

He ran out to his Jeep and jumped in, stowing the gun behind his seat. Anthony suspected he was scared— probably even terrified—and he just couldn't feel it yet. He hadn't stopped shaking. It wasn't the time to freak out. Later, the shock of what had just happened would probably sink in, and he could really freak out.

At the moment, though, he had a purpose, and that was enough to keep him moving.

Chapter 13

Drip...drip drip...

Elise's head throbbed in time with a distant beat. Her shoulders and ankles ached. Her eyes felt sticky.

Drip drip...

Where was she?

"James?" she croaked. Her throat was too thick and dry to speak properly. She swallowed and smacked her lips, rolling her tongue around in her mouth. "James?"

Drip...drip...

Something was running down her arm. She tried to lift her head against gravity, which seemed to have tripled while she was unconscious. The plain gray ceiling had a drain in the middle. The floor was covered in exposed beams.

Wait. No. That wasn't right.

Elise was hanging upside down by her ankles.

She squinted at her arm in the dim light. Blood trickled out of the inner corner of her elbow, trailed down her hand, and dripped off her fingertip. That sound was her blood hitting the floor. Never a good sign.

She relaxed and shut her eyes to collect herself. It wasn't

the first time Elise had been captured by a demon. This was like riding a bicycle. A hell bicycle made of damned skeletons and fire, but a bicycle nevertheless.

Counting silently to ten, she opened her eyes again to study the room around her.

It was empty. No furniture, which meant no obstructions to use as hiding places. She knew she must have been disarmed, but she double checked her waist anyway. Even her holsters had been taken away. She wasn't surprised to find that the stone staff was missing.

Flexing her abs to sit up, she held onto her ankles and examined the bindings. Silk ropes. What kind of demon used silk ropes? They were pulled tight against the iron hook by her weight, but nothing prevented her from untying them. She lifted herself on the hook with one hand while she picked at the knots with her fingernails.

The loss of blood made her weak. She had to rest twice before she could unravel the knots enough to get her first leg free. The second was short work after that, and she lowered herself carefully to the floor.

Changing orientation after being upside down for so long made her head rush. She braced a hand against the wall for a moment.

Deep breaths.

The only light came from the crack underneath the door. It looked like she was in an unfurnished, windowless basement, and her own blood was oozing toward the drain in the floor.

She finally got a good look at the wall she had been hanging on, and she jerked her hand back. The sigil from Lucinde's forehead had been painted in blood on the wall. It stretched from floor to ceiling. Elise had been hanging in the middle of it.

All that blood couldn't have come from her. She searched her body for injuries and only found a nick in the veins of each arm. It was already clotting.

She sniffed it. Definitely blood.

Someone moved on the other side of the door.

Elise crouched behind it, twisting the ropes around her fists and stretching them tight to form a garrote. Her heart wasn't even beating fast. A strange kind of calm settled over her—the calm before the killing.

It swung open. She prepared to jump.

And Ann stepped in.

Elise brought the ropes down in front of the witch, yanking them against her throat to pull her back against Elise's body.

She wrenched the ropes back. Ann choked.

"Elise—"

Turning her fists to tighten the ropes, Ann's words became incoherent gurgles. She slapped against Elise's hands as they sank to the floor together. The witch's feet kicked helplessly against the concrete.

Elise nudged the door open with a toe to look in the hall. Empty. Shouldn't there have been something guarding her?

Doubt crept in as Ann's struggles grew weaker. What if James had sent her?

Ann gave strained spluttering noise.

Elise released her. She collapsed.

"What are you doing here?" Elise asked, crouching over her body. She gave Ann's legs and sides a brief pat, searching for weapons, and didn't find anything.

The witch sucked in several hard breaths. Her ruddy face had broken out in sweat.

"They aren't kidding when they say you're like a human

weapon, are they?" she gasped. "That *really* hurt. I thought you were going to kill me."

"I was," she said. There was no point dancing around the subject. "I thought you were working for Death's Hand. Did James send you? Is he okay?"

"James is fine for now." Ann sat up and smiled.

The situation felt completely wrong for a rescue. Elise wrapped the rope around her fists again. She recalled seeing those bright blue eyes under a ski mask at the cemetery—the same eyes that smiled at her now.

"James told me you're an herb witch," Elise said. "But you're the necromancer, aren't you?"

Ann shrugged. "Kitchen witchery is easy to fake." When Elise tensed, she held up a hand like it could stop an attack. "There are more than a dozen fiends in the house above us."

"Why?"

"I'm not a fighter. It makes sense to have guards."

"No. Why are you working with Death's Hand?"

She stood and dusted herself off. Ann's color was returning to normal. "*Vedae som matis* doesn't think I should tell you very much. She's usually right about things. Look, I like you a lot, Elise. I could have drained you dry to paint that sigil, but I used mostly pig's blood instead. We don't have to fight. There's enough room in the new world for both of us."

"New world?" Elise tried to make herself sound calm, even though she was watching the doorway and mentally calculating the odds of escaping twenty fiends unarmed.

"Sure. I know you're in Reno because of the Warrens, and you thought all the power from them would prevent your enemies from locating you remotely...right?" Ann didn't wait for a response before continuing. "But that protection doesn't come from the Warrens. There are angelic ruins below them."

She already knew that, but having her suspicions confirmed made a sick kind of chill settle over her.

"So this is a takeover."

"*Vedae som matis* is trapped in Hell, Elise. You know what it's like down there? It's…well, it's Hell. All she needs to break through to this side is a corporeal body, and then we can build a kingdom together." She took the stone staff out of her pocket and gave it the kind of loving look most girls would reserve for a boyfriend.

Her opinion of Ann immediately shifted from "this girl is misguided" to "this girl is insane."

Ann stepped forward, holding out a hand. "We can still be friends. When *vedae som matis* takes over, she'll need a council, and I can suggest you and Betty if…"

"If what? If I agree to be a blood donor?"

"No," she said. "I've got all I needed from you. My house is done being anointed. *Vedae som matis* was right about that, too. Your blood is really potent."

"You can't use me as a vessel. I'm not a witch."

Her smile went painfully wide. "Who says I wanted you? I poisoned James for a reason, you know."

I am the cold kiss of Death…

Elise joined her fists together and swung, bringing both down on Ann's head.

The witch screamed as she fell, bringing up her arms to protect herself. It wasn't good enough. Elise kicked her in the face, and her nose snapped. Blood sprayed across the concrete.

A gray blur hurtled into the room, striking Elise in the stomach with all the power of an oncoming train. Her back slammed into the wall.

Over the fiend's head, Elise saw Ann try to push herself up, then collapse again.

Elise kneed the demon in the stomach, pushing it away from her. She ran for the door, but the fiend grabbed at her shirt with its clawed hands. She stuck her hip out and used its own momentum to throw it over her leg. It lost balance, and Elise jumped over Ann, pausing only to pick up the staff.

It made her hands burn, so she stuffed it in the back pocket of her jeans. She ran up the stairs and burst through the door to the first floor of the house.

The walls were lined with pictures. None of them featured Ann.

Something scuffled in the basement behind her.

Elise darted to the nearest room, throwing the door open. Empty bedroom. There was a bookshelf in front of the window. She opened another door—closet. Its shelves were covered in fragments of bone.

The fiend launched itself out of Ann's room, and she dodged. It hit the wall instead, and the drywall cracked.

"Get the kopis!" Ann shrieked from the other room. "Get her!"

Elise rushed into the darkened living room. It stank of brimstone and blood, and a trio of possessed corpses sat beside the battered couch. They didn't register Elise's appearance, even though she recognized two of them as the ones she had fought in the cemetery the night before.

But the pair of fiends huddled in the corner in the shadow of the television, eating a bloody scrap of meat, didn't fail to see Elise.

One of the fiends darted at her, and she backhanded it, sending it flying into the wall.

Fire burned a path down Elise's thigh. She cried out. The

second fiend flung shreds of her jeans from its claws and slashed again, but she leapt away just in time. The backs of her legs bumped into something, and she stumbled. Her thigh gave out.

Elise hit the ground. The possessed ones animated and stood, staring at her with empty eyes.

She scrambled to her feet as they lunged, kicking a fiend squarely in the face. It flew backwards with a little squeal, striking the lone window through the curtains and sliding to the floor.

Elise flung open the front door, and light flooded into the living room. The remaining fiend recoiled, covering its bulbous eyeballs with tiny scarred hands.

She hurtled outside into fresh air and freedom. She ran to the end of the street and stopped short—Ann's house was on a hill overlooking the city, and below the hill stood Our Mother of Sorrows cemetery.

The other houses on the street were silent, seemingly unoccupied, but the sky was gray and growing darker by the minute. Black thunderheads rolled down the mountains toward the late afternoon sun. Once the sun disappeared, there would be nothing keeping the fiends from following her.

The possessed ones didn't care about sunlight. Something scraped behind her.

They were coming.

Elise's feet pounded against pavement. Her right twitched. The fiend's claws hurt like a son of a bitch, and the staff in her pocket hummed with furious energy.

The street behind her grew louder. More scraping, more motion. Elise's leg wouldn't go as fast as she needed it to—every time she set down her foot, her leg buckled and the best she could manage was a striding limp.

She glanced over her shoulder. Three possessed ones chased her, and they were picking up speed. Worse yet, Elise could feel the demonic presence of the fiends—they were vulnerable to bright lights, but that didn't mean they couldn't run blind. And Ann was furious enough to make them do it.

A Jeep passed the other end of the street and stopped at the corner.

"Elise!" The Jeep backed up, made a hard turn, and pulled up alongside her backward. Anthony stared at her from the driver's seat. "What's going on?"

"No time to explain," she said, grabbing the car's frame and hauling her body up. She didn't even wait to be fully inside the car before waving at him. "Go, Anthony!"

He adjusted his side mirror. "What are *those*?"

She clambered into the passenger's seat. The sense of the servants was almost overwhelming, and she didn't need to look to know they were coming up on the Jeep. "Drive, damn it! Drive!"

Anthony slammed his foot on the gas. The tires spun out, and the engine red-lined.

Then he found traction, and the car shot down the street. Elise was thrown back into the seat. She gripped the roll cage, twisting around to watch the street recede behind them.

He threw a hard left turn without slowing down. The Jeep felt like it was going to roll, but it barely kept its tires on the road.

The fiends couldn't keep up. Even better, there wasn't much traffic, so they didn't have to stop. Elise dropped back again and ripped her jeans open even wider to see the damage. Three parallel gashes marked the side of her thigh, hip to knee. Although they burned, the wound was shallow.

"Oh God," Anthony said, staring at her leg.

"Get to the studio, and take the back roads," Elise ordered, reaching into the back seat to search through his junk. She found an oil-stained polo with a university logo on the breast. "Are you attached to this shirt?"

He shook his head, and she dabbed at her wounds.

"Elise, what in the heck was—shit!"

Anthony slammed on the breaks. She hit the dashboard hands-first.

She looked up in time to see a hand swipe at her over the windshield, white eyes and a pale face dripping with blood pressed against the glass.

"Don't stop!" Elise yelled, pushing the hand aside when the servant reached for Anthony. He slouched low in his seat. "Faster!"

The engine roared. She pulled herself up on the windshield, hauled back, and punched the servant with all her strength. He didn't register any pain, but his one-handed grip on the roll cage weakened.

Anthony swerved, and Elise fell against the side of the Jeep. The possessed one tumbled off the hood.

Elise watched him roll down the asphalt. A truck several car lengths behind them swerved to avoid him as it turned the corner. The servant picked itself up, and then Anthony and Elise turned a corner as well. He disappeared.

"What the *fuck* was that?" Anthony asked as Elise plopped back down in the seat again. His chest was rising and falling rapidly as though he had been the one running. His face and knuckles were white. "That looked like—I mean—was that a *zombie*?"

"Not exactly. I have no idea why you were passing that street, Anthony, but thank God you were. I'm not sure I could have out-run them. I think they're getting stronger."

"Oh my God, they're still back there, aren't they? Ann lives up there! We have to go back, she might be—"

"Fuck Ann," Elise said. "She's fine."

"I'm going to take your word for it. I have seen the weirdest shit today," Anthony said. "Do you want to tell me what's the hell is going on?"

She studied the strong line of his nose and jaw in profile. He was focusing on the road, but the veins standing out on his neck belied how much of an effort it was for him not to stare at Elise.

"You know how you were saying you wanted to be a part of my life?" she asked. He nodded, knuckles white. "Wish granted. Now get me back to the studio."

Part 5: The Twelfth Hour

Guatemala – August 2004

When James woke up in the condo, he was partially healed, and totally alone. Elise's swords were gone.

He wasn't sure if it was instinct or Elise's history of getting into trouble that told him something was wrong, but he didn't bother waiting for her to return. He stuffed what was left of his Book of Shadows into a bag, slung it over his shoulder, and hobbled out the door with his makeshift crutch. He could barely feel his knee as magic knit the ligaments back together. Every time he took a step, it tried to buckle under him.

Worse yet, it was still raining, and as dark as night even though it was afternoon. The ground was slick and muddy. But slowly, deliberately, he made his way toward town.

He tensed when he saw two figures coming up the road toward him. When they drew close enough for him to realize they were human, he still didn't relax.

One of the men was built like a cinderblock, and the other was a boy with a shotgun strapped to his back and nervous eyes. "Where's Elise?" asked the first without prelude.

"Who are you?" James asked, raising his voice to be heard over the blasting wind.

"The name's Bryce." The cinderblock jerked his thumb at the other man. "This is Diego. McIntyre said Elise needs our help. Here we are."

So they were kopides. Both of them. "I thought McIntyre was coming himself."

"He couldn't make it," Diego said with an accent so thick that James barely understood him.

"Well, you're too late. She's already gone. She's gone into the undercity—looking for that clock."

"So she's dead," Bryce said.

James's fist clenched on his walking stick. "No. She's alive." He would know the instant she died. It hadn't happened. Not yet. "But that could change quickly. We have to find her."

Bryce looked excited at the prospect of going into the undercity. He grinned, and James saw that he was missing most of his teeth. His skin had the tough, scarred look of an old farmer even though he couldn't have been thirty yet.

"Fucking fantastic," he said. "Tell us what to do."

He opened his mouth to respond.

James!

Pain flared down his flesh. Burning silver spikes flayed his skin, baring his bones as the jungle blurred and darkened around him.

With a roar of pain, James staggered. A pair of hands kept him from falling.

"The hell—?" someone said.

But James was lost in a black pit of agony. Smoke burned his lungs. Hot stone dug into his spine, and metal bit his wrists, chafing until they went slick with blood.

No. Not *his* wrists.

A fist struck him across the face. His vision cleared in time to see Bryce rearing above him with his hand raised for another blow. "Stop," James said with a shudder. Elise's silent cried echoed through him. He hadn't even know she could scream.

Bryce lifted him and set him on his feet like he was a child. Diego gave James his dropped crutch.

"What's wrong with you?" Bryce asked warily. His hands flexed as he stared around at the trees, as though waiting to be attacked.

"It's Elise. Something is happening to her. She's—"

The pain blazed again.

James...James...

She was chained. Bleeding.

"What should we do? Tell us how to help," Diego said. His hands were trembling.

Help? They wanted to *help*?

He took a moment to size them up. Bryce looked as dumb as the mud beneath his feet, but he was pure muscle. Diego wouldn't be nearly so useful—he was too scared. He wouldn't last long in the undercity, and James wouldn't make it far with his ruined knee, either. And he wanted that shotgun.

"Sorry about this," James said.

He dropped his walking stick, pulled a slip of paper from the Book of Shadows, and seized Diego's arm.

Electricity leaped between them. Diego's skin turned ashen gray, and he collapsed, dragging them both to the ground. Bryce shouted and drew his gun, but James held up his hands.

"He's fine," James said. "He'll be okay. He's unconscious."

Careful to stay out of arm's reach, Bryce checked Diego's pulse. "What did you do to him?"

"I borrowed his strength to heal myself." And to prove it, he stood up—slowly, no need to tempt the trigger finger —and stripped the bandages from his knee. It didn't hurt anymore.

James expected him to argue. There were so few living witches that rivaled his power that most people weren't aware such healing was even possible. But Bryce looked angry, not disbelieving. "Are you nuts?" he asked. "Now there's only two of us!"

"And I wouldn't have been able to go anywhere without healing first. Tell me: would you rather descend toward almost certain death with a scared boy, or the aspis who just defeated him with a single touch?"

Bryce couldn't seem to find a reason to argue.

Elise had no idea that she could hurt so much without passing out. Time made no sense anymore. Had it been minutes? Hours? Years?

Had the clock struck twelve yet?

Brilliant white pain burned through her bones. Blood raced down her skin from a thousand shallow cuts.

She was a roast pig on a spit. She was a rabbit being skinned. Pillars of fire raced along her spine, arced through the sky, scorched the earth.

When she thought it couldn't hurt worse, the knife dug in somewhere new, and it did.

"Amazing how well kopides heal," a voice said. "You may not even scar."

The words jangled in her ears. She screamed and

screamed. Blood swirled past her head, filling the cracks in the stone, and flashes of black blurred her vision.

The tip of a stone knife scraped against her breastbone.

You may not even scar.

Her head swam. She had no blood. No skin.

The goddess of death held something over her, and it dripped warmth on her face, and Elise thought she recognized the strip of pink dotted by freckles and—*oh God.*

The world couldn't end soon enough.

James ran through the jungle. He didn't see with his eyes; he saw with Elise's. He saw a limp hand in front of her on the floor. He saw pooling blood. He saw iron chains and bare, dirty feet.

Pain. So much pain.

He muttered under his breath as he ran on his repaired knee, even though he wasn't sure she could hear. "I'm coming—hold on—stay awake—"

Bryce crashed gracelessly through the trees behind him, panting and swearing. Like many bulky, muscled men, he didn't seem to have focused on his cardio health. He couldn't keep up.

The rain poured around them, salty-sweet like the ocean. Trees swayed in the wind. James's shirt stuck to his back, and he hugged the shotgun to his chest to keep from catching on the foliage.

Where was she?

James tried to follow the feelings Elise radiated, but it was difficult. Her mind made no sense to him. Maybe if they had been piggybacked—maybe if she wasn't in so much pain—

A mark on a tree caught his eye. "Wait!" James called.

Bryce stopped and leaned on his knees, gasping for air. "What?"

A signpost was carved into the trunk of the tree. It was a marker from one demon to another, indicating the direction of the undercity.

His eyes tracked the signpost to the next tree, and the next. There were small marks all around him. They led back toward town. How could he have missed them?

"This way," James said.

He doubled back, climbing toward the road. Bryce followed as well as he could. "Hey!" he shouted. "We got company!"

James turned. It was hard to see through the motion of the trees in the wind, but something was moving higher on the mountain. Dark shapes.

"Demons?" James called back.

"A whole fucking century of 'em!"

He ran faster, the Book of Shadows bouncing on his back in its bag. He didn't like his odds against a centuria of demons—over eighty of them—not even with Bryce's help.

As he followed the marks closer to town, he began to hear yelps and howls. They were getting closer.

"It's in there," he shouted, pointing at a shop the markers indicated as the entrance. Bryce was hurrying to catch up, but he was still a hundred meters back. "I'm going down! Can you hold them off?"

The kopis responded by drawing his gun.

James dove into the shop and went into the basement. There was a trap door. It was open, but the stairs had collapsed.

James!

Elise was screaming again. She wasn't far. He could feel her through the earth, through the collapsed paths, just a couple miles away but completely unreachable.

Gunshots fired outside the shop. Bryce shouted.

Fear dragged on James's heart. What was he supposed to do? How could he get to Elise when the only entrance to the undercity was blocked?

He shut his eyes, trying to see through their bond again. *Where are you? How can I reach you?*

Through her pain, he glimpsed a bone scepter and a stone knife. James fought to push back the sounds of fighting above him and focus on her vision, trying to see beyond the bare knees of the goddess.

A wall. Smoke. Window. And beyond that, pyramid. It was tall. The chamber, and the clock inside of it, was huge.

James's eyes flew open. She wasn't at the end of a labyrinth of demonic undercity—she was just under the surface, in the jungle not far from him.

He quickly paged through his Book of Shadows, seeing how many battle spells he had left. There weren't many. The simple ones—casting fire, blasts of air—were almost gone. Everything else that remained were the powerful spells his aunt told him not to mess with. Horrible, deadly spells. He'd been carrying them around for years.

Whispering a short prayer, James ripped a handful of pages out of the Book and flew up the stairs to street level.

Bryce blocked the doorway with his body. Another one of the leathery gray demons had its teeth clamped down on the arm of his leather jacket. Dozens more demons rushed down the street.

James barely had time to register the sheer number of bodies before they crashed upon them. He was lost in a rush of blood and drool and growls. He dropped the shotgun. "Get down!" he shouted to Bryce.

The kopis threw himself to the ground, and James threw a scrap of paper.

Power ripped from him. A dozen hearts stopped beating at once.

They fell like dominoes, but James didn't stop to watch it. He grabbed Bryce by the arm and hauled him to his feet. "Move," he said as the surviving demons clambered over their dead brethren. "Now. Hurry!"

The men sprinted across the road and into the jungle again. James could still hear Elise in the back of his mind, but it was faint. After another minute, he couldn't hear her at all.

"Why aren't we going down?" Bryce asked.

"We are going down," James said. "But we're not taking the stairs."

After an eternity of pain, Elise awoke. She tried to sit up, but her hands couldn't find traction. She slipped on something soft and slick. She looked down to see that it was a face with gaping eyes and no jaw.

Gasping, she jerked back. Something dug into her leg—an exposed rib.

There was nowhere safe to move. She slid to one side and rolled on top of a hairy chest with no head. When she slipped to the other side, her hand fell on a scapula.

The realization that she was in a pit of human meat came upon her slowly, and it was followed by emotional silence—a yawning void of feeling. Elise took one shuddering breath and stopped fighting to get away.

She settled back on the corpses and looked up at the

steep walls around her. It was dark, but the occasional blast of flame revealed jagged rock. She could climb out. The clock was still rocking the earth with every beat of its human heart, and it sounded close.

She was still in the chamber. She was not dead.

But given all the pain she felt in her torso, she almost wished that were not true. No amount of emotional void could numb her cuts. Elise was slick with blood—both hers and that of the bodies—and she felt like she had gone through a cheese grater.

Her shirt was nothing but scraps, her weapons were missing, and there was a stab wound on her side. She flinched when she remembered the goddess burying the knife in her body. It was the last thing she remembered before waking up.

She must have missed all Elise's important organs, but the goddess hadn't known that before leaving her for dead. Thrown her in a pit of bodies. Forgotten her.

Elise decided to consider herself lucky.

She counted to ten and crawled to the wall of the pit. The clock continued to tick.

Digging her fingernails into a jutting rock, Elise climbed to the top with her teeth grit. Stretching her arm to find another handhold hurt her stab wound. Putting her weight on one leg to push made the bites on her hip burn.

She rolled over the edge and scrambled to the shadows on all fours, finding a dark corner to crouch before examining the situation.

Elise could see the back of the clock. It was only a hundred feet away. Her side of the chamber was empty aside from the pit, sheltered by half-rotten columns, and the occasional blast of steam from the floor grates made enough smoke to conceal her.

She couldn't see many of those ugly gray demons around the clock, but she could feel them. There were hundreds. The goddess of death was talking to them, but Elise didn't stop to listen.

She made her way to the other side of the chamber, sticking to the shadows, and climbed unseen onto one of the platforms with the dead cultists.

A flash of silver caught her eye. The goddess had dropped her staff of bone and was carrying one of Elise's falchions as she paced across the dais.

There were four humans huddled beside her. It looked like a family. Their wrists were chained to the clock.

So that was the sacrifice. Elise wondered what it was about those people that made them a better sacrifice than her, the greatest kopis, who barely ranked as demon food. It would have wounded her pride if she had any.

She needed a plan, but she didn't have any idea of how to cross the room through a hundred demons, prevent the sacrifice of four humans, and stop the clock with numerous injuries and no time. She didn't even have her weapons.

Of course, that was fixable. If she could get one of her swords, she could bury it in the heart of the clock. It was the only thing she could imagine that might stop it.

Her time to plan ended. The death goddess stopped speaking and whirled with the stone knife. It plunged into the neck of the man at her feet, and blood spurted from his throat.

Elise leaped off the dais, launching herself toward the sacrifices.

But it was too late. With a few swift strokes, all four lay dead in front of the clock. The minute hand groaned into the twelve position, and the first bell chimed.

James found a place in the jungle where the trees swayed and the ground vibrated beneath his feet. The clock was below him, and Elise with it. He was certain.

But he also had a hundred demons following him.

He and Bryce had evaded some of them in the jungle, but not enough. The kopis fired randomly into the horde behind him. Whether any of the bullets hit their targets didn't matter—there wasn't enough ammunition to kill them all.

Stopping where the vibrations were strongest, he tucked the shotgun under his arm. "I need a minute!" James yelled as he scrambled up a tree. "Hold them off!"

Bryce didn't respond. His fighting style completely lacked Elise's grace, but there was no denying the accuracy of his aim or the power of his swinging fists. He was a force of nature.

"Hurry up!" Bryce shouted.

James wedged himself between two high branches, selected a couple spells from his Book, and took out a pen. He muttered words of power under his breath as he drew new spells.

The rocking earth shifted. The tree shuddered, and the air grew thick.

A bell chimed.

The reverberations above the pyramid were so powerful that the entire ground tipped. Bryce lost his footing. The demons swarmed over him. He didn't get a chance to scream.

James tried not to watch as they overtook him. One demon leaped onto the trunk of his tree, then another, scaling it with their stubby claws.

He carefully folded three of the spells together. A hand swiped at his foot.

Then he threw the pages into the air.

The earth split with a dull thud, ripping open beneath the trees while the first bell continued to toll. Hot air gusted through the hole. Demons slid into the earth.

Holding his breath, James leaped off his branch.

Twelve bells. Four minutes. Elise was out of time.

One.

A dozen demons plowed into Elise like athletes piling onto a football. The back of her head cracked against the ground.

She jammed her elbow into a biting mouth and jabbed her fingers into an eye. The bell vibrated through the temple. It shook her blood, her bones.

Elise lashed out with a foot and felt it connect with something. It didn't do any good. There was no light under the pile of demons, no sense of gravity.

That was when the roof collapsed.

Two.

The rubble didn't crush Elise. But it did crush the demons on top of her.

She shoved her way out of the pile. Dirt and rain showered through the hole in the ceiling. Beyond it, the sky changed. Gray faded to crimson as Hell and Earth began to merge.

Elise gasped and coughed through the dust. Half of the centuria had been crushed at once. Nothing so much as touched the clock.

A hammer swung. The bell struck again.

Three.

The third chime was louder than the first two. Her skull ached, and even when she jammed her hands against her ears, her brain rattled.

Something moved on the dais. The goddess had survived.

More demons began climbing toward Elise over the rubble. She stumbled toward the clock, slipped, and almost fell.

Her hand caught the side of the dais. The vibrations traveled up her arm and down her spine as she dragged herself onto it.

The goddess was laughing.

Four.

"It's too late," said the death goddess. "Hell is come upon Earth."

That face. That laugh. Elise's wounds ached with the memory of the knife. "Shut up," she growled, raising her fist for a strike.

"Elise!"

She looked up. James climbed down from the surface, carefully making his way along a tipped column. The first thing that occurred to her was that his leg was fixed. The second was that he had a shotgun. Where had James gotten a shotgun?

The goddess saw him. She stopped laughing.

"Catch!" he yelled, tossing the gun.

Elise caught it, balancing it awkwardly between her hands. She'd only held a shotgun once before. Her father had taught her to shoot, but she hated them.

Still, she was armed. It was better than the alternative.

She whipped the butt of the shotgun across the

goddess's face. Her head snapped back.

Five.

The sky turned virulent red, and the world was falling. Elise's senses screamed—demons everywhere, all around her, like she had felt in Dis so long ago—and the air tensed like something was about to snap.

Demons were climbing toward James. She was helpless to join him.

The goddess regained her footing and came at Elise, falchion raised. She braced the shotgun against her shoulder, took aim, and fired.

The goddess's leg became a mess of red below the knee. She screamed in Latin. Elise smiled.

Six.

Elise tried to pump the shotgun so she could fire again, but the mechanism was stuck. Didn't matter. She preferred the personal touch anyway.

She tossed the gun aside and ripped her falchion out of the goddess's hand. The twin was next to the sacrifices. Elise grabbed it, too.

Holding both of her swords was like having her arms reattached. She was complete.

Seven.

Elise thought her skull might split in two.

The chime shook James off the pillar, dropping him in the crowd of waiting demons.

"James!" she shouted.

No response.

The dais rocked with the pendulum. She scrambled to keep her footing as the goddess lunged. Her stone knife slashed through the air and sliced into Elise's arm, deeper than before. She cut into muscle.

The air thickened, darkened, grew sour. Air gusted from

the grates. It stunk of sulfur, like the planes of Hell.

A man screamed.

Eight.

The goddess was fast. Too fast for a woman with a ruined leg. She twisted and spun, meeting the blades of Elise's swords with her stone knife, swift and agile and skilled beyond imagining.

She deflected every swing, every strike. The ritual knife was a blur. Blades met, and Elise shoved her away. She couldn't take down a goddess.

The clock was her last chance—the only way she could stop the collapse of the wall between Heaven and Earth.

Nine.

The goddess flashed in front of her. The knife bit into Elise's injured side. She cried out, and her voice was silent under the bell's roar.

Pain seared through her body when the goddess shoved her against the clock. Elise's ears rang. Her vertebrae shook and scraped against each other.

The stone knife slashed open her brow. Blood cascaded down the side of her face.

Rain showered upon them. It tasted like acid.

Ten.

Her back was against the clock. She was *right there*, and she couldn't do anything to stop it. The goddess's stinking breath heated Elise's face as she smiled, baring bloody teeth.

If she couldn't reach the heart of the clock, there was another heart she could reach.

She kicked the goddess away. Just enough to have room to move.

A wave of demons crashed against the dais, clambering over the edge. Their mouths were bloody. Elise wondered if any of that belonged to James.

Eleven.

She plunged her sword into the goddess's chest.

The heart in the clock exploded blood, splattering against the inner workings. The hammer shattered.

The dais pitched and everyone fell.

The twelfth bell never rang.

When the eleventh bell died off, Elise was the only one left standing.

She clutched her sword in both hands as though it was her last line to life. Its blade dripped, her knuckles were white, and her gaze was empty. Her mind was a thousand miles away.

The pendulum no longer kept in time with the seconds. Its hand slowed with every swing.

Nearby, gray matter slipped out of a crack in a demon's skull, oozing across the tile. It trickled into one of the iron grates and dripped onto underground fires a hundred feet below. Brain hit flame. It gave a hiss and smelled like barbecue.

Barbecue. Her stomach lurched.

The sword slipped from Elise's fingers. Metal clattered against stone. The death goddess was sprawled at her feet, her necklace of skulls shattered, and her face had lost all its malice in death. She almost looked human.

The fires darkened and the heat faded.

Elise's eyes rolled up to the ceiling. Her fingers twined through the curls at her scalp as her mouth opened in a silent cry. She had screamed too much earlier in the night and no longer had a voice.

Her knees weakened. She collapsed.
The clock's pendulum continued to slow.

James pushed the bodies of demons off of him. Emptying every page of the Book—even the terrible ones he had sworn never to use—meant they had died in a thousand ugly ways. Ruptured organs. Suffocation. Burning from the inside.

His foot caught the pentagram-marked binder as he climbed free, but he didn't pick it up. He didn't want to look at it. He never wanted to cast a spell again.

The clock wasn't ticking with that terrible pulse anymore, and the sudden silence made his ears ring. Coughing, he slipped to the bottom of the pillar. "Elise?" he called, voice muffled in his ears.

He nudged a demon's body onto its back. The slash of its mouth gaped open, and the remaining air in its lungs sighed out with a whiff of sulfur. Covering his nose and mouth with his arm, he moved forward. James scrutinized each body he passed, half expecting to see Elise beneath them.

The room depressurized, and the demons began to rot.

Their skin dissolved to reveal bone. Their chests spread and tore. Organs twisted like worms within their guts as they vanished. One by one, they rotted away until the only body left was that of the goddess in the front of the room.

A glint of steel caught his eye. His gaze moved from the sword to the legs beside it, and he realized the goddess wasn't alone.

"Jesus Christ..." He scrambled onto the dais. Elise's skin was shredded and her chest was blackened with blood, and his stomach flipped when he realized it was all hers. "Elise—oh, Lord, Elise..."

Her eyes fluttered open. "James?"

"Are you all right?"

She sat up carefully, wincing. "I'm not the one with a sword through my chest." It wasn't funny, but he laughed. Even a hint of humor after that fight was enough to drive him toward hysteria. "Let's not do this again."

"I couldn't agree more." He helped her stand, and then picked up the sword she dropped. Elise turned to leave. "Don't you want the other one?"

She glanced at the falchion buried deep in the goddess's chest. Her lip curled. "No. Hell can keep it."

The bladed clock swung once more, and it stopped midway on the down stroke, forever frozen between *tick* and *tock*. The earth shook.

"We need to get out of here," James said.

Slowly, painfully, they climbed to the surface. Night had fallen, and the rain had stopped, leaving the air sticky and hot. They staggered almost a quarter mile before collapsing.

Elise shuddered like a tree in a hurricane. Her wounds looked agonizing.

"Can you heal me?" she asked. Her voice came out in a raw whisper.

"I'm sorry. I have nothing left."

She nodded without speaking. Her face was very pale.

They stared up at the vast black sky together. The clouds thinned, revealing stars and endless black sky. They waited until the sky faded to the deep navy of false dawn, and the sounds of night were replaced by birdsong.

When the sun broke the horizon, the light shone in Elise's hollow gaze.

They had won, but James couldn't help but feel they had lost something much worse than their lives. She sagged against his side. "Never again," he murmured into her hair. "Never again."

Part 6: Sacrifice

Chapter 14

"James!"

Elise burst through the apartment door. The air inside was stale having the windows and doors closed all day. Nothing had changed since she left—paper spells were strewn across the kitchen table, and a rug was rolled neatly against the wall. There were even vacuum lines on the carpet from the last time James cleaned.

"I could use you at Motion and Dance, Betty," Anthony was saying into his cell phone, trailing behind Elise. "There's something going down. Elise is messed up and I'm confused and I need someone sane. Yes, you're sane. What? God, *shut up*. Just get over here, okay?"

Elise jiggled the handle on James's door, and it didn't open. She found the key on top of the molding for the bathroom door. The tumblers fell into place with an audible *click*.

James's bed was empty. She cut her gaze to the window —open—to the mess of papers and books on the floor. The sheets on his bed were a mess. Stephanie sat at his desk. She gazed blankly at the window.

Anthony came up beside Elise and peered over her

shoulder. "Was there a fight?" he asked.

Elise gazed at the exposed mattress. Red drops blotted its surface. She ran her fingertips along one of the spots, and rubbed it between her finger and thumb. She didn't need a forensic expert to know whose blood it was.

"Stephanie," she said. The doctor didn't look at her. "Stephanie. Dr. Whyte."

Slowly, so slowly, she looked over to Elise. "They took him," she said. Her voice was the kind of calm that came from having reached a point of such hysteria that she didn't have any emotion left. "Those...things. They came through the window. I cracked it to get some air."

Elise hauled Stephanie out of the chair and slammed her into the wall by the door. Anthony gave a startled cry and stepped forward, but she shot him a look that froze him mid-step.

"Are you working with her? Did you let Ann in? What the *fuck* did you do to him?"

Stephanie's face crumbled. "I didn't do anything. James was resting peacefully. I got a phone call and after I hung up, *they* came in. They knocked me out. I woke up and..." She wouldn't look at the bed.

"Who called you?" Elise demanded.

"Ann. She said she had a question for James."

"Did you tell her to come in? Did you tell her to take him?" She pulled back a fist, but Anthony caught it.

"Elise!"

He peeled her off Stephanie. Elise jerked her arm out of his grasp, but she didn't move to attack again.

The doctor adjusted her shirt, neatened her hair, and broke down into tears.

"I don't understand," she cried. "What *was* that?"

Stephanie sobbed for a good long minute, and Elise

waited, drumming her fingers against her thigh. When the doctor showed no sign of letting up, she made a disgusted noise.

"This isn't helpful. Where did they take James?"

Stephanie sucked in a hard breath, straightening and grabbing a tissue to blow her nose. The tears stopped as suddenly as they began. Long breath in, long breath out. When she spoke, her tone was measured and even. She enunciated each word with great care. "I have no clue. I was unconscious."

"What were you doing all day?"

"I woke up a few hours ago and waited for you. I didn't know what to do," she said. "I think—I might go home."

"She's in shock," Anthony whispered.

"Fine. Get out of here. Have a drink and lay down or something. You're not doing any good," Elise said. Stephanie left without saying another word.

Elise stared at the spot of blood on the bed, her gaze narrowing until she saw nothing else.

James was gone. Ann had him, and Elise had been *right there* the whole time.

"I'm going to fucking kill her," she said.

Daylight waned. Clouds darkened what little sun remained. One moment, the air had grown still, and the next, rain poured out of the thunderheads. Lighting sparked over the mountains in the distance. Rain filled the streets and the people of the city took shelter inside.

Inside Motion and Dance, a storm also began to break within Elise.

"He's not here," she said.

"Who?" Betty asked. Her friend Cassandra had given her a ride as soon as Anthony called, but Elise's attitude made her wish she had taken a minute to put on full body armor first.

Her roommate paced the dance hall like a caged animal, limping on every other step. Her eyes were darkened pits of fury. She had become the spirit of vengeance itself, barely contained by human flesh.

Anthony cradled his forehead in his hands as he leaned against one of the mirrors in the main dance hall. He had stopped trying to talk when Elise almost punched him for it.

"Who's not here?" Betty repeated.

"James. She took him." She struck the palm of her hand with a fist. "I shouldn't have left so fast. I should have searched the house. I should have…"

"Hey, calm down," Betty said, touching Elise's shoulder. Her skin was hot. "Talk to me, girl. What's happened?"

"Ann has kidnapped my aspis for ritual sacrifice to a demon goddess of death."

Betty shook her head. "Yesterday, I would have said you were crazy. Today—well, you're still crazy, but it's contagious. What's an aspis? Demons? Is that what that gargoyle thing was?"

"That was a fiend." She flung herself into the chair, shredding her jeans along the hole to turn them into half-shorts. Betty leaned in to examine the gashes on Elise's legs. The blood had smeared, and the wounds were raw.

"I hate to state the obvious, but…"

"Yeah, it doesn't look good," Elise said. She pressed a towel emblazoned with the "Motion & Dance" logo against her injury. They were intended to be used by sweaty dancers. Elise's blood soaked through the cloth quickly, obscuring the logo of the ballet man wrapped around the ampersand.

"So what's this about zombies?" Betty asked.

"They're not zombies," Elise replied impatiently. "They're the dead, possessed by a demon called Death's Hand, and reanimated to do her evil bidding."

Betty began laughing again. When she saw that nobody joined her, she stopped. Elise's eyes were cold. She was serious. Deadly serious. Betty deflated. "Oh, jeeze," she said. "I can't believe Ann's evil. I mean, lazy Ann? 'Let's eat ice cream after working out' Ann?"

Elise dropped the towel in the trash can. "The one and only." She moved her leg experimentally, watching the gashes.

Betty spun on Anthony. "Why aren't you as shocked as I am?"

"We were attacked by some kind of mutant this morning, and then a dead body with bleeding eyes attack my windshield," he said dully. "My ability to get shocked has eloped with my sanity and run away to Africa."

"I think I need the Reader's Digest version of what's going on," Betty said.

"I don't have time for this. I need weapons and I need to bring all kinds of pain down on Ann." She snapped her fingers at Anthony. "You're taking me in the Jeep. Now."

"Fine."

Betty hurried after them as they went for the front doors. Elise spoke as she limped along.

"So here's what I told Anthony: I'm James's exorcist friend. When working with Lucinde, I stumbled across a demonic plot to ascend to Earth from Hell. Ann is a powerful necromancer and she's on his side. Now they're planning to sacrifice James. Good enough for you?"

"Wow. Uh. Okay. If Ann's got James, why can't we just walk in and take him? I mean, we've worked out with Ann. She's not exactly formidable."

"She has a small army. We can't 'just walk in' unless we deal with them first."

"Oh," Betty said.

Anthony opened the front door, letting in a wash of the moist air.

A small figure stood silhouetted against the rain. She wore a slicker too big for her tiny body, and she stepped inside without being invited. The girl pushed back her hood, revealing a face with white eyes and cheeks tracked by blood tears. Her skin was pale, almost papery.

Betty took a step back, covering her mouth with a hand. The little girl had a black symbol on her forehead, and her veins pulsed visibly beneath the skin.

Elise sucked in a hard breath. "Lucinde."

"It's like that zombie I saw earlier," Anthony muttered. "But...it's a kid."

The child's blank eyes focused on Elise. Her mouth dropped open.

"I have James," she said. Her mouth didn't move, and the woman's voice that came out sounded like a recording. "You have the artifact of *vedae som matis*. Let's be adults about this. I'll cure James of the poison, return him to you, and leave the area. You won't hear from us again. Just give back the staff."

Betty glanced at Elise. She was watching the girl with her lips set in a hard line.

She went on. "I'll take everything with me. You can return to living a normal life. I'm sorry we ever had to fight like this, Elise. I wouldn't have chosen it. I want to meet at Our Mother of Sorrows at ten o'clock tonight. Send your response with my servant." Her mouth clapped shut, and she stood, immobile, with her hand extended.

Anthony shuddered. "That's freaky."

"She looks like a demented doll," Betty agreed.

"Do you have that notepad in your purse?" Elise asked. She sounded calm, but tense.

Betty gave her a piece of Hello Kitty stationary and a green pen. Elise scrawled out a message and stuffed it into the girl's hand, which closed on the paper. She hid it inside her rain slicker.

Her mouth dropped open once more. "Thank you."

Lucinde walked out with a mechanical gait. Elise lingered in the doorway to watch her go. "Ann's actually willing to trade?" Anthony asked. "The way you were talking earlier, it seemed like James is too important for her to let go."

"He *is* too important," Elise said. "She's not going to let go of James now that she has him. I'm not going to return the artifact either."

"But you said…"

"I lied."

"Oh."

"I'm going to have to meet Ann, exorcise her servants, kill all the demons, and take James back," Elise said. She laughed harshly. "No big deal. I don't even think it's possible to perform a mass exorcism. It's never been done before."

Betty's eyes lit up. "We could do some exorcisms."

"You wouldn't have any idea what to do. There has to be another way."

"We could clone you," Anthony said in a "you're all crazy" tone of voice as he stalked away. "It's no more insane than everything else that's happening!"

Elise took something out of her pocket, and Betty recognized it as an MP3 recorder. "That's not a bad idea, Anthony," she said. "But first, I have some business with a lawyer and his wife."

When Elise reached the Ramirez house, Marisa was loading her car, sheltered from the rain by a blue poncho. Her face was red, but her eyes were dry now, and she carried two suitcases under each arm. She flung them into the back of her Hummer.

"Can I help you?" Elise asked.

Marisa jumped. "Oh—Elise. I didn't see you there."

She took a step toward the garage, but Elise moved in her way. "What's the rush?"

"I can't stay here," she said. "Augustin's...angry. Throwing things. I'm going to go live with my mother." Marisa took a deep breath. "We discussed divorce even before what happened to Lucinde. My bags have been packed in the garage for weeks now. But with what's happened recently..."

"Your daughter has gone missing," Elise asked. "Somehow, she got possessed again. I don't see how that could have happened unless someone surrendered Lucinde to the bad guy."

A look of panic shot across Marisa's face. "What?" Her hand fluttered at her breast, and it was only then that Elise noticed the bruise from her collarbone to her shoulder. "Are you—are you saying that Augustin let someone hurt our baby? *Madre de dios*...it makes sense. He's so angry!"

Elise frowned. "Has he been beating you?"

She jerked the poncho closed over her chest. "Yes."

Marisa swallowed hard. "Yes, he has. He's gone crazy."

"Where is he?"

"Augustin is inside. Don't make me go back."

"Okay. Stay with your mom for now. I'll find Lucinde, and I promise she will be safe," Elise said.

Marisa gripped her arm. "I never meant for James to find out we were having problems with our daughter. Do you understand? I always meant to keep things private. Your involvement—his involvement—was an accident. I'm so sorry."

"Go. I'll take care of Augustin."

She bit her lip. Nodded again. "Thank you. My mother's phone number is on the refrigerator. When you have found Lucinde—if you have saved her—call me. Please." Marisa got into the driver's seat and slammed the door shut.

She pulled out of the driveway as church bells tolled.

Elise went inside without knocking. She held her breath to listen for sound—something like the pattering of feet or an accidental brush of leathery arm against the wall. The living room was empty and silent. She glanced into the kitchen, but there was nothing there, either.

Elise made her way up the stairs, fists raised in the anticipation of an ambush. One of the family photos on the wall was askew, and another was missing entirely, making a gap in the long row of family history leading to the second floor.

There had been a scuffle upstairs. A decorative pot that had once filled a wall cubby was now in shards on the floor. Lucinde's door was cracked open. Elise pressed her back to the wall beside it, easing her fingers around the frame to push it open another inch and peek inside.

There were no fiends inside, no possessed ones, and no Lucinde. Only Augustin—sitting on his daughter's tiny bed and staring at the photo missing from the wall. He looked up at Elise and his eyes were full of hope. "Did you find her?" he asked. "Our daughter…"

"No, Augustin," Elise said. Her knife emerged from beneath her jacket, and she held it at her side. "I know what you did. Did Ann offer you money? Power?"

"What? Who is Ann?"

"You sold your daughter out. Your *own blood*."

He set the photo down on the bedside table. "Listen here. You may think you have some sort of—some *right* to come in and boss me around—but don't be mistaken. I'm still the man of the house, and—"

"I already got some of the story from your wife. Let me see if I can fill in the blanks." Elise shut the door behind her and stepped forward to stand over Augustin. "Ann gave you money. It wasn't a problem for you to betray your family; you don't like your daughter anyway. You couldn't even be bothered to be with her when I exorcised her. You get off on beating women, and—"

Augustin stood. He towered over her, and his face was dark. "What did Marisa say?"

"She told me that she's leaving you. Marisa loves her daughter very much, which is more than *you've* shown."

"I love my daughter, just as I love Marisa. I could never hurt either of them," Augustin said. He laughed bitterly. "I'm surrounded by crazy women. I thought Marisa would be different from my first wife, but then she started throwing things at me, just like Louisa did. And now you!"

Elise opened her mouth to yell, but a thought stopped her. "Wait. Marisa's not your first wife?"

"Now I think I should have let Louisa have custody of Lucinde," he said. He sat back down again with a moan. "Marisa's leaving me. I should have known…"

"If you didn't beat her, then why is she bruised?"

"Our daughter was possessed by a demon! Where the hell do you think it came from?"

"You're going to have to make something clear for me," she said. "Is there any reason Marisa would sell your daughter out?"

"She wouldn't," he said dismissively.

"Your story doesn't match hers. She told me that you've been angry and beating her and that you gave Lucinde up to the demon. Now you're telling me neither of you did it?"

"There's no reason for you to think we've hurt Lucinde. Yes, Marisa and I have fought. This isn't even the first time she's left. But we do not abuse our daughter."

"If you're lying to me…"

Augustin took the picture off the bedside table again, cradling it in his hands. "Leave me alone." His eyes burned through Elise.

She stomped downstairs to the refrigerator to look for the phone number Marisa left.

A single magnetic clip held a folded up paper that said *Give to Elise Kavanagh.* She unfolded it. The handwriting was loose and messy, and she jumped to the bottom— signed by Marisa—before going back to read it more carefully.

I never meant for things to get so out of control. I love Lucinde. Ann told me this would cure her heart defect and make her powerful, but instead she died and now I've caused too much pain. This isn't how I meant to get away from Augustin.

Several lines were scribbled out and illegible. The next readable line said, *She keeps everything in the attic. Tell him I'm sorry.* Her name was scrawled hastily beneath that, and the pen had torn through the paper on the last letter.

Elise's fist tightened around the note. Her hand shook. "You should have asked for help," she muttered. Marisa would never make it to her mother's house—demons didn't appreciate people who betrayed them.

She dropped the note on the kitchen table and left.

Chapter 15

Elise took James's car back to the studio feeling like she was in someone else's nightmare. The only thing that warmed her was the thought of those six words—*she keeps everything in the attic.* She knew where James was. Now all she needed was a miracle so she could get into Ann's place again.

Betty and Anthony were still working on her miracle when she got back. She parked in the lot and watched them moving around the studio through the windows. They were almost done with the Jeep. It was parked outside, and there was so much extra metal on it that it looked like Frankenstein's monster.

She knew she needed to go inside and help them, but Elise felt like she was frozen to the spot. She didn't want to tell them what Marisa had done, and she didn't want to have to answer the millions of questions that must have been bursting inside Betty, either.

Shutting her eyes, she pressed her forehead to the steering wheel. Everything was so much simpler when it had been just Elise and James against the world.

She took a deep breath before getting out of the car. It

took her a moment to realize she wasn't alone.

The three other people didn't make any noise as they slipped from the shadows of the building like oil oozing over water. As soon as Elise saw them, she stopped.

"How's it going, cabbage? Having a really dreadful evening, I hope."

David Nicholas.

Elise didn't respond. She recognized the woman on the left—it was the basandere from Eloquent Blood. Tattered pants revealed plump thighs and dirty knees, and a swooping neckline showed too many ribs between her surgically altered breasts. She had strung her iron chain through the loops of her jeans like a belt.

The basandere was meaner than she looked. Elise was certain of it. She would be as great a threat as the dark-haired man on the right, who looked so high that he wouldn't have felt it if Elise knocked his skull off his shoulders.

And then there was David Nicholas.

"What do you want?" Elise asked, even though she could tell by the way they moved to circle around her that they weren't there for a polite chat.

"You think you can push people around and not pay for it? First you walk into my office and stab me—and maybe I put up with it because I owe you money, sure. But then you interrupt my card game? Threaten me for information? Who the *fuck* do you think you are? Don't put up with that shit in this town, do we?" He jerked his head the other demons. "Make it fast."

The basandere reached, and Elise knocked her hands aside, jabbing her elbow into her gut to send her stumbling.

She spun smoothly and snapped a kick at the junkie's

face, but he ducked under it and grabbed her ankle. With a jerk, Elise's butt hit pavement. The shock of it jolted up her spine.

Before she could stand, a heavy boot smacked into her gut. Her ribs creaked. Her intestines mashed against her spine and her head bounced on the parking lot.

She rolled away from the next kick, gasping for breath, and got to her knees. A hand snatched her ponytail and jerked it back, nearly ripping the hair from her scalp.

David Nicholas drove the bony spike of his knee into her chin. Her teeth snapped shut on her tongue. The iron taste of blood flooded her mouth.

Elise lunged for him, but her hair was held tight. The junkie threw his arms around her. He could barely restrain one arm with his whole body. When he felt her shove against him, his face paled at her strength, but he held firm.

"You don't know what you're doing," Elise groaned as the basandere pulled her to her knees using her hair as a handle.

"You're a bully, bitch," David Nicholas said. "I'm taking out the trash."

He punched her. The ridges of his knuckles made fire blossom across her face as her head snapped from side to side. He didn't hit hard—she had been beaten by worse. But it had been years. She almost forgot the sweet pain of it.

Her lip split. He hit her eye, and her vision blurred.

"She's not even fighting back!" the basandere said, shrieking with laughter.

David Nicholas stepped back, rubbing his knuckles. He looked disappointed at Elise's lack of reaction. She sucked on the blood in her mouth and spit it out.

"You done?" she asked. "I have shit to do tonight."

His face twitched. "I'm nowhere near done yet."

He brandished a knife with a blade like a straight razor. A cold calm settled over Elise, numbing her pain. She hated to lose a customer—but she hated to lose her life even more.

The junkie shifted to grab her other arm. She head butted him hard enough to snap his nose and send blood spraying down his lip. He sprawled out in a parking space.

Metal flashed. She ducked, tearing her ponytail out of the stripper's hand and leaving a fistful of hair behind.

David Nicholas's knife blew past her ear.

She twisted and yanked the chain out of the basandere's belt loops, popping two of them.

Everything slowed.

David Nicholas flashed through the shadows to Elise's other side, and she could almost track his progress through the darkness. Wisps of smoke followed him as he vanished and rematerialized.

She whirled, shoving the basandere out of the way, and whipped the chain toward David Nicholas as he reappeared.

It wrapped around his neck, catching him before he was completely corporeal.

She jerked.

His head disconnected from his body.

He flashed into black smoke again, knife clattering to the ground.

Elise snapped her arm to wrap the chain around her fist. The basandere screamed and ran at her, flashing blood-red fingernails. Elise backhanded her with the chain. Something cracked—something important—and the stripper went limp.

The junkie reached for the knife. His hand shook.

"Get the fuck out of here," Elise spat. Blood spattered on her chin.

He was gone before she could unwind the chain.

As soon as her levels of adrenaline dropped, the pain came roaring back. Elise didn't realize how much her body hurt until she fell to her knees beside the basandere. She thought the stripper was probably dead. She didn't care too much.

Elise evaluated her physical condition. Between the blood loss from Ann anointing her house and these new wounds, she might not return to full strength for days.

James didn't have days.

She got back to her feet with a groan. Pain radiated from the top of her head down to her ribs, like every bone was fractured.

"Hell of a time to collect on a debt," she muttered.

Elise threw the basandere in the trunk of James's car. She swallowed a handful of the ibuprofen he kept in the glove box and checked her face in the rearview mirror. Her face looked like hamburger.

Great. Just great.

She slammed the car door shut, turning.

David Nicholas stood in front of her.

He moved an instant before she did. His hands closed on her shoulders, shoving her back against the car. Elise's head thudded against the metal.

"You killed one of my girls," he said.

"It was self-defense. What are you going to do about it? Call the cops?"

Loathing twisted David Nicholas's features. "I should sell you into slavery, that's what I should do. You and that succubus bartender *bitch*."

Elise grabbed his wrists. Her fingernails dug into his

234

wrists like they were sponges. Decapitation didn't do the nightmare any favors.

"Look," she said, carefully enunciating each consonant, "you and I can fight all night if we want, but it's a waste of time. You paid your debts with a bad check. You pounded on me, and I won this round. Let's call it even."

"Why should I do that?"

"Because I'll kill Death's Hand if you leave me alone for the night."

His expression dissolved into a grin so wide that the corners of his lips nearly touched his ears. "I just kicked the shit out of your skinny ass. You think you can take *vedae som matis*?" She nodded without returning his smile. He released her shoulders. "I like the idea of letting something else kill you."

"Only because you can't do it yourself."

David Nicholas swung, but she was faster. Before he could get a hand on her throat, she knocked his arms aside and pressed his own knife against his throat.

The nightmare froze.

"Try me," she whispered.

"Hey! What's going on?"

Anthony rushed out of the studio. David Nicholas's black eyes flicked to him, then back to Elise. He stepped away from her, lifting his hands.

"If Death's Hand doesn't kill you, we'll finish this conversation—and we'll do it under the eye of the Night Hag, you understand?"

Elise tossed his knife to him. "Won't that be fun?" she said flatly.

He vanished before Anthony could reach them.

So much for *that* customer.

"Jesus Christ! What happened to you?" he asked,

grabbing Elise's shoulders to steady her.

"Don't touch me. I'm fine."

Anthony scanned her injuries, from the rapidly swelling black eye to her bruised cheeks and swollen lip. He ran his fingers through the hair that had come loose from her braid.

"Why didn't you call for help?" he asked.

She swatted his hand off. "I told you not to touch me. Is the Jeep done yet?"

"No, but—"

"Then you and Betty need to finish it. I'm going upstairs to get my sword. I'll be back down in ten minutes, and we're going to leave."

Her legs buckled under her when she hit the stairs. Anthony wrapped an arm around her waist.

"Whoa," he said. "Let me help you up."

Elise turned a cold gaze on him, letting all her pain and frustration show in her eyes. He jerked his hand back. "I told you not to touch me."

He followed a step behind her as she ascended to James's apartment. She managed to keep her hands steady when she unlocked the door.

She leaned against James's wall as she lifted the hem of her shirt to examine her stomach. Red welts had risen on her skin, and she probed the edges gently. Even a light touch made her wince.

"What can I get you?" Anthony asked.

"Bandages. They should be in the bathroom cabinet."

He disappeared, and Elise took a ritual mirror off the kitchen table to take another look at her face. In the minutes since she had last looked, her eye had nearly swollen shut. Her lip was bleeding.

She moistened a rag in the sink and washed off the

blood. By the time Anthony returned with the bandages, her skin was clean, but there was no help for her shirt.

"Thanks," she said, pressing a fistful of ice to her swollen forehead. "I don't think I'll need it after all."

Anthony folded his arms as he studied her, and Elise studied him back out of her good eye. She didn't appreciate being scrutinized.

For the first time that day, she noticed he was wearing a nice button-up shirt and clean jeans, although working on the Jeep had gotten his hands dirty. His hair was even combed back. It showed off his full lips and dimpled chin. And he was muscular, too.

Elise wondered how long he had been so handsome. They had been neighbors for over two years, and she had known him as an acquaintance for four, and she had never seen him as anything but Betty's kid cousin before.

"Elise?"

She realized he had been speaking, and she shook her head to clear it. It made the bruises on her face throb. "Sorry. What?"

"You got pretty beaten. Are you sure you don't need bandages?"

"Yes."

She twisted to check her back in the mirror, and the movement sent pain lancing up her spine. She squeezed her eyes shut.

"Careful," he said.

"On second thought, I need you to look at my back and tell me how bad the injury is. Okay?"

He nodded. Elise turned her back on him and lifted her shirt over her head. She could feel him looking at her. Her cheeks got hot, and she was glad he couldn't see it.

Her heart was beating fast, but it was probably from the

adrenaline of the fight. Probably.

She heard him step closer. "Hmm," Anthony said.

"Well? Do I need bandages?" she asked, keeping her tone level.

"You're scraped up, but it looks mostly like bruising."

"How about on this side? It hurts more." She turned and lifted her arm so he could check her ribs.

His fingers traced over the bruises on her side. Elise closed her eyes as chills prickled down her shoulders. "Same here. That looks painful." Warm breath blew over the back of her neck, tickling the hair behind her ear.

Elise hadn't been touched like that in years. Her body's reaction was almost violent—the way her stomach muscles jerked, the heat that flushed her face, the warmth between her legs. "That's not helping," she said, and her voice shook. It actually shook.

She turned to face him, and Anthony's cheeks had a warm flush. There was a certain intent darkness in his eyes as he focused on her. His gaze couldn't seem to make it above her lips, which was good, because her handful of ice had melted down her wrist and left her swollen eye exposed. "Huh?"

"You're not helping," Elise repeated. One of his fingers hooked under her bra strap.

"Oh," he said. His hand ran down her bicep as he lowered the bra strap. He dipped his head to trail his lips along the exposed skin. "I thought you said you didn't want help."

"Anthony…"

"Yes?" he murmured, pushing against her until her back bumped against the wall. She relaxed against him, letting the pressure of his body hold her suspended.

She half wanted to forget the danger pressing on them—

and the danger James was in. But when her eyes opened, she saw the Ansel Adams photo over Anthony's shoulder, and the memory of the time her aspis bought it shattered the illusion of peace.

Anthony's hand slid over a bruised rib, and she flinched as pain stabbed through her side.

"Sorry," he said against her neck.

Elise took a deep breath and planted her hands on Anthony's shoulders. She could have thrown him across the room, but she made herself shove gently. "This isn't the time."

He caught her wrists. "We've got a few minutes."

"Anthony. Not now. I'm serious."

"But later?"

"The odds are pretty good." She smiled a little. "At least fifty-fifty."

He kissed her again, but this time, it was only a brief touch of his lips on hers. "I like my chances." He took her hand, giving it a gentle squeeze. "Can I ask one question?"

"You can ask."

"What's with the gloves you're always wearing? Is this some kind of weird demon hunter thing?"

Elise's mouth snapped shut. "Go see Betty. I still have to grab something, but I'll be right down."

"But you said I could—"

"You can't ask that," she said. "Go."

His tongue darted out to wet his lower lip. Elise was a lot more interested in the look of that than she liked to admit, but the heat building inside of her dissipated at the thought of James.

"See you in a minute," he said, voice husky. He straightened his shirt and moved to go back downstairs.

"Anthony?"

He paused in the door. "Yeah?"

"You look really good." As an afterthought, she added, "I'm sorry I missed our date last night."

A brilliant smile illuminated his face. "Thanks, Elise."

Once Anthony had gone downstairs, Elise had trouble remembering where she dropped her shirt. She didn't have any other, cleaner clothing left at James's apartment, so she pulled it back on to cover her injuries.

The painkillers were starting to kick in. Lifting her arms over her head ached, but it was hardly debilitating.

She rolled out her shoulders, touched her toes, and reached for the ceiling. Full mobility. Painful, but workable. David Nicholas picked a bad time to take out his frustration on her.

If only Anthony had come a couple minutes sooner. She could have skipped a beating and saved her time. Elise pushed the thought aside. There was no point in regretting what she couldn't change.

Taking a set of keys out of James's desk, she went into the spare bedroom that used to be hers before she moved in with Betty. Now it was an extension of the library in his room, with a cozy chair for reading books…and a gun safe bolted to the wall.

James didn't own any guns.

She twisted a combination into the lock, whispering the numbers to herself. Two. Twenty-five. Nineteen. Nine. And eight.

Nothing happened when she twisted the key in the lock until she passed her hand over a charm James had welded to the side. The tumblers fell into place with a heavy, muffled *thud*.

Twisting the lever, Elise opened the safe.

Once upon a time, James and Elise hadn't had thousands

of books. They hadn't had an apartment or a duplex or furniture. In fact, they hadn't even had a spare pair of pants between them. They'd had a handful of cash in various currencies, two tattered backpacks...and swords.

Elise's old chain of charms—which had since been replaced with newer, shimmering chains and tokens—was pooled at the bottom of the safe, and her sword was mounted against the back wall. Three feet long and gently curved like a waning sliver of moon, the falchion had a leather-wrapped hilt worn perfectly to the contours of Elise's hand. She had rewrapped it a hundred times after a hundred battles in the twenty years since her father gave it and its twin to her.

"A falchion is meant to be wielded with a shield," Isaac had said as Elise studied her birthday presents with grave seven year old eyes.

"Then why two?" she asked.

"Because you don't need a shield if you kill everything that approaches you."

She still wondered if that meant Isaac never intended for her to have an aspis. Elise got the impression he would have disapproved of her partnership with James, and the lengths to which she would now go to recover him. She didn't care. Her father was a bastard anyway.

The magical engravings on the blade shimmered with more than the light when she took it in her hand. Elise swung the kopis through the air, slashing it at an invisible enemy. It felt strange to wield without its twin.

The back sheath was in a drawer at the bottom of the safe. Elise slung it on like a backpack and had to loosen the straps to make it fit.

Sheathed, the hilt of the sword protruded over her right shoulder. She flipped her hair back to hide it.

When she examined herself in the bathroom mirror, she couldn't see the sword, and the straps of the sheath looked innocuous enough. But her swollen, bruised face was all too familiar.

Elise didn't realize she had lashed out at the mirror until her reflection fractured. Glass sprinkled on the countertop.

"Damn it, James," she whispered as her knuckles bled through her gloves.

This was all his fault.

If she started hunting again, there would be no going back. No second retirement. Maybe she had been naïve to think she could have left it the first time.

She swept out of the apartment and didn't look back.

Chapter 16

Ann clenched her fist, and the city grew silent.

The matter of calming people was simple. Press magic against the right part of the mind, and a person would grow lethargic. Press again, and they became all but comatose. Another press…well, it would be a long time before someone woke up from that.

Ann had once been too weak with her akashic magic to calm a single person, but it had grown easier with time. Now, with the full force of *vedae som matis* behind her, she felt she could silence the world itself.

But the world was not her goal. Even the entire city was more than she needed for the time being. She envisioned only the surrounding neighborhoods and lulled them to silence. Normal people would panic if they saw Ann's demons and reanimated dead on the streets. With a calm laid over them, they felt nothing. She could operate in the day as easily as the night.

She was so *powerful* now. The universe's energy flowed through her veins, hot as molten lava.

Rain sluiced down the attic's lone window. The fading gray light was barely enough for Ann to make out her surroundings, but she knew her workspace well. She could have navigated it in absolute darkness. The only new addition was the pale form on her work table—a man so tall his feet dangled off the end.

Ann found her pen and nibs exactly where she had left them on the desk at the end of the attic. She paused to glance in her small ritual mirror—her nose was twisted, swollen, red, and her eyes were rimmed with dark purple bruises. Elise had mangled it with a few well-placed kicks, and Ann wasn't the right kind of witch to heal it.

She collected the special ink *vedae som matis* had instructed her to make and took it to the table. She studied the face of James, her high priest, in half-darkness. The poison worked so deep into his body that organs began to fail, and he looked very old. Deep lines furrowed his skin, accenting the faint hints of gray at his temples. His temperature was so high that Ann could feel it from inches away. The edges of his lips were blue.

The poison made it impossible for him to escape while Ann prepared, but once he housed *vedae som matis*, the demon would burn the illness from his blood. He would heal in moments, and James would be the perfect vessel. With maintenance, his body would last for centuries to come.

And Ann would be right there to witness it.

"I need my straight razor," Ann said as she shook the ink bottle, and her smallest helper, the girl once known as Lucinde, went to find it. "And a light, please."

The lamp on her desk clicked on. The room was filled with a pale pink glow. A huge sigil anointed the floor, drawn in the same mixture of blood that marked the basement.

James didn't stir when Ann touched the silver nib to his

forehead. She drew intricate symbols on his face, repeatedly checking both to make sure she was drawing them correctly.

She cleaned a clumped fleck of red ink off James's brow and let her fingertips trace on his skin. Ann couldn't wait until her mistress had a body at long last. She was grateful that they had failed to prepare Lucinde properly. Ann could ignore a man's body as long as it was *vedae som matis* inside. She wouldn't have been able to deal with her mistress appearing as a five-year-old.

Ann moved down his body, writing the specific marks of transference on each critical point of his flesh. In order to preserve James for as long as they could, she had to inscribe over two dozen marks. She drew one carefully on his left shoulder atop a brilliant white scar he bore just over his chest.

Her smallest helper returned with the straight razor.

"Thank you," she said, brushing her hand across the top of the child-servant's head. "You can go sit in the corner again." Ann didn't watch to make sure she would obey. They always did.

Ann flipped open the straight razor and sliced it through the waist of his pants and down the legs. The cloth fell open as a snake shedding its skin.

A twinge of guilt clenched in Ann's gut as she cut away his trousers, removing James's last semblance of dignity. Although she had never been close to her high priest, or even that fond of him, she knew he and Elise were close. It was obvious they adored one another. She would be devastated.

The kopis is the enemy, Death's Hand reminded Ann, brushing her mind. *She will not share in our vision. She will not accept your offer to join us.*

Ann didn't reply. Betty wouldn't share in her vision, either—or so *vedae som matis* insisted. Death's Hand had deployed a fiend to kill Betty without asking Ann, and now one of her creatures was dead. She was still angry, but she sensed the demon's jealousy—the worry that Ann would find she preferred human company. Ann tried not to feel too pleased with that. *Vedae som matis*'s jealousy made her feel wanted, and it was hard not to preen a little.

Marisa has betrayed us. I must kill her.

"No," Ann said. "I don't want anyone else to die if they don't have to. You know I'm still mad you sent one of our babies to attack Anthony and Betty."

Her voice turned soothing. *It was necessary. I knew they would get in the way, and if you could see what they are doing now, you would agree. They are coming to kill me.*

"They can't," she said. "They wouldn't."

But the demon had already subsided from her mind, leaving her with a sense of the inevitable. Marisa wasn't a big deal anyway. She had served her purpose. *Vedae som matis* wouldn't kill anyone that didn't need to die—right?

She resumed preparing James, trimming the thatch of pubic hair over his genitalia so she could properly access the skin beneath. She carefully tried not to look at his naked body. Ann wasn't interested in the sexual sense, but it was so *distracting* trying to draw so close to a penis. She suppressed the insane urge to giggle.

He would be ready soon. She would only need the anointing oil, and perhaps a few herbs…

The clock chimed. Ten o'clock. Elise would be in the cemetery soon.

Ann smiled and continued to work.

"How's it looking?"

Betty leaned on the Jeep's roll cage to support her elbows, peering through a set of black binoculars. She hummed at Elise's question, lips pursed.

They were positioned in the driveway of a sports complex across the street from Our Mother of Sorrows. Even though they had been parked at the edge of a busy road for twenty minutes, not a single car had passed.

The view from their side of the five lane road wasn't good—the statue at the entrance of the cemetery was in the way, along with a few well-placed trees, and Elise could only barely see the illuminated angel statue in the back of the cemetery through the obstructions. "Hmm," Betty said, fidgeting with the focus. "Interesting."

"What?"

"It looks very black. Almost like it's nighttime and I can't see anything."

Elise grabbed the strap. "Hand them over. You don't know what you're doing."

"I'm not using them wrong and I can do reconnaissance all on my own, thank you very much!"

Anthony made an irritated noise and slouched in the driver's seat, folding his arms. His feet sloshed in the half inch of water that had collected at the bottom of his Jeep.

It was hard to maintain a good mood outdoors in the middle of a rainy night, and Elise felt like she had been here, doing the exact same thing with James, just hours ago.

Elise took the binoculars from Betty's eyes.

"Hey!" Betty protested.

"It's almost ten. We don't have time for this." She gazed through the eyepieces, searching for the street lights around the cemetery. At first, all she saw were tombstones, and then she began making out moving shadows behind them. The shapes were faint, but she could guess what she was looking at.

She lowered the binoculars. "The possessed ones are already here," she said, passing them to Anthony.

"What does that mean for us?" he asked.

"It bet it means Ann and James are there."

"Does that change the plan at all?" Betty asked, dropping into her seat.

"She's probably ordered her servants to take the artifact as soon as we show up. So no, this doesn't change anything. We stick to Plan A."

"I hate to be a party pooper, because you know I'm your girl whenever you want to be destructive, but don't you think Plan A is a little noisy for an ordinary neighborhood?" Betty asked. "*Somebody* is bound to wake up and call the cops."

"Ann lives nearby. I think she's been casting a calming on her neighbors in the surrounding streets. It's the only way I can figure she can get away with sending out her servants without drawing attention."

"A calming?"

"It's a kind of spell that compels people to go to sleep," she said. "James can do it to one or two people at a time. With her soul bound to a demon, it wouldn't be hard to do it on a broad scale."

"So I get to break things?" Anthony asked.

Elise nodded. "You get to break things."

"That's almost cool enough for me to stop being completely petrified," he said. "I do have to wonder, though—why did we bring that thing with us at all?"

"The demon is in it," Elise said, patting her pocket. "Part

of it, anyway. It's watching. If we left it at Motion and Dance, we wouldn't have demons *or* Ann to fight here at all—they would be at the studio. We're not that important."

"They tried to kill me," Betty said, bracing herself against the additional bars they had welded to the roll cage. "I'm way important."

Elise sighed. "Do it, Anthony."

Chapter 17

Just meters away, the possessed ones wandered through the cemetery. They moved aimlessly without acknowledging one another, vacant eye sockets glazed with mucus.

Occasionally, one of the servants would pass by the grave in which his body had lain, and he would pause, the faintest hint of recognition lighting up his face. Then the light would fade, and he would shuffle off once more.

The old grave markers were soaked and dark, and water puddled in the eroded faces of the more recent headstones. A breeze rustled through the trees, and fell again moments later. Our Mother of Sorrows was silent.

And then, distantly... "Woo hoo!"

Crash.

The fence smashed open and Anthony's Jeep exploded into the graveyard.

Elise's recorded voice roared out of the speakers bound to the front. The large crucifix forming the hood ornament blazed in the darkness. A length of fence stuck to the crude cowcatcher, and it clipped a shambling old woman, sending her flying.

"*Crux sacra sit mihi lux, non draco sit mihi dux!*"

Pain roared from the throats of the possessed ones. They twitched and flailed as though taken by a massive seizure, clawing at their own faces. Blood spilled underneath their nails, unable to feel anything but the pain of St. Benedict's prayer.

Anthony peeled through the paths of the cemetery at twenty miles an hour, skidding around tight corners intended for pedestrians.

"*Vade retro, Satana, nunquam suade mihi vana!*"

A shaking body—a teenager, only a boy—clawed at the side of the Jeep. His hand caught, and he was dragged alongside them, fighting to climb on board even as his entire body shuddered with pain.

Elise drew her sword from underneath her hair in a single smooth motion. Her chain of charms was entwined between her fingers and the hilt.

The engraved symbols on the blade flashed as she swung. The blade sliced into the boy's wrist. He fell to the earth missing a hand.

"Oh, man!" Betty exclaimed, leaning back to kick at his still-twitching fingers. "Gross!"

Elise swept to her feet, bracing her legs against one of the seats. "There!" she called, pointing to a cluster of possessed ones near the center of the graveyard. "At your nine o'clock!"

Then her hand faltered, fell, as she realized what she was seeing.

"What?" Betty asked. She got to her feet, barely keeping her balance, and followed Elise's gaze. Her jaw dropped open. "Holy…"

There were so many possessed ones the ground seemed to seethe. Elise had grossly miscalculated how many servants Ann could have had—she'd clearly had several years to work up a collection. One dozen, three dozen. Maybe more.

The vessel of *vedae som matis* hung heavy in her pocket, growing so hot that it nearly burned her leg through her jeans. It snapped her out of her shocked reverie. "Be careful, Anthony," she said, climbing into the front seat. "Ann and James might be in there somewhere. Take out the edges first."

His response was to slide into line with the crowd and shift the old Jeep into a higher gear. He was grinning. Elise could only hope he would still be so thrilled when he was cleaning the blood off his car later.

Elise's voice continued to roar from the speakers. "*Ipse venena bibas! Crux sacra sit mihi lux, non draco sit mihi dux!*" The verse echoed amongst the tombstones and rattled the branches on the trees. They passed the ragged woman in the half-torn sundress, and as soon as the voice hit her ears, her spine went rigid. She fell to the ground, shaking, and Elise watched her pass with a critical eye.

"They're not getting exorcised," she said. "Damn."

"What?" Betty asked, leaning up on Anthony's seat.

She gestured to the servants. "The exorcism phrase isn't enough. It's hurting them, maybe even paralyzing a few, but on its own it can't actually free them."

"Hang on!" Anthony cried.

The Jeep shuddered as though it had struck a cement wall. Elise was flung forward onto the roll cage, and a body hit the windshield.

The glass cracked, splintered. Betty screamed.

The body that struck their windshield slid off, but more rose out of the darkness, falling under the wheels and being flung to the sides. They were helpless to run. All they could do was get chewed by the wheels of the Jeep as Anthony fought to keep control and Elise searched for James.

The speakers crackled. *"Crux sacra—lux, non draco sit mihi—retro, Satana—"*

One of the possessed ones leaped at the car, clawing for Elise's jacket and the burning weight in her pocket. She threw herself out of its grasp, straddling the seat to keep her balance.

Her blade flashed. Blood sprayed.

The speakers made a static noise once more, and then died. *"Ipse venena..."*

Silence.

"The cable under the dashboard must have come loose!" Betty said.

A servant slammed into the hood of the Jeep, and it shuddered. This time, the man didn't slide away. He found grip near the windshield wipers, hauled himself higher, and pulled back his arm.

His fist punched through the glass.

Anthony cried out, falling to the side in his seat to avoid the groping hand. The car swerved, but Elise kept her balance. She brought her sword down, slicing into the possessed one's already-bleeding arm.

"We need the speakers!"

Betty crawled between the two front seats underneath Elise's legs. "I can reconnect it. I just need a second to find the break!"

The servant groped blindly and found the steering wheel. He wrenched it to the side as Anthony slammed on the brakes.

Betty squealed again. The three fell into one another, a jumble of legs and arms and confused bodies.

The Jeep lurched to a halt, and a man climbed over the side. His fist struck Elise in the face. Her injured cheekbone exploded in pain. Her vision blurred and darkened. She swung blindly and felt her sword connect.

Something warm splattered on her. It wasn't the rain.

Her vision cleared, and she saw her sword had sunk into the side of his neck. She pulled free and kicked, sending him over the side.

"Holy crap!" Betty exclaimed, untangling herself from Anthony.

"Fix the speakers," Elise said. She reached over the windshield and swung at the possessed one reaching through the cracks. Her sword connected with his back, but didn't cut. She took a deep breath, and began to shout. *"Crux sacra sit mihi lux, non draco sit mihi dux. Vade retro, Satana! Nunquam suade mihi vana. Sunt mala quae libas, ipse venena bibas!"*

The crucifix engraved in her sword blazed to life. The possessed one shrieked, jerking its arm out of the windshield and falling off the hood of the car.

More servants took his place, swarming the Jeep. Elise would kick one off, only for another to take its place climbing over the side. There were dozens. No matter how fast she swung, she couldn't keep up with them.

Anthony slammed the car into gear, but the wheels spun out in the mud.

"Betty…" Elise urged.

"I think I found it!" Betty announced from under the dashboard.

The Jeep's wheels found traction, and the car leapt forward, mowing down a pair of servants who had been coming up on their makeshift cow-catcher.

The speakers crackled, buzzed, and Elise's voice roared

out of them once more.

"—*dux. Vade retro, Satana! Nunquam suade mihi vana!*"

Screams rose from the graveyard, as inhuman as the sounds that came from a slaughterhouse. "Success!" Betty cried, pumping her fist.

"Take this," Elise said, shoving the stone vessel into Betty's hands as she emerged from under the dashboard. "Ann can't perform the sacrifice without it, so it's safest with you. I trust you. Don't go far. I might need help transporting James."

Her friend nodded, cheeks flushed. "They won't get it without a fight!" Betty declared.

"Wait," Anthony said, power-sliding around the stone angel to a stop, "where are you going?"

"Ann's not here, so James isn't here," Elise said. "Ann lives across the street. I'm sure they're in there."

"You can't go alone."

"I'll be fine."

Elise prepared to leap down into the cemetery, but Anthony caught her hand. "Wait," he said, and he pulled her to him and kissed her. He was forceful, desperate, as though afraid it would be his last chance.

And then she jumped over the door before he could catch her again, disappearing into the night. She caught a glance of his face before she went—an expression of admiration, adoration, and fear.

Now that she no longer had the vessel, the servants ignored Elise. They followed the Jeep, and Anthony gave them a good chase—he weaved in and out of the path, and the bigger spots in between the graves, driving over several of the shorter headstones as he made a line for the exit. The possessed ones couldn't keep up.

The storm overhead broke with slaps of thunder and

lighting. Elise flipped her braid over her shoulder so she could sheathe the sword, and she ran toward Ann's house...and James.

The night grew darker.

One by one, the street lamps flickered and went out. A line of shadow crept up the street. The few people still struggling to stay awake began turning off their lights and going to their bedrooms, oblivious to the world around them. The heavy rain clouds that had briefly parted to reveal the moon's crescent covered it once more, and the shadow's hand gripped the Earth.

A single oil lamp illuminated Ann's room as the neighborhood's electricity turned off. Her outline was thrown against the wall in stark relief, a huge monster of a woman with massive shoulders and tiny legs.

The shadows beside her twisted and writhed. Ann's fiends covered every square foot of her house, silent and hungry. She passed the trap door, carrying the oil lamp to the altar, and peered down the ladder. The demons covered the floor below, and the floor beneath that as well. Elise wouldn't be able to get in without getting ripped apart.

Ann set the lamp beside James's leg and faced her altar, standing with her back to the open window.

The fiends touched her legs and stroked her arms and rested their heads on her feet. Some touched James, too, but he didn't stir. The high priest was unconscious.

She spread her arms wide. "Listen up, guys," Ann said. "Every beginning is the end of another. Tonight we leave behind the world we have come to know together for the past several years. Tonight we march to the ruins and transform everything. Tonight, you become the children of the new world."

Their lips quivered. They drooled.

"The city will be ours, and soon, this whole world will too. Why return to Hell under the law of another when we can have this Eden? You all deserve freedom. You deserve flesh. You deserve Earth."

Something clattered downstairs.

Ann cut off, frowning. She perked her ears, listening to the reports the fiends whispered into her mind when something happened. But there were no comforting voices from her demons—only a complete mental silence.

Elise.

"Take care of her, please," she said.

The fiends piled down the ladder, leaving the attic empty except for a handful of fiends and the two humans.

Ann rested her hand on his forehead. His pulse throbbed in his temples, rising and falling like the heart of the ocean. He was beautiful with symbols of transference and death painted upon his body. He was so lucky.

She took a step away from the table and began walking a slow circle, speaking quietly as she went. Ann drew runes in her mind and called upon spirits at the north, the west, the south, and the east—spirits few humans called in fear of their power. Her dominant hand pointed to the floor, and she felt rather than saw the energy burn an invisible path on the wood.

Ann clapped, and the circle of power erupted around them. James's eyes almost fluttering open.

"Did they get her?" Ann asked one of the fiends.

But before she could make out any reply, a dark shape darted out of the corner. She spun to see curtains flapping in the open window.

Nobody was there.

A fiend shrieked.

Elise stabbed again, driving her blade through the skull of the demon to silence it.

The weapon shocked Ann into silence. It wasn't just steel and leather—it coursed with magic, enchantments, prayers. It glowed in Ann's vision, both beautiful and terrible. She recognized it. Death's Hand had its twin.

Elise jerked her blade free, and a spray of blood spattered to the floor. The kopis decapitated the fiend's body with one smooth blow of her sword, and she kicked the head across the floor to Ann's feet.

Fresh blood flowed down the sharp edge of the sword. Elise's skin was flushed, her eyes blazing. *Vedae som matis* may have been the Goddess of Death, but Elise was the goddess of fury—and even with the power of a mighty demon at her back, Ann felt afraid.

And when Elise spoke, her voice burned. "Give me back my witch."

Chapter 18

"Elise," Ann said. "Put the sword down."

Elise's eyes flicked between Ann and the nightmare of an altar with James as the centerpiece. His nakedness was a shock, but not nearly as horrifying as the black demon runes looping over his skin like the brands burned into the flesh of the fiends.

"Not until you let him go."

The necromancer scooped up the head at her feet. "Let him go?" she asked, cradling it in her arms as blood dribbled out the neck. "You killed my fiend."

"That will be nothing compared to what will happen if you don't give me James."

"I offered you a trade," Ann said.

"We both know you weren't serious." Elise took a deep breath. "We don't have to fight, Ann. This is between me and *vedae som matis*."

"I know," she whispered. "I know."

Ann straightened suddenly. Her head tilted, as though listening to some distant voice Elise couldn't hear. And then she began to smile.

"We have company."

The trap door banged open. Fiends jumped inside, dragging two larger shapes with them. For an instant, Elise half-hoped they were injured, struggling servants—but servants didn't fight and swear like these two.

The fiends threw Betty and Anthony to the floor. One of them ripped the pocket off her jacket, and the stone vessel thudded to the floor. Betty struggled, trying to take it back, but the fiends held her arms.

"Hey, get your hands off me! I'll punch you! Don't make me do it!"

Ann cradled the staff against her shoulder like a baby. "This night just got so much better."

Elise moved. Blood splattered on the walls.

The fiends holding Anthony fell. She sliced again, and the fiends holding Betty also fell. Intestines spilled onto the floor in a wash of red and yellow fluids, stinking of brimstone.

Anthony jumped to his feet. He punched another fiend in the eye. It keened, stumbling backward, and he hauled Betty to her feet before returning his attention to the little demons.

Elise twisted and jabbed, skewering a small demon on her sword. Something hit her wounded side. The breath rushed out of her lungs.

They hit the ground and rolled, and then it seemed like all the fiends were on top of Elise, clawing at her, grabbing and biting. The demons were nothing but shadows in the darkness of the room, blotting out all the light. She felt stubby teeth sink into her arm, and she threw the fiend off, struggling to stand. She was just a little too slow, a little too weak with the injuries David Nicholas inflicted.

Between the legs of an attacking fiend, she saw Betty fly at Ann like a manicured beast, her fingernails flying. Ann shrieked and Betty leapt onto her back, dragging them both to the ground.

Elise pushed away a fiend and swung blindly, feeling blade connect with body and hoping it was going to do damage.

Kicking off another demon, she flew to James's side at the altar. His closed eyes looked like they were bruised.

He stirred at her touch. "Elise?"

"Let's get you out of here, huh?" she said, throwing her jacket over his body. She felt around the ropes binding him to the table. "Hang on, it's going to take me a minute to figure out these knots."

"Finish the fight," James rasped.

She took a moment to plunge her sword into a fiend's stomach when it broke away from the others to attack. "I'm not leaving you behind."

"Ann will get away, Elise."

"She's not going anywhere. Betty's got her."

He gripped her wrist. His eyes had darkened, no longer that perfect shade of ice blue. A thunderstorm roiled in his gaze. Elise's fingers went still on the lock. "Trust me. I'll be fine. Get Ann."

"Okay." Elise pressed her boot knife into his hand. "If she gets close to you—kill her."

The room was in turmoil. Anthony thrashed in the grip of several fiends, but he wouldn't relinquish his position over the trap door, which he had locked. He bled from a gash near his hairline. The other fiends had turned their attention to the fight between Betty and Ann, which seemed to involve a lot of slapping and hair-pulling.

Elise smiled faintly. A slap fight. That was new.

And then a blade flashed from nowhere, and Elise's smile disappeared. Ann's hand cracked against Betty's skull with the flat end of the hilt.

"Betty!" Anthony roared.

Elise leapt forward, but the trap door suddenly exploded underneath Anthony. The force threw him forward into the waiting arms of the fiends, and the servants from the cemetery began to climb inside.

One by one, the attic filled with the possessed ones. The man from the hospital, his female partner. A burly, tattooed corpse Elise hadn't seen before. And then Lucinde.

Ann stomped to the front of the room again, standing beside the altar. "Restrain them!" she ordered, and three of the servants came forward, grabbing Elise's arms and dragging her to the end of the room.

A fiend ripped the sword from her hands and dropped it out of reach. Another dragged Betty's lifeless body to her side. It took two of them to restrain Anthony.

The rest had to hold Elise.

A knobby fist sank into her side, making pain explode through her body. She staggered and fell to her knees. Claws raked down her bruised face and smacked into her jaw.

Through blurry eyes, Elise saw James raise a free hand with the knife.

The motion drew Ann's attention. She slapped it out of his hand.

"This was going to be my night of glory. This is when I was going to show *vedae som matis* that I'm good enough for her. Don't you realize what you're ruining?" She slashed her dagger along the wound she had carved on his belly. Fresh blood began to trickle down his side.

Elise struggled, but the possessed ones held her in place. "You better not—"

Ann pointed the knife at her. "Shut up. I don't want to talk to you anymore."

"He doesn't deserve to die.!"

"Do you think he's a good man?" Ann asked as she sprinkled herbs over his head.

Elise swallowed. "The best I know."

"Then you don't know him as well as you think you do," Ann said. She traced her bloody finger down the bridge of his nose. "He's never told you the truth. You would let me kill him if he had."

Betty sat up, holding a hand to her head. "Ugh. What did I miss? Did we beat that—" Anthony threw a hand over her mouth.

Ann pulled an owl's skull from underneath the table. Sharp teeth that birds had never possessed on Earth filled its mouth. She laid it on James's chest.

"And now I can repay my debts to the Hand of Death," she said. Her voice was hushed, reverent.

She smashed the skull on James's chest. Pieces of bone flew everywhere, and blood seeped forth beneath it. She smeared it across James's solar plexus.

Elise's muscles were liquid. Every time she moved, little hands dug into her wounds, burying their nails into muscle.

If only David Nicholas hadn't attacked.

If only Elise hadn't provoked him.

If only she were a little stronger...a little faster...

Ann turned her back on them. She raised the dagger high, smoothing her hand over James's brow. Shadows rippled off her body.

Elise felt the press of Betty and Anthony's eyes on her. They were waiting to see what last-ditch trick she was going to pull out of her hat, like she was some hero from a movie with a plan always in place.

But she didn't have a plan. She couldn't think, or

breathe, and she couldn't move with so many demons holding her down. She met Betty's gaze, and she saw her best friend's worried countenance dissolve into terror.

The stress of the last days built inside Elise, growing and swelling until she felt her ribs might burst. Exorcising Lucinde. Fighting the possessed ones in the cemetery. Losing James, and finding him again to realize he had been all but gutted like a pig and left poisoned. Her new life destroyed; her old life returning like an unyielding cancer.

I'm not ready for this.

Ann. Lucinde. James.

The witch shifted her grip on the dagger so its blade faced down.

Elise threw herself against the steely arms of her captors, but they were unyielding. "Ann! No!"

Her hand came down. The dagger buried into James's chest with a *crack*.

His mouth opened in a silent gasp, eyes blank.

For an instant, there was no reaction. The world was reduced to the space between Elise and James—so close, just inches away, and yet utterly impassable. Elise's breath caught in her lungs. Her pulse roared in her ears.

Betty let out a sob, deepening the silence rather than breaking it.

James's chest hitched, and blood spilled over his lip.

"James," Elise said. She was so cold.

His head lolled to the side, looking beyond the wall of servants to his partner. Their eyes met for a breathless instant, and his mouth formed a single word: *Elise*. No sound escaped his bloody mouth. His teeth were red.

The light behind his eyes faded, and that was all. His body sank into the table, muscles relaxing one by one until there was no sense of life in his face, his body.

And that was all.

"Berald, Beroald, Balbin, Gab, Gabor, Agaba," Ann was saying softly, her hands moving over James's body. A bracelet of bird bones dangled from her wrist, brushing against his bare stomach. "Berald, Beroald, Balbin, Gab, Gabor, Agaba…"

The world receded, slipping away from Elise. Her ears were ringing and her heart was thudding and she *knew* that James was dead. She could have been a thousand miles away, and she would still know with absolute certainty. It was as though, in his passing, a part of her had died, too.

The scar on her arm from the binding ritual that tied them together as kopis and aspis burned.

Dead.

Anthony was muttering under his breath. It sounded like prayer. The valley of the shadow of the death. She took another step back, and the fiends finally released her. Betty was on her knees. Anthony was beside her, holding his cousin's hands. They were pale and shocked and Elise barely even registered it.

James's eyes were empty.

"Balbin, Gab, Gabor, Agaba, Berald…"

She didn't feel pain anymore. She didn't feel anything at all. A glint of metal caught the corner of Elise's eye.

"…Beroald, Balbin, Gab…"

She dropped.

The hands of the possessed ones reached for Elise, but she rolled under their grasp and took her sword. She came up on her knee in one smooth motion, plunging it into a servant's stomach until the hilt slammed into flesh and the blade burst out its back.

She freed the sword with a jerk of her wrist and kicked

the servant to the floor. It fell, lifeless and gaping.

Ann spun. Her jaw hung open. "That was mine," she said. "You little—"

Elise spun, burying her sword into the belly of a nearby fiend, tearing it out its side with a gush of blood and mucus. It dripped down the blade and onto her gloved hand.

"Plan B," Elise said. Her voice was dead.

The attic exploded in motion.

Fiends and servants alike dove for Elise. She dropped to her knees and slashed, slicing through hamstrings and driving her blade into torsos regardless of whether it belonged to a demon or had once been human. Her ribs ached and she thought something was broken and she didn't care.

Blood splattered on the walls. Someone screamed.

James's empty stare remained fixed on the wall.

Elise kicked, punched, and dodged entirely on instinct. She let her long-unused muscles twist her out of the way of blows just in time, feeling claws whistle past her cheek and slice into errant curls.

Something sharp sliced down her arm. She chopped off its hand.

Anthony fought behind her with less grace but no more regard for what he was fighting. His fists flew, making sledgehammer noises against flesh.

Elise threw herself around him, ducking low to stay out of the way of one of his blows even as she gutted another enemy. A body. It had once been the man from the hospital, but now he was mulch. He hit the floor in several pieces, and Elise's foot squelched on a piece of steaming intestine as she spun to attack another.

And she came face-to-face with Lucinde.

The little girl didn't look human anymore. The symbol on her forehead burned, and she reached for Elise with little hands that almost looked like the fiends' claws.

But her face registered in Elise's numbed mind. She froze mid-swing.

A fiend struck her in the side, sending them both bowling to the floor beneath the altar. Its slavering mouth flashed at her face, and she blocked it with her forearm. Its teeth buried into her flesh.

She used its own grip on her to slam its head into the underside of the table. She smashed its head twice, and it released her.

Betty had crawled between two bookshelves and covered her head with her arms. Elise couldn't hear her over the beat of her own heart, but she knew her friend was screaming, crying.

Another clawed hand came at Elise. A flash of her sword. Dismembered.

She rolled out from underneath the table, throwing a high kick into the face of a possessed one. Its head snapped back, and it stumbled into a set of shelves. Glass alembics and vials shattered against the ground, raining tinkling shards of glass across the wood floors.

"You idiot!" Ann stormed around the altar with demonic energies swimming in her wake. She burned with black fire. The tangled hairs on her head stuck straight out in every direction as though repelled by her flesh. "I've won! Can't you give up already?"

Elise's couldn't think of a response, so she didn't speak at all. She swung her fist, clenched around the hilt of the sword. It cracked against Ann's face and her head snapped back.

Ann slashed at her with the dagger stained by James's

blood. Elise dodged it and kicked her in the head. Ann fell.

She rolled onto her belly, scrambling for the knife as Elise loomed over Ann's supine body.

"Get up," Elise said.

Ann's fingers brushed the hilt of her knife. Elise stomped on her hand, grinding with the heel of her shoe. Ann's bruised eyes were round and frightened.

Elise lifted her foot long enough to kick her in the ribcage. The witch cried out.

"You said this is your night of glory. Get up!"

Ann almost made it to her feet before Elise's knee connected with her temple. The bone made a sickening noise like a rotten tomato splattering against concrete. Her eyes were empty before she hit the floor.

This time, the witch didn't stand.

"Fight me," Elise said, but there was no response.

She faced the room. The trap door had been shut again, and all that remained in the room were a half a dozen bodies scattered across the floor. A handful of Ann's remaining servants had teamed up against Anthony, slamming him to the floor.

Elise began to move toward him—but a wall of demonic power struck her full force. Fire ripped through her body. Pain arched her back, and her sword fell from her fingers.

She clutched at her head as wave after wave of energy shattered her thoughts and twisted her brain, making her eyes explode with black lights.

Voices swam through her skull.

Crux sacra sit mihi lux...

I am the cold kiss of Death, and you can never defeat me.

Elise was on the floor, but she didn't know how she had gotten there. She stared up at the raftered ceiling, the bars of heavy oak casting dancing lines against the ceiling.

The breeze twisted through the window and extinguished the oil lamp with a pinch of its invisible fingers.

But the attic was not dark.

A man towered above her. Every inch of his bare, sweaty skin was bared to the attic, and his eyes welled with tears of blood. Thick veins bulged under his skin, crawling up his arms and neck onto his face. His muscles bulged as though they had been shot full of testosterone. His pulse visibly pounded in his throat, erection full and straining in a bed of trimmed black hair.

A symbol swam to life on his forehead and multiplied, spreading down his body. As it passed the painted marks, they flared with black shadows. The distant fires of Hell reflected on the marks.

The witch usually made a sound like chimes in Elise's skull when he was around, soft and powerful. Now he thrummed with the power of *vedae som matis*, and the air around him trembled.

"James," Elise whispered.

Chapter 19

Death's Hand surveyed Elise with James's eyes. She tensed, expecting him to attack, but he stared at her without moving. His face twisted with a tangled mix of emotions.

Emotions? Could a powerful demon *feel*?

The silence of the attic around them was broken by shuffling feet. The possessed ones left Anthony's body to flank Death's Hand, heads bent in submission. Lucinde knelt with her small head resting against his knee.

The fiends crawled on their bellies to his feet. They laved their black tongues along his ankles, his calves, pawing his hips and stomach. Death's Hand didn't acknowledge any of them. His gaze remained steady on Elise, as though he was in no hurry to do anything but *look* at her.

Vedae som matis lifted a hand. She flinched.

Ann's body lifted from the corner of the room behind the altar, where Elise had left her. Her limbs lifted, and her legs twitched, but her head remained slack on her shoulders.

She came forward without taking a single step. Her toes dragged against the ground. Ann's face was blank and her mouth hung open. Her every motion was unnatural, as though she was a puppet with invisible strings. By the time she stopped moving just beside Death's Hand, Elise was certain she was dead.

Ann spoke. The language that spilled from her lips made no sense to Elise, foreign and guttural and inhuman. Foamy saliva dripped from her bottom lip as though she were an ancient Pythia controlled by a demonic Apollo.

Death's Hand gestured once more. Ann shivered, and when she spoke again, it was in English.

"Kopis," she said. It came from her throat, her vocal cords, but the words belonged to *vedae som matis*. "I have been eager to see you and your aspis, who thrived as I struggled to rebuild my withered soul from the brink of nothingness."

Another gesture. A fiend skittered from behind Death's Hand and opened one of Ann's drawers, withdrawing a long object wrapped in cloth. It supplicated itself at James's feet. He took the item from the fiend's hands, giving it time to scurry back before unwrapping it.

Steel glinted in the dim firelight.

"You recognize this, I'm sure," said Ann's body. Death's Hand turned the sword in his hands, hefting it by the hilt to examine the line of the blade. Someone had cleaned the falchion. It was in perfect condition. "Here we are again. Little has changed in the ensuing years, except you are fleshier. You have fattened upon the spoils of victory and comfort while I have floundered."

Elise finally found her voice. "You can't have James."

Death's Hand made his lips smile. "No?" Ann's chin quivered, and blood dripped from the corner of her mouth. "It is difficult to campaign on Earth. Things in Hell are much simpler. There are many complications. You and your aspis are a complication. What a coincidence that he would be a suitable vessel. It is fate."

"Fate," Elise echoed.

Blood pulsed in James's veins. "Or something like that."

"What about Ann?"

"She will survive in this form." The gesture *vedae som matis* made with the sword encompassed James's body, but not Ann's. "I have absorbed what I need."

"She was in love with you."

He rested the sword behind him on the table, out of Elise's reach. "She lives in me now. We are closer than ever before. She would prefer it this way." There was almost a hint of love in that voice.

Elise took a step away, inching closer to her sword where it lay next to a bookshelf. She could feel the bulge of the charm-draped chain in her pocket. "Anyone that's been possessed can be exorcised."

Vedae som matis nodded, acknowledging the challenge.

Ann's corpse fell, no longer necessary. Elise threw a hand toward her engraved sword.

The room exploded into black stars.

Elise was smashed chest-first into a wall. Hands gripped her wrists, pinning her in place.

His face buried in her shoulder, and pain erupted in her collarbone. She screamed and tore free.

Elise put several feet between herself and Death's Hand before she touched the wound on her shoulder—and realized she had been bitten. Blood gushed from the raw flesh underneath her fingers. The inside of her body felt like the inside of fresh steak.

She turned. Blood dribbled down James's chin as a small chunk of her shoulder disappeared between his lips. His throat worked as he swallowed.

272

Elise lunged for her sword. She scooped it into her left hand and stood in the same smooth motion, twirling just in time to see James flying at her. She dodged and raised the sword. Her blade slashed across James's arm in a spray of blood that splashed across her chest.

Vedae som matis barreled into Elise and knocked them both to the floor.

She took their weight on her uninjured shoulder, trying to bring around the sword to slash at him again. Death's Hand didn't give her a chance. He grabbed her wrist and crushed it in his hand until Elise could feel something pop.

Her fingers went slack, and he ripped the sword out of her grasp, shifting his weight so his entire body pinned her to the wood. He stank of blood and decay and brimstone, and very faintly like Ivory soap.

Elise struck him with her right hand, but he grabbed her other wrist and pushed both of her arms to the ground. His body burned like a furnace.

She twisted her head away from his sulfuric breath. Death's Hand buried James's face into her shoulder, the same one he had bitten before. Elise fought harder, but it was like struggling against rock.

His teeth found her wound around the shoulder of her shirt. Something pinched, tore. She grit her teeth and refused to scream.

James's weight shifted just slightly, and something pressed into Elise's leg. Her charms. She squirmed around enough to see her jeans, and a glimmer of metal told her they were sticking just slightly out of her pocket.

"*Crux—crux sacra sit mihi lux,*" Elise panted. "*Non draco sit mihi dux. Vade retro, Satana, nunquam suade—*"

Death's Hand threw his head back, roaring. It tore through Elise's ears, and she screamed with him as her eardrums thrummed.

He ripped at her jeans, tearing away the pocket. The charms spilled out onto the floor.

James's teeth sunk into her shoulder again, and he worried at her flesh like a dog with a bone.

She beat her fist against his head, his shoulders, his hand where it pinned her other arm to the floor. He paid no attention, growling deep in his throat. She reached for the charms, but he shoved them out of reach.

Elise twisted and writhed, and all she could do was worsen the agony where he bit into her.

Vedae som matis pushed her shirt aside to get a better taste of her shoulder. The pain grew from agonizing to indescribable. His teeth scraped against bone.

I will not scream.

Her back arched, and he pulled his head away. A small strip of skin dangled from his teeth. The burning told Elise it was part of her neck.

Death's Hand began to lower to her shoulder again, and Elise felt faint. She wouldn't be able to remain conscious through another second of that horrible chewing, and if she passed out, the pain would be the last thing she ever knew.

Elise reached back. Her shoulder screamed.

Her hand flexed around a shelf on Ann's bookcase, and she *pulled*.

The shelves came down on Death's Hand, on Elise, and the books rained around them. The heavy wood of the shelf struck James's shoulders.

He roared his terrible roar once more, rearing to shove the shelves off of himself. The space between them was slight, but it was enough for Elise to throw all of her weight into him and push him off-balance. *Vedae som matis* tumbled away.

Elise scrambled to her hands and knees, closing the inches between herself and her sword. Her hand closed on the leather-wrapped hilt.

Relief washed through her. Adrenaline overrode the pain enough for her to lift it.

She turned as Death's Hand swung, but her head spun as she moved and dizziness swept over Elise. Blood loss slowed her. He knocked her blade aside and she felt the metal bury into his forearm.

Blood fountained from his arm and splattered against the floor. As Elise watched, the wound closed, healing without a trace.

She took a deep breath and pointed the sword at James. "*Crux sacra sit mihi lux*," she gasped, pressing her hand harder over the wound on her shoulder. It grew more agonizing as it dried out and sent fire racing down her nerves.

Death's Hand smiled. It was James's smile, warm and friendly, as though he was beginning to assume her partner's habits.

She reached inside herself, searching for that wellspring of energy that James would always touch when they piggy-backed. It wasn't magic. It was older, primal—the force of a kopis and exorcist. "*Non draco sit mihi dux. Vade retro, Satana, nunquam suade mihi vana.*"

She took a mental hold of the power inside herself and tore it open.

Elise's senses exploded. It hit James, still in the clutches of *vedae som matis*, and kept going, sweeping through the servants and wrapping its invisible fingers around them. It poured through her sword, through her charm necklace, and she felt her energy curl around the demons with metaphysical fingers.

Vedae som matis screamed. The demon's voice ripped through James's throat, but Elise's power had taken a life of its own and it wasn't done.

Wind blasted through the open window, and papers around the room went flying, swimming in circles around and around Elise and James. Vials tipped and shattered, carpeting the wooden floors in shards of colorful glass and ceramic. James's hair stood straight up from his head, swaying as though he was submerged in the ocean.

His bleeding gaze cut through the chaos. He didn't speak—she wasn't sure he even could—but she could feel the fury of Death's Hand.

Elise kicked him in the face as hard as she could. He crashed to the floor, but his hand reached out and dragged her down with him.

He rolled on top of her and closed his hands around her throat.

She struggled, beating against his arms, but his muscles had turned into bands of iron. She shoved against him.

He didn't budge.

Blood thudded in her skull.

His bloody moth still grinned as the room grew dark. Her chest hitched with a desperate need for oxygen.

Elise had imagined dying before. She knew it could come in any number of ways. She never imagined it with James's hands on her neck.

Her legs might have been kicking, but she couldn't feel them anymore. Her brain was bulging against her forehead. Everything grew distant and dark, even her fingers, and she thought she might have gone limp.

James...

She wished she could tell him she was sorry.

"No!"

The pressure on her throat vanished.

Air stabbed into her chest, burning a path down her bruised esophagus.

Elise wheezed and coughed as color returned to the room, too vivid with the sudden intake of oxygen. James arched. His lips peeled back against his teeth and veins bulged at his throat. His muscles rippled, almost tearing. It was like his skull was trying to crack in half.

His nails dug into the sides of his head. "*Let go!*"

The voice belonged to James.

An internal battle wracked his body as he fought Death's Hand for control. Symbols swirled wildly over his skin. "James," she said, "James, look at me—"

But he didn't hear her. He twisted on the floor like he was burning in invisible flame.

Elise gathered both of her swords and stood over him, uncertain. She needed to help him, she needed to *save* him, but who was in control—James or the demon?

With another cry, he froze. His eyes fell on her.

"James?" she whispered.

His mouth was stained with her blood. "Elise, I—" James's expression twisted, and then stilled.

He was gone again.

Death's Hand thrust his fist toward the ceiling.

An explosion rocked the building. A huge roar filled Elise's ears, followed by a cracking like a glacier snapping off into the ocean. Fragments of plaster showered across the floor.

The entire roof ripped off the house and flung into the night with a blast of wind. There were no stars. Clouds boiled overhead as rain poured into the attic.

"James!"

His body lifted into the air. She leaped, clambering as high on the wall as she could to swipe at his feet. Elise wanted to catch him and drag him back. She couldn't exorcise him unless she could touch him. But an invisible wall had materialized around him, and her hand slammed into solid nothing inches short of his heel.

He dropped to the street outside, and Elise gazed hopelessly down at him, clinging to an exposed wall stud.

She dropped to the floor. The human servants had already gotten to their feet and disappeared down the trap door to follow Death's Hand. The fiends stirred again, like they were rousing from a long night of sleep.

Elise didn't want to give them the chance to move.

She took her swords—both of them—and plunged them into the heart of a fiend at her foot. She slashed and stabbed over and over again until blood coated her hand and spattered on her face and nothing stood in what used to be Ann's attic. There wasn't much left to kill. Almost everything had fled with Death's Hand.

Elise climbed onto what used to be a window, preparing herself to climb down the side of the building. Her shoulder burned, but she didn't care. She had to reach James. Maybe it wasn't too late, maybe she could—

"Elise—help—"

Anthony had come to consciousness pinned underneath one of the ceiling beams.

She hung suspended, her urge to follow James warring with Anthony's pleas for her attention. "Come on," he said, groaning as he shoved at the beam.

Elise sheathed one sword and dropped down. With their combined strength, it was easy to shift the weight of the rubble enough for him to slide out underneath. He was white with plaster dust.

Betty screamed on the other side of the attic. It was a single, constant shriek like the wail of an alarm.

Elise went to her, but when Betty saw her, she only shrieked louder and hugged her body tight into the corner. "Shut up," she said, kneeling in front of her. Betty tried to scramble back. Elise seized her wrist. "I told you to shut up!"

"Oh God, oh God, oh God—"

Elise slapped her.

Betty silenced instantly. Her free hand flew to her cheek. "Hey!" Anthony protested, but Elise turned her glare on him.

"You two need to listen to me. This is—"

A silent voice boomed through the air: *Sleep.*

"Did you hear that?" Anthony asked.

But before Elise could reply, she felt the command sucking her down into darkness, like she had a dose of narcotics injected straight to her heart.

Sleep…

Anthony and Betty's eyes went blank at the same time. She slipped to the side and went unconscious immediately. He managed to take a step toward Elise before his knees gave out and he, too, collapsed.

Elise shook her head, trying to clear the flies buzzing between her ears. "No," she said.

But it was like telling the sun not to set at the end of the day. Her eyes rolled up, and the world went dark.

Chapter 20

Time passed, and Elise awoke.

She rolled onto her side, groaning. Every muscle had stiffened. Her bloody shoulder felt like someone sawed into it every time she moved, and when she probed it with the tips of her fingers, she found blood caked over the injury.

With a jolt, she remembered James's flight from the attic. She sat upright.

Anthony and Betty were still unconscious. Elise over and shook him.

"Get up. We have to get Death's Hand."

He rolled onto his back without stirring. She pressed her fingers to his throat and found a pulse. Anthony wasn't dead, but he was equally useless.

Elise supported herself with what was left of one of Ann's walls, shutting her eyes against the waves of pain that rocked through her body. Everything felt torn, bruised, and broken, but there was no time for self-pity. She had no idea how long she had been unconscious. Death's Hand could have been miles away already.

She scooped her charms out of a puddle of fiend blood

and lifted the trap door.

The house creaked and shuddered as she made her way down the stairs. A steady drizzle turned the pavement into a shining black lake in the night.

Elise ran down the hill and across the road to the cemetery, feet splashing in the puddles. Anthony and Betty had made it to the road outside before getting dragged from the Jeep.

The gas indicator was almost on empty. Her voice still crackled out of the speakers, quieter than before. "...*sit mihi dux. Vade retro, Satana*..."

She punched the power button to silence it. Elise had almost backed onto the street again before something strange caught her eye.

All the graves had been torn open.

Elise pulled herself up on the roll cage with her good arm to stare out at Our Mother of Sorrow's cemetery. Ann had raised several bodies from it over the last few weeks, but most of them had been untouched. Now every grave had sunk in on itself, pitting the grass and leaving piles of mud everywhere.

Her heart sank. Had Death's Hand resurrected *every* corpse as he passed? Elise didn't want to consider what that might mean. There were hospitals downtown, and more cemeteries.

And a lot of innocent lives.

Elise tore down the road, ignoring the speed limit. She approached tail lights and climbed the median to go around them.

The stoplight turned green. None of the cars moved.

She blew past the line and had to stomp on the brakes. A group of cars and trucks had stopped in the middle of the intersection, causing a minor accident. The drivers were all slumped over their steering wheels.

The calming must have spread far enough to stop everyone on this side of town. The streets were completely blocked. Elise pounded her steering wheel, biting back a curse.

She wove the Jeep carefully around the intersection. It looked like there had been parties celebrating finals at the university, because the sidewalks were covered in students sprawled out in skirts and heels. A few had even passed out in the middle of the street.

The Jeep's engine spluttered. The fuel indicator had dropped to the empty line. Elise made it another two blocks before it died, stopping in front of the school of art. The bar across the street had its lights on, and she could see everyone inside asleep on their tables.

"Shit," she muttered. "Shit, shit, *shit*."

She jumped out of the Jeep. The instant her feet hit the ground, she could feel the presence of Death's Hand.

Sleep...

Elise muffled a yawn. It weighed heavily on her, but it wasn't as strong as it was in the attic. Something about being a kopis—or maybe the particular kopis bound to James—seemed to make her resistant to the effects of the calming spell. The bite on her shoulder burned all the way down the scar on her arm. She wondered if James's scar burned, too.

Something flicked through the darkness up the street, and she reached her good arm up to one of the swords on her back. Giant eyes shone at her in the darkness, spotting her in the street.

Another pair of lights reflected behind it, and then another, as their heads turned to look at her.

She couldn't fight one fiend, much less three. Not with

her muscles stiff and a ragged wound on her shoulder. Not with her aching ribs, which stabbed with pain every time she breathed.

With no other choice, Elise darted down the street and crouched behind a car and held her breath. The occupant inside had his cheek mashed against the damp window. Blood trickled from the corner of his nose, trailing down the glass like rivulets of rain.

The fiends yipped and growled as they scurried from the houses to the street.

Shutting her eyes, she rested her head against the side of the car and tuned out her pain to reach out and *feel* where the fiends were. She matched the noises—the scraping of claws, the brush of leathery flesh against branches—with the sensations in her gut that said they were behind her, just feet away. Something gave a heavy huff as it searched the air for her scent.

Elise eased around another car, trying to keep her feet from grinding against the grit of the pavement. Rain tapped out a rhythm on the sidewalk.

She peered around the tailgate of a truck, trying to see through the purple haze of night to the shadows she knew had to be there. Four fiends. There were four of them, even though she couldn't see them.

Creeping out another inch, Elise turned to look on the other side of the truck.

A slathering mouth opened in a wide, hungry grin.

Elise jerked back with a shout. She went for her sword instinctively—wrong arm—and pain flared down her back.

She fell with a splash. The fiend lunged.

Planting a foot in its gut, she snapped a second kick into its chin. It screamed. She kicked again and got an eyeball this time. It exploded like a pustule and splattered all over its cheek.

A dozen other fiends scurried to life at its scream.

Elise clambered to her feet and ran. Every pound of her feet jolted through her wounds. It burned through her body, like little strikes of lightning on her nerves.

Behind her, fiends dug their claws into the earth in pursuit.

Too many cars. Elise had to weave in and out, and the demons were climbing over them. They were gaining.

She cut across into the parking garage, which was mostly empty now that the semester had ended, and emerged on campus on the other side.

For a half second, she thought that people were still awake. Human figures moved down the paths toward the university buildings, slow on their feet and unperturbed by the rain.

But then Elise saw that many of them had only rotten scraps of clothing, and that some of them were rapidly healing—muscles wrapping around exposed, dusty bone before fat and skin rippled down their limbs.

She had to stop and stare at the power of Death's Hand. There were dozens of bodies—maybe hundreds—just where she could see. It was like they were being sculpted from flesh and blood as she watched.

And then the closest heard her running, heard the growls of the fiends echoing in the parking garage, and they turned to look at her.

Several hands reached for her at once.

Elise shoved them off. She elbowed a woman with no bottom jaw, kicked off a teenage girl with a gaping hole on the side of her head, and stumbled out into the open.

The healing corpses were sluggish, but their bodies

made a great barrier between Elise and the fiends. She turned a corner around the building, leaving the demons struggling to get around the bodies.

There were more corpses further south. They were headed downtown. When Elise ran past them, they made half-hearted grabs for her, but she ducked out of their reach and was soon forgotten. They were too busy answering the same call she was—the call of Death's Hand.

She left campus and went for the casinos. The lights were still on, marching in lines down the sides of buildings and flashing titles taller than she was. They cast colorful, dancing shadows on the immobile cars and slumped pedestrians.

The closer she got to him, the louder his voice became: *Sleep*.

It was James's voice, but it was not James speaking. Anger knotted in her heart.

Elise didn't stop to look at the mangled cars down on the freeway as she ran over the bridge, shoving past the body of an old man. He pitched over the railing.

She had almost run past a casino with corpses clustered by the front door when she felt the presence of Death's Hand shift.

He was inside.

The servants of Death's Hand had all stopped on the street to stare at the casino as though they could see through the walls to their master. They were spread out several blocks south as though they expected Elvis to burst through the front doors for an impromptu concert. None of them noticed her now. They were all absorbed by the silent call.

Elise tilted her head back to look at the glimmering sign over the door. Craven's. Somehow, she wasn't surprised.

Beneath her feet, deep under the streets, Eloquent Blood would be blasting music. And miles below that twisted the Warrens. Death's Hand was marching for the ruins.

Elise stepped over the body of a security guard to get inside. There was a huge bite wound on his arm, much like the one on her shoulder. Blood shone on his shirt.

Inside, the air was thick with smoke and the molasses-thick sense of evil radiating from Death's Hand. Slot machines jangled and clanged and sang enticing songs. The keno boards on the wall were frozen halfway through a game. Cocktail waitresses were sprawled out with drinks spilled in their hair and on their skirts.

Elise saw motion in one of the mirrored walls, and she jumped behind the bar for cover. She stepped on a bartender and he groaned softly.

"Sorry," she muttered, crouch-walking to the end of the bar as quietly as she could manage.

When she made it to the end of the bar, she could see around the next row of slot machines, and the source of the motion became clear.

A broad, bare back was crouched over the body of an unconscious waitress. His shoulders twisted and jerked. The distortion of the mirror almost kept Elise from seeing what he was doing—almost.

Death's Hand dipped James's head again to rip into the waitress's side, digging in and pulling back to swallow. Blood coated his face and hands.

His power grew with every swallow. He was stronger now than he had been in the attic.

Much stronger.

He straightened with a fistful of ragged flesh in his hands, studying it with calm, black eyes as though evaluating a cut from a butcher. The symbols on his flesh were so thick now that she could see almost none of James's skin.

Death's Hand reached out his other arm. She hadn't noticed him take the stone staff when he fled from the attic. Maybe he hadn't—maybe it had followed him—but he clutched it now, and it had *grown*. It extended from his right arm, as tall as he was and twisted with demonic runes. They grew from it like branches. The stone oozed over his knuckles and wrist like lava, melding with his arm so they were one.

He aimed the stone staff at the floor, and the building rumbled. The bottles on the bar rattled. The earth shook beneath Elise's feet.

A mighty *crack* thudded through the air, and a giant slot machine with a colorful wheel shattered across the brightly-patterned carpet. The floor split. Death's Hand gestured, and a chunk of floor the size of a sedan lifted.

Elise slowly drew one of her swords with trembling fingers. The blade whispered in its sheath, so softly that she barely heard it beneath the tearing of the earth.

Death's Hand froze.

She tightened her hand on the hilt.

She saw him drop the chunk of flesh in the mirror. She watched him face the bar. She watched him move toward her one step at a time, his feet inches above the carpet. Her shoulder burned.

Elise couldn't struggle with him. She would lose.

She only had one chance to end it.

"*Crux sacra sit mihi lux,*" she whispered, and her charms began to glow at her hip.

Death's Hand stood on the other side of the bar.

Elise jumped to her feet, swinging her sword—and he caught the blade.

The force of his power slammed into her.

A cacophonous buzzing resonated through her skull. The sour tang of blood exploded in her mouth. Her teeth strained against her gums, trying to rip free of her jaw.

The muscles in her arms shook as she pressed against him. Her blade cut into his hands, sending blood dripping down his arm and onto the floor. It sizzled and evaporated.

Hatred filled James's eyes. She felt the floor crack beneath her feet.

The bar fragmented and tore away from them. She couldn't release her sword. Her muscles had locked up in the grip of the demon's power.

Her vision darkened at the edges. Slot machines began falling behind him, but all she could see was his furious gaze and his bloody mouth and feel his hand gripping her shoulder. His fingers dug into the wound. Elise tried to cry out and found she could barely move her mouth.

He challenged her silently. *Try to exorcise me. Just try.*

The energy between them swelled. Her intestines writhed within her like maggots. He pulled the blade forward, drawing her against his body, and his skin burned like fire. His sweat steamed.

"*Non—non draco—*" Her tongue was thick. She couldn't speak. It felt like hot oil dripped off his flesh, spattering against her.

The stone of the staff began creeping over his hand to her skin, locking down over her shoulder.

Death's Hand was going to take her. She could feel needles of stone piercing her skin. Ichor spread through her muscles.

The casino was suddenly gone behind him.

The edge of her blade bit into his stomach, and Death's

Hand smiled.

"Non draco sit mihi dux—vade retro, Satana—"

Her power slid off of him. He was impenetrable.

Plaster showered around them, and rain began to drip through the holes. The stone locked into her bones.

The symbols on her kopis glowed, and then flickered.

You're out of time, Elise, Death's Hand said, and now he spoke directly into her mind. She could feel the weight of him oppressing her. He was going to kill her and fill her body and—

"—nunquam—suade mihi—vana—"

His fingernails scraped her wound beneath the stone.

"Sunt mala quae libas—"

Elise *couldn't* kill James, she couldn't do it, and Death's Hand knew it. Her blade cut him, but it hurt her far worse than it could ever hurt him.

But it's not James, not anymore, it's a demon—I can't do it—

His face spasmed.

For an instant—no more—Elise saw James in there. His eyes softened. His smile faded.

The power of Death's Hand lifted for an instant.

It was long enough.

"—ipse venena bibas!"

Bile rose in her throat. The power shut her throat and plugged her nose, roaring like drumbeats in her ears, snapping over her skin.

She tore the second sword from its hilt and plunged it into James's heart.

And everything became silent.

Death's Hand's eyes widened until she could see white at the very edges.

Elise," he said in James's voice, sounding stunned.

And then he threw his head back, and a soundless

explosion rocked the ruins of the casino.

Waves of raw energy slammed into her, one after the other. Elise was flung against the wall as if swatted aside by a giant hand. Bottles of alcohol rained down on her, knocking into her elbows, her hips, and she threw her hands over her head to protect her head.

The mirrored walls fell. Glass exploded on the ground. The shelves slammed into her shoulder blades and pinned her to the floor.

A wind rose, knocking over the last of the slot machines. Dark energy blurred around James. A seizure shook his body. He clawed at his arms with fingernails as the black symbols cascaded off his flesh and vanished into the air.

James screamed wordlessly as the power of the exorcism rushed Death's Hand toward the passages between Earth and Hell.

His fists slammed into the ground and an invisible string drew him up by the solar plexus, arching his spine. His heels kicked helplessly against the ground. Her sword jutted toward the sky, lodged in his breastbone.

With a sick popping sound, Death's Hand was wrenched completely from James.

He stopped screaming.

Elise could feel the bodies animated by Death's Hand throughout the city. She could feel the demon in them, the little bits of *vedae som matis* left behind. She fought to push herself onto her elbows, gripping her first sword, but she couldn't support her own weight.

"Servants," she gasped, and the words were whipped into the tide of power. "Return to the Hell in which you belong. Be gone!"

The cord binding Elise to James snapped, whipping away from her body and lashing into the ether. Death's

Hand faded away with a piercing scream. Every servant standing in the streets outside collapsed.

The wind died, leaving the casino in silence.

Elise fell to the floor.

And just like that, it was over.

Slowly, the city began to awake. Car engines came to life again. Pedestrians got to their feet and looked around in confusion.

Nobody moved in Craven's. Not the sleeping gamblers, who died when Death's Hand ripped the building apart. Not Elise, who was in too much pain.

What was left of the ground was cool beneath her cheek. Adrenaline drained slowly out of her in the space of many long minutes, leaving her muscles liquefied. The wall crushing her was heavy, and the shards of glass beneath her were little stars of pain in her stomach and thigh and arms.

She wasn't inside herself at all anymore. That pain belonged to someone else.

Elise never wanted to move again.

She half-dozed, somewhere between asleep and awake. Elise thought there was something she still needed to do, but she wasn't sure what. The casino was still.

Something dripped into her eyes. With a groan, Elise wiped it off, and then she planted that hand on the wall and pushed it off her body. One of her swords was near her leg. She picked it up as she stood. The blade was stained with blood—James's blood.

She worked her jaw around, trying to clear the ringing from her ears. She evaluated her injuries as she leaned on what was left of the bar for support. Blissfully, she seemed to have gone into shock. She couldn't feel her shoulder at all anymore. In fact, she couldn't feel anything else, either.

Lights on the surrounding casinos flickered. All the jangling slot machines were dead now. There were too many bodies to count. Elise couldn't seem to find it in herself to care.

She surveyed the bodies on the street, which she could see through what was left of the walls. One had been thrown to Elise's feet during the exorcism, and she could see that what Death's Hand had started earlier began to reverse.

The skin on the body's scalp shrank as it dried out. His lips drew back from their teeth in a shriveled grimace. Muscle melted away underneath his skin, and then that too dried, flaking and crumbling to white ash. His skull appeared in white patches, and then a burning odor filled the air, and his bones began to crack.

A fine webbing spread from his eye sockets and took over his entire skull like a window shattering in slow motion. Elise watched in distant bemusement as he became nothing but puffs of dust.

One by one, each body decayed and blew away, leaving the street empty.

Except for one body, laying in the middle of the sidewalk and surrounded by cratered concrete.

James.

She climbed over the rubble, almost slipping on a rebar as she made her way to his side. He looked like he had been thrown, too, but he had gone through a window. Her sword was still in his chest. She wrenched it free with a sick slurping sound.

Pressing her fingers into his throat, she held her breath. It was stupid, it was useless to hope, but she had to be sure.

There was no pulse, of course. Nobody could survive getting stabbed in the heart—not even the vessel of Death's Hand.

Elise bowed her head over his, pressing her mouth to the top of his head. His hair smelled like brimstone, plaster, and his shampoo. "I'm sorry," she murmured, eyes burning. "I'm so sorry."

Now she knew why she felt so hollow inside.

Was it supposed to hurt this bad? Was she supposed to feel like a fist had wrenched her heart from its chest, leaving a gaping void under her ribs? She had never felt such a thing. Not when her dog died as a child, nor when her parents left her with James's aunt because they moved faster without her. Not even when Pamela Faulkner died.

Her shoulders shook. She couldn't breathe. Elise tilted her head back, squeezing her eyes shut and gritting her teeth against the ache swelling inside of her gut.

A ragged wail tore from her, shattering the silence of the night.

Her fingers dug into James's chest, slippery with his blood. Becoming bound as kopis and aspis was an oath: to stand shoulder-to-shoulder in their battles, to protect one another, and when the time came—die together. She was supposed to guard him. She wasn't meant to kill him.

He gave up everything for her. Everything.

His skin cooled to the temperature of the air. Elise wanted to cover him in a blanket to give him the modesty in death Ann hadn't given him for the last few hours of his life. He shouldn't have to be naked and vulnerable when everything else had been stripped from them.

Elise's chest hitched. "James," she whispered.

And a voice whispered back.

Elise…

Her eyes fell on the stone staff. It was a few feet away in the crater, no longer alive even though it steamed slightly in the damp air.

All the mighty power of Death's Hand was gone, boiled down to a tiny flicker of demonic energy inside the cylinder. It gave a fraction of a roll onto its side, barely more than an inch.

Elise...

It was what was left of *vedae som matis*, but it sounded very much like James.

That tiny flicker of energy tugged at her.

Elise stepped away from James without thinking about it, sliding down one of the craters to reach for the stone cylinder. Her fingers hesitated just over its surface. She could feel the heat radiating from it.

It wasn't just demonic power. It was necromantic power, too—a little bit of the demon, a little bit of Ann, a little bit of James.

She glanced up at his body again, and the grief sliced through her anew.

He would never cast another spell. They would never have Sunday breakfast together again. She would never see him smile again, that special soft smile that she never saw him aim at Stephanie.

Unless...

She closed her hand on the stone cylinder even as every bit of her common sense screamed *no*! Elise had been tortured by the death goddess using the stone as a knife. She had felt it wrapping around her flesh as Death's Hand tried to possess her. It was the reason James was dead in the first place.

The flicker of light was fading fast.

She knelt over James, gripping the stone in both hands

as she studied him. His skin was gray. There had to be some way to use what was left of its power, but she didn't know what to do with it.

How did James do magic? A circle of power. Incantations. Elise wasn't a witch. She couldn't do any of that.

She leaned over him. The stone vibrated, and she touched it very gently to the wound on his chest.

Light erupted from the stone.

Shocked, Elise tried to let go, but her fingers stayed welded to its surface. Heat rushed through her fingers, up her arms, and into her body.

The symbols tracing the stone doubled and split from its surface, one set rising from the vessel in burning white lines. They swirled over her body and ruffling the little hairs at the back of her neck. The golden light filled her vision until she couldn't see anything around herself.

It wasn't *vedae som matis* she felt in that moment. It was something more, so much more, like staring into eternity, and the only anchor keeping her from spilling out into nothingness was her grip on the vessel. Some great beast pulsed in the beyond, rubbing past Elise through the marks. It wasn't demonic, or even angelic. It was something greater still.

The golden fire shifted from Elise's arms to her palms, glowing through her gloves. The power beat in time with her heart.

God, the *power*.

She felt as though she had never lived before. Wouldn't anyone kill to feel this energy for any length of time—to gaze into forever and clutch it in her grasp?

Through the light, she could see James sprawled on the ground, but she could see the dead for miles and beyond. It wasn't the corpses themselves—those had all dissolved with the exorcism—but a vast, endless ocean of souls, animal and demon and otherwise. They formed the Earth beneath her, and Life roared above her as the sky.

She could resurrect anybody. Elise could put her hands upon someone laid to rest a millennia ago and bring them back at a whim. She could touch any number demons she had sent to Hell and reanimate them as her own. She might even be able to improve upon what Ann had done— she could make them as alive as she was. Their hearts would beat for Elise.

James brought Elise down from her high. The instant she thought of him, the souls around her came into focus, and she could feel him clearly. His soul glowed brighter than any other in the vast ocean.

The power began to slip from her grasp.

She gazed down at his face, and even through the light, she could see the triangle of his jaw, the day-old stubble, the well-defined cheekbones.

Elise didn't really want power. She just wanted James.

Her hands overflowed with the symbols needed to call a soul into a body, to make the heart beat and the brain function. The magic wanted to be used, so Elise didn't try to resist. She laid her hands upon James's temples. She opened to him like a flower's petals parting to the sun, and the symbols from the cylinder flowed from the sword into her shield.

James's soul, torn apart so violently by *vedae som matis*, began to mend as Elise watched.

His heart beat once. Twice.

The rhythm sped until its steady beat matched her own. Elise's lungs expanded, and his inflated as well, drawing air through his lips and into his chest. It was strained, difficult at first, and she labored to breathe for them both, but it became easier with every breath.

The blood began flowing. Color faded into his skin, and warmth spread into his muscles and tendons. Electrical impulses sparked in the air between them, and something seemed to click on in his brain.

Her heart beat with his, one muscle in two chests. Slowly, so slowly, Elise's heart became her own again, but even as she left, his continued to beat. It wasn't as clean a cut as she would have expected. Some of Elise remained in James, and some of him remained in her, but when he kept breathing it wasn't her life that made his lungs work.

Only when his body functioned did his soul return. It drifted into him, as softly as a feather fluttering into the ground. It settled into his body with a soft sigh that curled through the room, and she suddenly felt as though a hole inside of her had filled. She was complete again.

James…

Eternity shut down, withdrawing from Elise. The burning glow of her hands flickered, then disappeared. The power blew out of her again. The gold light emanating from the stone died, leaving nothing but rock in its place.

The world went dark.

Elise sagged, suddenly weak. Her eyes cleared and she could see the casino once more. Everything was still.

And James coughed.

He rolled onto his side. His legs drew up into his chest, curling around the sword wound. Every cough brought a fresh groan of pain, punctuated with another cough when he sucked in the dusty air. "James," Elise said, reaching out to roll him onto his back again. Her hands were shaking.

He frowned up at her, brow furrowed with pain, confusion. His eyes were clear now the poison was flushed out of his system, but the stab wound in his chest trickled blood. "Elise?" James's jaw chattered as he spoke, his skin clammy underneath her bare fingertips. "What happened? What's going on?"

"Oh, James," Elise said, her voice cracking. She rubbed at the blood on his cheeks, wiping it away with her gloves, and then gave up, throwing her arms around his neck.

Her relief was so strong that she couldn't hold it inside. A laugh bubbled from her throat. James stared at her as though she had gone crazy, his hands clenched over his wound.

He would have questions later, and so would others. His resurrection would be a beacon that called to demons and angels for thousands of miles around them through a thousand dimensions. There would be repercussions.

But for the moment, Elise didn't care—not one bit.

He was alive, and nothing else mattered.

Chapter 21

The hospital released James the next morning. They were too busy to keep anyone longer than a couple of hours— the citywide coma had inflected tens of thousands of injuries, from car accidents to cigarette fires and people falling down stairs, and the hospital was swamped.

There was no accounting for the missing hours, but the news claimed that all the damage and dead were caused by an earthquake. It was a stupid excuse. Elise couldn't imagine anyone falling for it, even though the story was discussed worldwide as fact. She flicked through the channels on the hospital TV and saw it on every major news network.

"Can you believe this?" Elise asked, shutting off the television and dropping the remote onto James's bed. He was dressing behind a curtain while the nurses prepared his bed for the next patient. "Who comes up with this stuff?"

"Lord only knows," he muttered.

Stephanie stopped by to drop off a few forms and brush a kiss over his lips. "I'll visit you as soon as I can," she whispered, lingering in the door. "Maybe I should take you home."

"He already has a ride," Elise said.

"You're both on enough hydrocodone that I think—"

"It's fine, Stephanie," he said. "Thank you."

But it was true that Elise and James were both unsteady on their feet as they carefully made their way to the parking garage. Normally, Elise wouldn't have taken any of the painkillers they prescribed to her, but the injury on her shoulder was bad enough that she caved in. She was still better than James. He could barely walk.

He sighed as she settled him into the front seat of the car, shutting his eyes.

"Do you need help with the seat belt?"

"I was stabbed, not paralyzed," he said, but he couldn't work up the energy to sound annoyed.

He fell asleep again before Elise reached the street. Being possessed by a major demon, exorcised, killed, and brought back to life seemed to be pretty exhausting. James hadn't been awake longer than fifteen minutes since his resurrection.

Elise was hardly any better. She situated James in bed and passed out on his couch, waking up ten hours later to find he was still asleep, too. She staggered back to her car and slipped into the duplex without waking Betty.

Before the sun rose, she was awake and gone.

She stayed at the office over the next week while her injuries quickly knit themselves, avoiding Betty and Anthony and the long conversations they would need to have. Brushing her teeth in the sink and sleeping stretched out on her floor, Elise took her solitary time to mend—and seek out new clients online to replace David Nicholas and Craven's.

But Elise couldn't stay in her office forever. James called her phone at least three times a day, and although he never left a message, she was sure he must have been getting irate. Betty was—and she texted about a hundred times to make sure Elise knew it.

By the time the next weekend rolled around, her face and body completely healed other than her shoulder, and she finally gave in to the calls.

Elise found the Motion and Dance parking lot full. The main dance hall was occupied by a dance fitness class, so she found James in the back room supervising a "creative ballet" class for preschoolers, which wasn't a dance class as much as a play group filled with girls in tutus. He looked healthy but pale, slumped in a chair in the corner to watch the kids bounce around in pink leotards with a long-suffering expression.

She took a few minutes to observe him silently. She had missed him over the week, even as she hid out in solitude. There was a little color in his cheeks and a hint of beard growth at his jaw. He looked like he had on any other day. Normal.

Something tense inside of her eased. She hadn't *really* thought she would come to find him a revenant—or something worse—but he didn't look like he had been hurt by her little act of necromancy at all. Elise stood behind his chair and cleared her throat.

"Isn't this Candace's class?" Elise asked, standing over his shoulder.

James looked up, and his eyes widened. "Elise!" He tried to stand too quickly and winced, gripping his chest. She grabbed his arm.

"Hey," she said. "Relax. Sit down."

"Where have you been? I haven't seen you all week."

"I've been healing." She pointed at the last of the yellow bruises around her eye. Showing him her shoulder would have been a lot more impressive, but he didn't need to know he had eaten her flesh.

James eased back into the chair, studying her face. "It must have been terrible if *you're* not healed yet."

She ignored the implied question. "Where's Candace?"

"Her husband dropped a pot of boiling water on himself during the, uh, earthquake," he said. "First degree burns. She's taking care of him. Excuse me, just a moment." James clapped his hands and raised his voice. "You! Penny! I told you no running!"

Elise had to hide a smile behind her hand. James liked children about as much as he liked food poisoning.

"I can finish out the class," she suggested.

He sagged with relief. "Thank you. I'll be in the lobby."

Elise supervised the last twenty minutes of creative ballet. She didn't like kids any more than James did, but she had "taught" the class herself while she was still in college, so she didn't mind doing it one more time. Trying to convince a dozen four year olds to *plié* was a great exercise in patience.

When the class ended, James and Elise sat together in the lobby as the parents took their kids away. His friendly smile looked authentic until the door swung shut, and then he grimaced.

"Those people would do better with a daycare than a dance class," he muttered.

"They pay the bills. Your children's ballet classes are about half your income."

"I suppose. Would you like to explain why I've seen Betty more this last week than I've seen you? As you can tell, I really could have used your help around the studio. And not just with classes."

"I thought you would have Stephanie nursing you back

to health."

"She's visited when she has time," he admitted, "but there's very little of that. Betty said you haven't been coming home while she's awake."

Elise shrugged, and then winced. Her bra strap rubbed against the bandages on her shoulder. "I have a lot of work to catch up on. I'm busy."

"Your work ethic couldn't have anything to do you're your roommate's incessant questions, could it?"

"That might have been a factor."

"She's been here every day. In fact, you missed her by a half hour," James said. "I've never realized anyone could be so damn inquisitive about demons. If you wanted to tell her the truth, you could have also had the decency to make yourself available for questioning."

"I'll keep that in mind for my next earth-shattering revelation," she said.

Something in her voice made him give her a sad smile. "What happened that night?"

"Didn't Betty tell you?"

"She didn't have all the details. I don't remember anything after our investigation at the cemetery myself, except bits and pieces of trying to sleep that evening."

That was a lot of empty ground to cover. Elise sighed and leaned her head on his shoulder. "It was Ann. She was working for Death's Hand. She tried to fight me, and they both lost. I don't want to talk about it."

"Betty told me as much, but that doesn't explain why I'm healing from several major injuries. Or what happened to almost two hours of everybody's life."

"Your wounds aren't that major. The doctors said they missed your major organs." Of course, Elise was confident that she had actually punctured one very significant organ, but resurrecting him had healed almost everything. "I have a question."

"Yes?"

"Ann said that you hadn't told me the truth yet. That there was something about you that would…" She trailed off, gazing at the smooth line of his nose and the curve of his chin. *Ann said I would want you to die.* "She said you hadn't told me something."

"Demons are liars," James said.

"She wasn't a demon. I'm not sure she was evil at all. I think she was…confused."

"Then she must have been confused on this point as well. I have no idea what she's talking about." He spoke forcefully, and his hand tightened on hers. "You know you can trust me, Elise. I would never lie to you."

"I know," she said. "I know."

They sat together in silence, watching the cars empty out of the parking lot. It would be at least an hour until the belly dance class, which was taught by an instructor named Kendall. They didn't need to wait. But Elise didn't feel like moving, and she doubted James did, either.

"I'm glad you came back, but you didn't need to avoid me. You can tell me everything when you're ready."

"I wouldn't stay away for long." She took a deep breath. "What do you think?"

"About what?"

"Do we…" Elise picked at her thumbnail, avoiding James's gaze. She swallowed. "Are we going to have to run again? Should we go into hiding?"

She could feel him watching her. He gave a heavy sigh. "Do you *want* to run?"

It was a question that had been prying at her all week, no matter how hard she fought to distract herself.

Running would be the smart thing to do. Performing a huge exorcism—and having a city filled with the walking dead—ruined any chances they might have had of hiding.

But Elise had her job, and so did James. More importantly, it surprised her to find that avoiding Betty and Anthony all week made her a little lonely. Elise didn't want to leave them. For the first time in her life, she had friends. Real friends. People willing to go to battle with her. People she would die for, if she needed to.

"No," she said. "I don't want to go."

The corner of James's mouth twitched into a smile. "Good, because neither do I."

She thought that response would make her feel better. Instead, Elise felt they had just agreed to do something very unpleasant—something potentially deadly.

"Then we'll stay," she said with a tone of finality.

They sat together in silence, hands clasped, until the next class came in and life resumed its normal routine.

Somewhere very far away—somewhere very dark—someone else listened to that conversation.

It had been a long time since He had seen Elise, or heard her speak. He had dwelled in darkness for some years, and although he could not tell if it had been ten or ten thousand, he longed for the succor of light—however momentary.

And then it came in a single burning, brilliant moment. He felt her power and saw her eyes blazing with fury. He saw her fist clutching the sword as she plunged it into the heart of a demon. From another time, another place, He saw her anguish.

He had found her.
He saw it was very good, and He smiled.

Dear reader,

I hope you've enjoyed Death's Hand. The story continues in book 2 of the series (The Darkest Gate), which is available now!

If you'd like to know when my next book comes out, visit my website to sign up for my new release email alerts. I hope you'll also leave a review with your thoughts on the site where you bought this book—I can't wait to hear what you think of it!

Happy reading!
Sara (SM Reine)
http://authorsmreine.com/
http://facebook.com/authorsmreine